BACK to the FRONT

BACK to the FRONT

Suri

PARTRIDGE

A Penguin Random House Company

ISBN: Hardcover   978-1-4828-3846-6
            Softcover   978-1-4828-3845-9
            eBook   978-1-4828-3844-2

Print information available on the last page.

To order additional copies of this book, contact
Partridge India
000 800 10062 62
orders.india@partridgepublishing.com

www.partridgepublishing.com/india

To
Maa and Paa,
Thank you for your belief.

To
Daa and O2,
You are my strength.

CONTENTS

CHAPTER 1

October 2009

Beep . . . beep . . . beep . . . beep!

'Major sahib's vital signs are steady at the moment. Please continue prayers to the mighty Allah for his speedy recovery.'

My involuntary senses were activating. I was breathing. It took a few moments to gather myself. I could breathe, hear, feel touch on my skin; lying on my back, I was fragile and frail. It was impossible to distinguish life and afterlife. Trying hard to open my eyes, I couldn't. Scared, I wanted to scream out loud, incapable again. My face was completely draped; I couldn't move my lips or open my eyes. The only area uncovered was a narrow slit below my nose. But in between all these adversities, I could feel life. The beep sound helped me decipher I was in a hospital. There was some movement around me but nobody was yet aware of my awakening. I shifted my hand to draw their attention. Unfortunately, nobody spotted it, being under a sheet of cloth. Next time, I was determined for somebody to notice. I gathered all my strength and waved, somebody sighted it, and I heard a loud shout, 'Doctor! Doctor, please come inside, double time. He's moving.'

I sensed some commotion and a rush towards my bed. Checking my pulse, a heavy mature voice said, 'Janaab, major sahib, welcome back to this world. Madam-ji, many congratulations, we have every reason to believe that the major is waking back to his life after a month in coma.'

Heaps of crying followed instantly. Somebody was weeping, holding my feet. Some kid's cries were also audible.

To prevent further damage, the doctors had to take control of the situation.

'The patient needs rest. We will try our best to make sure he recovers at the earliest. Please cooperate. Let us analyze his condition, for which we request all of you to leave.'

Happy to discover life, I was too weak to comprehend and dozed off within moments. The next morning was eventful. The place was full of activity even before I woke up. Lying helpless, I could not interact with anybody. People were coming closer, touching me, praying in whispers. None of them were family. Saakshi was not around; neither were Mum or Dad. The environs were unfamiliar. After many departed, an elderly voice said, 'Good morning, major. I am Dr Taufiq. Please accept my salutations and appreciation. You have been comatose for almost twenty-eight days. You were in very bad shape when you arrived at this hospital. I guess you had a very close encounter with an explosive. The blast had almost blown you apart. You had multiple injuries and your upper half was badly wounded. The face and torso had suffered maximum damage. We had to conduct multiple operations and procedures to keep you alive. We are very glad our efforts are showing. You have had plastic surgery on your upper body and scrotum. Your face was disfigured beyond recognition, for which we have performed cosmetic surgery. So there might be changes in your facial features but we tried our best. You have to thank your loving family who has been praying to the Almighty all this while. I won't trouble you much and will leave you with the family but congratulations once again for this wonderful recovery. Thank you.'

Explosive! Damage! Plastic surgery! I was confused to death. For a moment, death seemed to be a better option. But God had other plans. Suddenly a woman crashed on my chest, wailing out loud. Two kids joined her.

'I am so relieved, Mazhar. The mighty Allah gave me the strength to believe you will come back. The kids haven't gone home since you are here. Afaaz, Inshaa, come to Papa.' The next moment, two small hands touched my chest, sobbing. I was distraught.

Who are these people? Who is Mazhar?

My mouth is shut, my eyes are strapped, my hands are tied. I am hurt, I am in pain. I was alive just a few moments back.

I am also human. I too shed tears.

Nobody noticed them, as always.

The next couple of days were spent nursing me back to life, getting used to the pain and medication.

As I was unable to experience the world around, one thing that put life back in a living corpse were memories.

CHAPTER 2

October 2001

I was a young, free-spirited individual. My father lectured students in college and my mother lectured us at home while taking care of our chores. My elder brother was the scholar of the family who satiated parents and the society with his high grades. This provided me some space to explore the sporting side. I participated in every sport my school would compete in. I was better at my football and cricket skills but didn't mind chipping in with anything that came my way. Not only in sports, I was also part of science projects, adventure treks, annual day events, drama competitions. So the idea was to find ways to reason logically for missing classes. But my brother always made sure I scored respectable grades. I was small and lean in my school days but the college vibes made me work out for some muscle mass.

I also gained height in these years and reached 5 feet 11 inches. The school cricket team that travelled together stuck together. We teammates were best friends and close confidants. We shared everything under the sun. Our tiffins, our notes, our pranks, our crushes, our music, our dreams, all were up for grabs for this close-knit circle.

With the festival of Diwali approaching, the buddies met up for the shopping spree. Since our adolescence, Diwali was one festival the whole country celebrated with equal fervor. In the early years, festival shopping was one big family outing, starting in the chaotic lighted gullies and ending up with a dinner at an Udipi restaurant. But college changed it all. Now the college boys went shopping all by themselves. During one of such evenings, we friends debated on career options after board examinations. Somebody aspired to be an engineer, somebody's mother wanted him to be a doctor, lawyer, CA; many different aspirations were in consideration. None of these dreams excited me. Then AD came up with a brilliant suggestion.

'Why don't we try army?'

'Army?' I enquired enthusiastically.

He explained, 'After you study engineering or management, which itself is a huge task, you need to find a job. This job will help you earn a salary and then begins the daily struggle of travel chaos, peers jealousy, colleague competition, deadlines, timelines, office politics, a never-ending saga of sorrow. We slog all our life to own one apartment for the family, a car for leisure, a holiday to plan for. At the end of the day, after all the struggle, if we are privileged to achieve our goals, there is still no assurance of appreciation or gratitude. The criticism and displeasures along the way are icing on the cake. At one point in time, we consider, is it worth the scuttle? On the contrary, the kind of life defense services can offer is unparalleled: huge houses, lots of servants, postings at exotic locations, subsidized provisions, sports to explore all your life long, the works, coupled with an apparent high of serving the country so obvious praise. Being an ordinary citizen, if you try to live the quality of life the armed forces provide, you have to make more than a million annually. I know I can't make that amount of money in this crazy competitive world. So I am opting for the army, it suits my sensibilities.'

Wow! AD was so sorted. I always looked up to AD. A great bowler who led our team to many victories, he was tall and huge like the great South African Allan Donald. His real name was Amit Dangar: Ami for his family, AD to his friends, and Donald to fans. He suggested being sportspersons; we should pursue something that keeps our sporting passions alive. I concurred.

AD and I had always been the best of friends. He resided two blocks away so we were together in every activity. We were classmates since kindergarten. We attended tuitions together, practiced cricket alongside, loved the same junk food, and had crushes on a single actress. We spent all day in school, on ground, sports training together, and even had dinners at each other's home. We had so much in common and so many secrets to share that we had developed a secret lingo for us to communicate. Both being big-time Bollywood buffs, we were always fascinated by the Mumbaiyaa language. We called our version of English as Mumglish, a simple modification of attaching *Bey* before the first vowel of the word and ending it with a *rele*. So a regular 'Hi, how are you?' would become 'HBeyirele, hBeyowrele Beyarerle yBeyourele?'

This Mumglish was our secret code of communication for disclosing results, planning pranks, discussing women and scheming against opponents. This invention was our weapon in dismantling our opponents and haters. We used it very effectively in general public but nobody could ever gather a whiff of it. We were proud to be the only proponents of this unique language in the world.

During one of such Diwali family dinners I disclosed the defense career plans to my ma and pa. They were a little surprised but supportive.

'If you believe you can join the defense services and serve the nation, we would be proud of you beta,' they concurred.

I was thrilled. AD and I studied hard for the entrance exam and sailed through. Along with the physical tests we were subjected to the group discussions and personal interviews. AD and I were tailor-made for this stuff. We topped most of the tests. One sunny afternoon, a letter arrived from the Union Public Service Commission (UPSC). I couldn't garner courage to open it, asking my mother to do the honours. She took a moment to read it herself and then with a soft tone announced, 'Mr. Rajeev Suri, you are selected for the National Defence Academy (NDA).' Ecstatic, overjoyed, I was jumping all over the place.

I was selected. I immediately picked up the phone to call AD. His number was busy which made me anxious. Within moments, the phone rang; it was AD.

'DBeyidrele yBeyourrele lBeyetterrele Beyarriverele?' (Did your letter arrive?) he enquired.

'YBeyesrele!' (Yes!) I replied.

Then what followed was mayhem. We both were screaming at the top of our voices. I rushed out to meet AD and ran into him midway. He too was sprinting towards me. We hugged each other.

'JAY AMBE, AMBE BHAWANI MAA. HEE HAA HOOO. JAI DURGE. DURGE BHAWANI MAA. HEE HAA HOO!'

Yelling our victory slogan, we shared our signature chest bump. The world was our playground. That evening was a pandemonium amongst friends.

The National Defence Academy (NDA), Khadakwasla in Pune was our dream destination. It is the premier institution for training of defense services; from here candidates are sent to army, air force, and navy as per their performances or preferences. Our families drove us to the NDA. Leaving the chaotic civilian life behind, we were curving towards a new dawn. Already on cloud nine, we were mesmerized with the roads leading us to foggy mountains. It was like a dream come true. The institute was every bit of what we heard, the stone-walled buildings reminding us of Victorian grace, the roads so spic and span as if they were washed daily. The garden was so well maintained it seemed the shrubs obeyed the disciplined life of the institution.

And then was the moment of truth . . . the national flag! A gracious larger-than-life flag was hoisted on a sky-high post, the tricolor fluttering in clear blue skies. It was a picture etched in my memory forever. No matter what religion, gender, or region you belong to, the moment you enter this esteemed property, all the inhibitions and attachments are foregone. This is where an individual is converted from a civilian to a soldier whose only belief is nationalism. It is a training which transforms men into gentlemen, grooming the cadets on mental, physical, and intellectual levels. From deep-sea diving to music, carpentry, debates, and fine arts, this institute imparts training for everything under the sun. Along with the brains, you need a tough spine and rigid determination at a very tender age to help you go the distance.

We enrolled and the first makeover was obviously the haircut. AD and I were small-time rock music enthusiasts. Though we never enjoyed real heavy metal, we flaunted long tresses faking the rock look. But this was the last day of false identities. A day later, all the students appeared identical, same, similar. Here you shed all past glories and stories, stand on equal ground, shoulder to shoulder with your friends, breathing the motto of the institute: 'Service before self'.

The morning parade, the physical exercises, extracurricular activities were apt. This stuff never tired me. As my brother advised, scoring good grades was always important so I concentrated in academics as well. I thoroughly enjoyed becoming a soldier. In fact, I realized I was born to be a soldier.

CHAPTER 3

October 2009

Waking up from slumber every morning was like rousing in the afterlife. Nobody could notice my awakening until I made a gesture. No vision, no communication. Ironically I was not dead, waking up to a life wrapped up in bandages. It was almost a week before I could start observing and learning things. Getting used to daily errands with such confinement was a mammoth task. So wonderful is the human mind and adaptability. If one of our hands is hurt and bandaged, the other hand takes charge to execute the activities we never thought it could accomplish all alone. We learn to work like an acrobat. We can button up a shirt with one hand, we can type efficiently with the only hand; in fact, we manage to talk on the cell phone, eat a burger while driving a car, all simply single-handedly. Now since my speech and vision were impaired, my hearing and touch senses were enhanced tenfold. I could hear things from far away and recognize people around from their touch.

Determined to rise, get back on my feet, go back to Saakshi's arms, hug my parents good night, I couldn't just wait and wane.

The pain was a constant companion now. Epidural helped a lot. I observed a woman religiously taking care of me, calling me Mazhar. So I am Mazhar. Two lovely kids calling me Abbu hug me repeatedly. I was unable to understand anything or to tell them who I am. The family loved me and I couldn't help but love them back. They took utmost care of me day in and day out. A brawny muscular man was always around, though. He performed all the trivial tasks. He washed me, fed me, cleaned, me and put me to rest. I was not new to atrocities. But one pain reminds you of the other.

CHAPTER 4

May 2003

Camp Rovers they call it. The infamous Camp Rovers was a legend amongst cadets at the NDA. Its epithet was the Hike of Hell.

We assembled in our military fatigues, just like any regular morning. It seemed like a routine drill. We had been doing it over the past two years and were habituated. Our physical training instructor, Major Singh, was at his imposing best. We congregated on the parade grounds and to our astonishment the company commander arrived with all his cavalry. This was something big. The murmur amongst cadets began anticipating the gravity of the event. Commander Namboothary occupied his place behind the dais, and in his signature thunderous tone greeted the company.

'Good morning, cadets, welcome to Camp Rovers! Many of you might consider this as just another training drill. But, gentlemen cadets, in these next five days you will rediscover yourself, reinvent endurance, befriend fatigue. This is not just a physical test but it really boils down to how far your mind can carry your body and for how long, in the time of real crisis! The five days that you all will spend together, helping each other through those grueling sessions will teach you the sense of camaraderie. This strong sense of brotherhood and bond that gets created between your course mates is a bond, a sense of responsibility that is to stay with you for the rest of your lives, so all the best and try maintain this smile and enthusiasm till the other side of the camp. Major Singh will take you through the better part of the day.'

This was an inspirational caution of the times to come. We exchanged concerned glances.

'Good morning, cadets,' Major Singh roared. 'Point 988 is your destination. I will not disclose the distance today. These numbers will hardly matter in the next few days. It is the journey that you will undertake, the activities that you will undergo which will transform you rough stones into glittering diamonds. You will start believing in your ability and capabilities like never before. It is a strong willpower, determination to excel, and above all, the fear of punishment that will take you to 988.'

Anxiety and concerns were aplenty but excitement and exhilaration superseded everything.

All cadets were given a 15-kg backpack in addition to the 3-kg rifle we carried. And we set sail. The first few hours were spent getting accustomed to the weight on the shoulders, the trek through the terrain. All the cadets were smiling and making merry, trying hard to hide the displeasure within. As the sun reached overhead, the first onslaught of soreness began. We were strictly restrained from taking off the backpack. Around nightfall, we arrived at the first camp, where we had the opportunity to put the backpacks aside, enjoy only one glassful of water, place our bottoms on the ground for exactly four minutes, and then get back on our feet with the gear. 'Move on' was the call.

We progressed into the night, when the temperatures dropped to bring some reprieve. But the marching did not stop. As darkness descended, we started ascending a mountain. The perception of distance and depth was consumed by the fog around. After a little while, Cadet Trivedi, who was trailing me, advised, ''Suri, kucch bhi kar lekin don't look to your right.' (Suri, please don't look to your right.)

But the inquisitive human trait made me immediately peep right. I felt depth. The winds blew a little of the fog away. I observed a deep gorge, more than 500 feet deep. Our pathway was just a tiny corridor not more than 12 inches wide, on the edge of the mountain and a deep valley on the other side. One minor slip and it would be a roller coaster for life. The climb continued. As the night advanced, our bodies started talking to us. Every tiny little corner and muscle was shouting out loud. The body juices were draining. Somewhere in the middle of the night, we were privileged with two loaves of bread and sugar water. This got back some life in the limbs. Seeing fellow cadets fighting it out also gave me the strength to carry on. There was a training site in the middle of a jungle. We were made to go through our routine drill and complete exercise regime. Sleep deprivation, food scarcity made our daily tasks feel mammoth. But we didn't have a choice. The food served here was like straight from a refugee camp. The next two days were comprised of all the workouts and drills we had learned in the past years at the academy.

During the next night walk, rain gods smiled on us. Well, smiled would be an understatement. They burst out laughing, and hence a cloud burst. It was barely visible amid the heavy downpour. At the next camp, we saw several slum-like structures. Major Singh, at his authoritative best ordered the teams to build a shade with anything that could be found, in an hour's time. So the next hour was spent collecting sticks and leaves and bamboo and shrubs to build an overhead structure. By the time this shelter was built, it was time to advance. We had been slogging for fifty-two hours nonstop. The contingent was drained. Many were already sick but Major Singh with a rock-solid look on his face, thundered.

'This is what you are. This is what you can deliver. This is your capacity. Now this is the time for real training to begin. Here on every hour that you are awake, every task that you perform, every goal you accomplish will extend your belief in yourself. Now it will be your mind over matter. Your willpower will hold and carry you to the end. Welcome to the power of the subconscious mind!'

So this was the beginning? Wow! Such inspiring words renewed our vigour. We were looking forward to the oncoming challenges. There comes a point in every struggle where we lose faith, drop our weapons, and bow out. Here our mind takes over, reminds us of the pleasant triumph of accomplishment. So 'Bring it on' was the mood in the company. Many who had fallen sick got back on their feet and were ready to face life.

Food was better at the next camp: semi-cooked meat. Many of the cadets were vegetarians and averse to eating veal. But they didn't have a choice. Once again, Major Singh was supremely commanding.

'On a battlefield you don't choose what you eat, you eat what is available. Meat, insects, animals, snakes, roots, flowers, fruits, leaves are not just food. They are sources of energy to keep you alive. You are alive because the country needs you. Nobody will question what you consumed to survive but will applaud you survived. So I don't want to hear the religious jargon, gulp down what is offered or else be ready for a confrontation with the commander back at the academy.'

During evening brief, we were informed this would be the last night, and next morning, we would reach our destination, peak 988. We had a sigh of relief. Four nights and days of extreme exertion had made us weary, but the joy of completing one of the toughest training camps was unparalleled. We started the hike at night. The pathway was all marshy because of the rains. Now we were used to this and it seemed a casual stroll. A few of us—AD, Trivedi, Jagga and me—were trailing behind the company. On one of such tricky corners on the edge of a hill, we had to hop, hold the grass, and climb a rock. The whole contingent had just passed through the same route, making it slippery. The instructor had advised us to grip the blades of grass closer to the roots to ensure a firm support. Cadets who passed ahead loosened the grass, while the rock smeared in muck made the hop all the more difficult. In between this scuttle, during his attempt AD slipped and slid straight into the ravine. It was a dreadful moment. We watched him helplessly sinking down the pit. It was dark around and we couldn't gauge the depth. Within moments, we called for him, and to our relief, he replied.

'Abbey kucch to jaldi pheko. Mera haath phisal raaha hai.' (Please throw something to grab on to. My hands are slipping.)

We removed our belts, tied them together, and lowered them. But AD was a heavily built boy. The weak belts were unable to sustain his weight. In the meanwhile, Trivedi ran across to get help. AD was sliding down, and it was certain death if we couldn't rescue him. I got hold of some tree roots, branches, shrubs, and lowered my feet. They reached him and offered a better grip than the belts. So he caught hold of my boot and hung on. I was holding on to random shrubs and had a 70-kg man suspended from my feet, in middle of one of the toughest camps, and this happened on the last night. I was exhausted and depleted. But I didn't have a choice. I had to hold on. Jagga was trying to help but AD was on the other side of the rock, making him inaccessible. Every passing second was a torture. The shrubs were cutting through my palms. My limbs, which were already lifeless, were pulled down in despair. Within a short time, aid arrived but they took a little while to understand the situation and act upon it. In between this, my hands started bleeding, inflicting the worst pain I ever experienced. But the life of my best friend was at stake and I had to persevere. Darkness descended in front of my eyes; I fainted as help started working AD out of that gorge. These were the worst few minutes of my life. But they instilled my confidence; if I could withstand this pain, I could endure any agony.

I was almost dead when I craved for life. Today I am alive in the middle of nowhere and I wish for death. Death is such a surreal feeling. Every person on the planet experiences fatal encounters and near-death feelings many times over. And when the moment comes calling, all these experiences render me useless.

C H A P T E R   5

November 2009

Life was getting back to normalcy, slowly but surely. The bandages were still intact but my hands and feet were moving. It felt great to be alive. I could hear, very loud and clear. Resuming my daily activities, I was trying to learn and observe things. Who was this Mazhar? The lady who supposedly is Mazhar's better half was a devout Muslim. Her Koran recitals were comforting. Deeply devotional, I also joined in her prayers.

She used to come closer, lean over, and kiss my bandaged forehead every day. I could feel her silky tresses stroking my skin, her soft hands holding mine. She used to massage my feet, lay her head on my stomach and murmur, have long conversations with me about the family and the kids. With my health recovering, she stayed for late nights at the hospital. It was almost three weeks since resurrection. I was still on heavy painkillers and antibiotics to fade away the injuries, physically unfit but these adversities didn't matter much where stimulations were concerned.

One of such evenings, she let go my help.

'Aaj aap ghar jaa sakte hai, janaab ke saath hum hospital mein raat guzaarenge.' (You can head home today, I will spend the night in hospital with janaab.)

The lady was restless over the past few days. Her heavy breathing and warm touches were obvious. That evening after the doctor was done with his routine check-up and the nurse with the usual injections, I was lying on my bed, blank as always. But now I could touch and feel things. The lady occupied a chair beside me. She started caressing my hand and her behaviour was edgy, fidgety. My eyes were shut and mouth sealed. All I could do was to drift with the flow. She started gently fondling my palms and I was immediately aroused, being in the field for long, deprived of a woman's touch. This pleasure was comfort on a battlefront. Her hands were soft and full. Slowly she placed her face on my palm; I began to feel her warm skin. She must be a beautiful woman. She had large eyes and a pointy nose. Her luscious lips sucked my fingers as she started gasping. I slid my hands along her neck, stroking the curvaceous body. The contours were accentuated around her bosoms and she had a very well-defined rear. As I was unable to reach far, she came closer and swayed herself to provide me a thorough touch of her shapely body. I was engrossed in the exploits but there was a major conflict between the male and the humane inside me. For the alpha male, being the character he's supposed to be, it was impossible to decline such a prospect but the humane in me defied the temptation. I couldn't venture beyond this, could not take advantage of a woman only because she had mistaken me for somebody else. No. I am not built this way. I backed out with an uneasy grunt. She immediately realized my discomfort and stopped her advances.

'Sorry, Mazhar, I know you are in a lot of pain. I shouldn't be doing this. But you know how much I love you and it's been so many months you were away from me. I will wait for you to be fit again. My love is strong, will wait for my time.'

She lay down on the little space on my bed. I put my arm across and embraced her. The body warmth was comforting. The moment transported me to memories.

CHAPTER 6

January 2005

As the company captain in the final year, I was responsible for the supplies of the whole academy. To hone our management skills, a team was formed every three months which managed all the provisions required for the academy. The NDA mess was one of the largest in the world, providing for almost 2,400 cadets four times in a day, with no compromise in quality. This particular month my team was in charge of coordinating with vendors, planning stock, preparing menu. Though this was a routine activity, it was humungous work at the back end to make sure every meal was delivered on time and tasted the best. One of these days, the rice served was of a substandard quality, which made the warden mad at the administration team. As I was the company captain, the onus in turn was mine. The vendor was summoned immediately. Furious, I resolved to cancel all his contracts for the rest of the year and tarnish his reputation beyond repair so he could never procure another contract. The next day, I was playing the role of the captain to its fullest, all ready to blast the vendor. Waiting for him in the company captain's chamber with the chef and other members, I was authorized to speak and take action on behalf of the academy. I was raging with fury.

The time scheduled was 11a.m. There was a knock on the door, and I thundered, 'Come in.'

The doors opened; along with the breeze walked in an angel. There was radiance from the door as she entered; the face was not visible, but the sculpted figure was impossible to ignore. Flaunting an angelic body in a short kurti paired with skintight denims, she made all eyes sparkle. The lady was tall, light-skinned, crystal-eyed with waist-long tresses flowing along her sides; she was an absolute diva. My eyes were glued, staring at her like an awestruck child, until an ogre following her greeted me. Abruptly, the harsh real world woke me. The next few hours were spent trying to understand what went wrong with the supply of rice, but the inferno had fizzled out. The gorgeous lady extinguished the blaze inside. Finally, we continued the contract, asking for a visit to the vendor's facility to examine and approve. The following day we went to the supplier's warehouse and there was the girl of my dreams. In the coming weeks, I unearthed reasons to visit the granaries in exchange for meeting the pretty girl. As I dressed prim and proper to impress the lady, my magic was working. I instructed the supplier that if he intended to continue the contract, the academy would need dedicated personnel to interact and coordinate with. I anticipated she would be handed the responsibility. In subsequent meetings, I discovered that she was the businessman's daughter and not an employee. Saakshi was her name and it seemed my world was complete. Training in the most prestigious academy of the country to serve in one of world's most coveted armies and the woman of my dreams was right in front of me. My universe was realized.

In subsequent days, she invited me to accompany her to her college's annual festival. She made a special request that I dress like an officer for the evening. Sundays were usually a holiday in the final years so I grabbed the opportunity to spend an evening with her.

'AD, Saakshi hBeyasrele Beyinvitedrele Beyusrele tBeyorele hBeyerrele cBeyollegerele. ShBeyouldrele wBeyerele gBeyorele?' (AD, Saakshi has invited us to her college. Should we go?)

'DBeyefinitelyrele.' (Definitely.) AD concurred.

Dressed in my full glory, I headed out with AD to meet the lady, feeling nervous and excited simultaneously. She was at the college gates, looking ravishing. The smile on her face when she spotted me in the crowd was worth dying for, a thousand times over. The lady had already swept me off my feet and today she made me her devotee. She was the most beautiful girl in that horde, with boys drooling all over her. AD and I were nervous getting in this crowd after being alienated from civilian student life for more than three years. It was a different setting altogether. There was chaos, randomness, confusion, and madness. Nothing seemed to be organized but everybody was having a gala time. We were out of our comfort zone so we decided to stick to the girl. She held my hand all throughout, flaunting me proudly to her world. I did receive some stern looks from the boys, but they were wise enough not to mess with an army officer. Her friends were flirtatious enough, trying to hit on AD, but he was rather shy of the attention. We spent too much time in a disciplined environment with big brawny men around. This was new but it was fun; it took a little while for us to get accustomed. As the evening passed, we got into the groove and started enjoying these new people and environs. AD particularly got very cozy with one of Saakshi's friends.

He enquired, 'Suri, cBeyanrele BeyIrele flBeyirtrele wBeyithrele thBeyisrele gBeyirlrele?' (Suri, can I flirt with this girl?)

'AD, yBeyourele dBeyontrele nBeyeedrele Beymyrele pBeyermissionrele.' (AD, you don't need my permission.)

As the music started blaring, the world around forgot discipline and regulations, and above all, they forgot they were humans. Chaos reigned supreme. Saakshi and I decided to escape from this wilderness.

Pune is a beautiful town and a heaven for students. It is a calm, serene, lazy, and 'I mind my own business' place. This college was located on the foothill of a temple mountain. The pathway leading to the temple was deserted in the evening. We hopped, jumped, and ran away from the crowds into solitude. I held her hand throughout the adventure and she gladly accepted it. We ventured to a cliff at a distance from the pathway to a corner of the hill, overlooking the college. The temperatures were pleasant on the heights. I was trained for this trek but Saakshi was tired and shivery. It was pitch-dark around. I held her hand, pulled her closer. The moonlight was glowing on her skin and her crystal eyes were shining like diamonds. She hugged me tight and I embraced her. It was a simple expression of love. The firm grip that she held me with communicated that she never wanted me to go, and my warm grasp conveyed that I would always be there for her. It was a brief moment and I was submerged for life.

After three rigorous years at NDA, it was time for the next move. True armed combat enthralled me.

The choppy seawater was not to my liking. Many fellow cadets were fascinated with flying and wanted to join the air force. But for me it was always the basic form of warfare. Humans are land animals. We are designed and evolved to fight on land. Any victory or defeat is finally conceded on the expanse of land. I had decided to opt for the Indian Army. AD was interested in leading the life of a spy. Like always, he was one of the top performers at the academy and was shortlisted for the Presidents Gold Medal in Overall Order of Merit. In open interactive sessions, he used to express his admiration towards the secret service. After his impeccable performance at the academy, our superiors recommended him for R&AW (Research & Analysis Wing). He was one of the very few cadets who was privileged to join the prestigious services. His accomplishments spoke volumes. After the glorious pass-out parade, we separated for the first time after twenty-one years of togetherness. With tears in our eyes, I proceeded towards the esteemed Indian Military Academy (IMA) in Dehradun, and he went on to pursue his dream of becoming a secret agent.

CHAPTER 7

January 2007

I was privileged to receive the Sword of Honor at the Indian Military Academy (IMA), Dehradun. The last twelve months at this academy were easier than the NDA. The regular graduates from civilian colleges who joined the IMA to serve the country had a difficult time altering their lifestyles. Many of us who continued from the NDA enjoyed watching the newbies' struggle. We had been through the drill for more than three years. It was relatively easier for us to excel. The training was more or less the same. The pass-out parade at the IMA was also a glittering ceremony and the day arrived for the real deal.

My first posting was on the Nathu La pass along the Sino-Indian border. After reaching Sikkim, I was posted in the army transit camp. Here I learned that the Indian army was actively involved in civilian activities as well. It was not a very sensitive war zone but sharing a border with one of sour neighbors (China) was not a very relaxed proposition. The freezing winds, the snow-capped peaks, the dense forest mountains made a very pleasant setting. I was a young recruit enjoying every bit of this adventure. Almost all soldiers at the camp used to pray to Baba Harbhajan every morning and visit the shrine of this holy man whenever possible. I observed that this god-man Harbhajan Singh was devoid of any particular religion, and army men of every faith and belief used to visit his samadhi. I was inquisitive to know more.

Born in the village of Browndal in the Kapurthala district of Punjab, Harbhajan Singh enlisted in the army at an early age and was posted on the hazy mountains of the Sino-Indian border near Nathu La Pass. On October 4, 1968, sepoy Harbhajan Singh was escorting a mule caravan from his battalion headquarters in Tekula to Dengchukla; he fell into a fast-flowing stream and drowned. The search for his body continued for a couple of days but was abandoned because of bad weather. Then Harbhajan Singh appeared in the dream of one of the sepoys of his unit, Pritam Singh. In the dream, he informed about his death and the exact spot where his body would be found. He requested for a samadhi to be built there. Pritam Singh dismissed the dream as an illusion of his grief for losing a friend. This wasn't considered serious until another member of the same unit had the same dream. Same dream, same instructions, same assurances—everything was similar, to the letter. It seemed a supernatural quirk that two people could hallucinate the same sequence of events. Taking cognizance, a search party was dispatched to the spot as described in the dream where they traced the late sepoy Harbhajan Singh's corpse. He was cremated with full military honors, and a samadhi was made at Chhokya Chho. In the dream, he assured them that he would always guard the area and never give up being a soldier. Soon, reports of a man seen patrolling the border began trickling in. Soldiers deployed in the area would talk of sightings of a lone uniformed man on a horse. Forces on the other side of the border confirmed these reports and claimed that they too had seen the ghost rider. Over the years, soldiers in the area began seeing Harbhajan Singh in their dreams, where he informed them about voids along the border or a lapse in security from where the Chinese could attack. His instructions generally proved to be accurate and the legend of Baba Harbhajan Singh grew. Legend also said that in the event of a confrontation between India and China, Baba would warn the Indian soldiers a few days in advance of any impending attack. During flag meetings between the two nations at Nathu La, the Chinese set a chair aside to honor Baba Harbhajan Singh, who had since become a saint.

Baba is respected and worshiped by every army man in Sikkim. They believe Baba would forecast accident in the valley much ahead of the happening. The story was too intriguing and I immediately decided to seek the blessings of the holy saint. The samadhi is reconstructed at the junction of Kupup–Gnathang road and the pathway leading to Menmoichu Lake as a part of the watershed memorial complex. I took the next transport to the shrine and was amazed to see a massive structure. Baba Mandir is a three-room structure. The central room has a large portrait of the baba along with other Hindu deities and Sikh gurus. To the right of the central room is the personal room of Baba. The room has all the household belongings required for daily activities, from clothes, shoes, toothbrush, and a neat sleeping bed; it is all well maintained. The uniforms are ironed and shoes polished ready for use. Caretakers of the samadhi swear that each morning, the bed sheets would be crushed as if someone had slept in the bed the previous night and the carefully polished boots would be soiled and covered with mud.

I was never a believer in any such supernatural legends but was not an atheist as well. Over the years, I learned to respect others' faith. Rarely did I toe the line but never offended or upset anybody's belief. But this year 2007, in the month of September, an experience altered my belief in mystical legends. On September 14 of every year, prior to the year 2007, Baba Harbhajan Singh proceeded on his month-long leave. Accompanied by a JCO, a subedar, and an orderly, a trunk full of Baba's personal belongings and a portrait boarded a train from Jalpaiguri to Kapurthala to reach his native village. A berth was kept reserved and empty throughout the journey. This year (14/7/2007) nothing of the journey was planned. There was unrest at the camp and the shrine. The government had reportedly retired the Baba and his pension was curtailed. But this did not stop the god-man from his predictions. He appeared in the dream of some soldier but this time he assured India a World Cup triumph. I was surprised to hear such a prediction and dismissed it as a hoax from people trying to keep Baba's legacy alive. Since the government retired him, I assumed he was now making predictions of international events to gain publicity. The desperation of Baba's followers was amusing.

It was the inaugural tournament of a new T20 format of cricket. India was sending across its youngest team ever. Indian cricket was passing through a nasty phase with four captains replaced in the space of two years. The veterans like Sachin, Dravid, and Ganguly opted out, leaving the team in tatters. The only names that could ring a bell were Sehwag, Gambhir, Yuvraj, and Dhoni. The average age of the Indian team was around twenty-two years, captained by Mahendra Singh Dhoni, known only for his prior two innings. India had no experience of playing this format of game. Before embarking on this journey,

India had played only one T20 contest. Dhoni was captaining a very young side and the country had minimal expectations of the team. A day prior to Baba Harbhajan's annual journey, 14 September, he appeared in the dream of some soldier and predicted India's World Cup triumph. Well, it was rather optimistic. Baba's journey was not scheduled for the year but it was the day of the India–Pakistan match, 14 September 2007. I was always a cricket enthusiast but since Tendulkar was not playing this tournament, the excitement had subsided. On the thirteenth, sepoy Arvind Singh spoke about the dream and India's victory. The Pakistan fixture must win the game for India stay alive in the tournament. I watched it in the army barracks with the whole company cheering for the country. The match ended in a tie and proceeded into the bowl outs. For the first time, such novel rules were implemented in the game of cricket, and surprisingly, India won the nail-biting encounter. Baba's followers were ecstatic, celebrating as if India had won the World Cup. I was happy but the young team deserved the applause. Baba had predicted the World Cup and not just one match. But the whole episode invoked much interest in the tournament so I decided to follow it diligently. The whole country, including me, was astonished to find this team in the finals, and yet again, the opponents were arch-rivals Pakistan. The whole country had come to a standstill when the game began. It's not a happy disclosure, but we were the weakest at the borders during the course of such matches. If China had attacked at this time, we would have been sitting ducks all locked into a small dingy room watching the live telecast. But thanks to the Almighty, the Chinese never understood cricket.

The final lived up to its expectations and the match boiled down to the last over. Pakistan needed thirteen runs in six deliveries. With an in-form batsman like Misbah-ul-Haq at the crease, it seemed like a cakewalk for the Pakis. But the whole country was praying otherwise. I recollected Baba Harbhajan's prophecy and prayed to him that if he existed somewhere, India would win this battle. And as luck would have had it, Dhoni handed the ball to the most inexperienced bowler. Joginder Sharma was a neophyte who had never participated in any nerve-wracking games before. India's only slim chance was that Pakistan was batting with its last wicket. Misbah had scored a half-century in the earlier game against India and was in a rollicking form. But Dhoni trusted his instincts. Joginder Sharma started with a wide ball, reducing the target to twelve runs in six balls. The whole country was reeling under pressure, and Dhoni ran up to his bowler to offer him some advice. Joginder's shoulders were drooping; the team dugout was hanging their heads. Misbah was practicing his next shot, looking relaxed and confident. The next ball was a dot, providing the whole country some relief, definitely some confidence to the bowler. And as luck would have it, in the next delivery, Joginder bowled the worst ball of his life, delivered a simple full toss which Misbah lynched on to and set it sailing over the ropes for a six. The target was reduced to six runs in four balls, an absolute easy achievable target. The entire country lost faith and so did I. All these god-men as just a farce, I concluded. The Pakistan supporters at the stadium went berserk celebrating a victory. Nothing on the planet is more depressing and saddening than to see India being defeated by Pakistan in a cricket match. The whole army barrack was pin-drop silent. Nobody spoke a word. The game was almost lost but Dhoni never looked defeated. He went back to his bowler and instilled faith in him with some magical words. Scoring six runs in four balls was just a mere formality. Joginder was on his mark, striding to bowl; Misbah was positive as always. I couldn't garner the courage to watch, prayed to Babaji once again.

'If you really exist, show me your presence.'

And who knows what influenced Misbah's decision; he attempted an over-ambitious scoop over the short fine leg and mistimed his shot. The ball flew up in the air and landed safely in Sreesanth's hands. Pakistan lost the wicket and also the match. More importantly, India won the World Cup. After 1983, after twenty-four years, Indians were the world champions. The entire country went crackers. I closed my eyes and thanked Babaji.

CHAPTER 8

November 2009

Each passing day was a victory and accomplishment. After a major injury, the road to recovery is one of the most amazing experiences. The patient has short definite goals. One day, the intent is to mobilize an arm while some day, it may be to take baby steps. The person tends to forget his aspirations, his ambitions garnered all through life. The only objective is to be fit and healthy again. In this sojourn, simple little feats deliver unparalleled happiness. One of such mornings when the doctor paid a visit, he was accompanied with a lady doctor who must have been a physiotherapist. She made me sit up and perform some exercises. Being bedridden for almost two months, my muscles were in limbo and it was very difficult to execute simple movements. My body had been through a lot of torture but my mind was determined. The physio recommended that I begin with modest exercises along with a small walk. I was desperately awaiting this moment. The next day, I requested the person aiding me to help me walk. He got me on my feet and the joy was indescribable. I felt like a toddler. With the bandages still wrapped around my face, it was a tad difficult but my training was to adapt to adversities. It was claustrophobic being confined in the same room, so in the next few days, I requested my wife to walk me outside. She held my hand as we stepped out of that room. Sniffing fresh air after months was great. As we were strolling, there was a lot of activity in the corridor. It felt pleasant to experience the world around. I could sense that the people were scared to see a bandaged face walking around. It was audible in their chatter as they made way for me. I was like a walking mummy. The sound of a television pulled me towards it, keen to know my whereabouts and happenings. I was confused why none of my family members had come to revive me. But such is the army life. I settled myself close to the television set, trying to hear the news attentively.

It was difficult to understand the language at first. I tried to concentrate; after a while, it made sense. The newsreader was talking in Urdu about the turmoil in the Balochistan area, the American drone bombings, political chaos in Pakistan, and the ongoing test series between New Zealand and Pakistan. Though all the events seemed interesting as I had been dead for two months now, I wondered why she was reading out news of Pakistan. There was a section of Kashmiris who supported Pakistan but why would they watch such news in a military hospital? Towards the end of the news hour, the woman bid good bye and mentioned the name of the station as *Islamabad*!

I was flabbergasted.

Islamabad? Am I in Islamabad? Am I in Pakistan? Am I being treated in a Pakistani military hospital? Do these people mistake me as a Pakistani? What on earth is going around here? Where am I?

I was dumbstruck, frozen in my position for the next few minutes. My wife shrugged me asking to get back to the room. In a state of shock, I wanted to shout out, exclaim to the world, disclose my real identity. But the bandages were not helping much. One moment I was angry and, in the next, helpless. All I needed in this hour of agony was Saakshi's embrace and to cry like a baby in her arms.

Sensing trouble, my so-called wife screamed for help; many ward boys and nurses came rushing to aid. They tried to wake me but I was inert, stagnant. It was impossible to accept the fact of being in Pakistan, mistaken as a Paki. I walked back to my room like a corpse with an empty head. The whole effort of waking back to life appeared to be a waste. What if these people discovered who I was? What would I reason when they saw me after the bandages were removed? Would they kill me? What about the family that's been caring and praying about me for all this while? What would happen to them? Back on my hospital bed, I had to recollect how I ended up in Pakistan.

CHAPTER 9

September 2009

After postings in the north-east corridor for a few years, it was time for the true calling. Many of my colleagues were posted in Kashmir, making me desire the same for long. When my transfer orders arrived to this dream destination, I was over the moon. Well, the family and Saakshi were not very excited, but they always were aware of my desire to serve in Kashmir. We had a few get-togethers with close family and friends before I embarked the journey. Trivedi, Jagga were already posted in the state. I was longing to meet them and relive some old memories. Landing in Kashmir was like a dream come true. Every individual who enrolls for the defense services fantasizes of his posting in Kashmir. It is a 24/7 live combat zone where everybody is a part of some action. I reported at the army headquarters in Srinagar and was privileged to be posted in Poonch.

Poonch is a beautiful town in the Indian-administered Kashmir, around 1,000 meters above the sea level bound by the LOC from three sides. The Pir Panjal Range separates the Poonch Valley from the Kashmir Valley. Surrounded by majestic snow-capped mountains, sprinkled with lovely lakes, flourishing in fruits, flowers, forests, and ancient historical monuments, the Poonch district offers the perfect backdrop for holidays. Poonch has witnessed history. When Alexander invaded India, he fought a war with Porus on the Dravabhisar plains of this region. It also finds special mention in the tales of the Chinese traveler Huein Tseng. After politicians defined the border between India and Pakistan, this place was largely hurt. Pakistan put up watch posts on all sides. Although it is an India-administered region, Pakistanis stare from everywhere.

The first few days were spent getting accustomed to the weather and new friends. I was a captain reporting to Major Thatte. The Paki camps were visible right across the border, a difficult proposition watching the enemy sitting gladly on our land which was handed over to them only because some politicians pulled a line across. It was fire raging inside with snowy temperatures outside. With winter's setting in, the nights were freezing. Indiscreet firing was an added attraction. Every moment, you had to be vigilant. A stray bullet might hit you for no good reason. Though the situation was at ceasefire, the army was always on high alert. The noose slackened during night hours. In these times, the infiltrators took advantage and sneaked in. As an outsider, I assumed anybody who crossed the border was a terrorist. But spending time on the ground taught me it's not just armed terrorists that cross borders. These places are a hotbed for the drug cartel. The quantity of narcotics that is traded across this LOC is mind-boggling. Moreover, it is widely believed that forces guarding the borders from both sides are hand in glove with these traders. Such traders are locals who earn only a fraction of the pie. They are miniscule couriers for big mafias who run the show. This makes the atmosphere around the LOC and at the army camp nerve-wracking.

The month of October was coming to a closure. The night vigil was my task. With a few soldiers, I used to venture into the dark, visiting bunkers along the LOC. These visits were not casual strolls. We had to infuse enthusiasm, inspire, motivate the soldier who stands in bitter cold, making sure his countrymen had a sound sleep. As we were passing from point 5387 towards 5388, my sepoy, Havaldar Yadav, noticed some movement along the barb fences. He was a veteran who had spent decades along these dreaded lines. Picking up the clamor, he started sprinting towards it.

'Ghooskhoriyenn . . . Aatankwaadi!' (Terrorists!)

He screeched. My team responded in a split second as we followed Yadav. Hearing our voices, the infiltrators were alarmed, leading to a commotion. Some of the terrorists ran towards the Indian side of the border while a few escaped on the opposite side. The fleeing group was aghast at their foiled attempt and started shooting randomly. One of the shots hit Yadav and he collapsed. This was way beyond my tolerance. I instructed a section of my team to follow the infiltrators on Indian soil while I decided to pursue Yadav's shooters on the Paki side. I was raging to bring them to justice. Along with Havaldar Sharma, I entered Pakistan soil, chasing the assailants. The terrain was similar but they were well versed with the turf. They jumped, hopped, crawled but we were equally determined. During pursuit, one of them collapsed in a pit. Sharma and I reached and shot him in the head. We spotted two more of them running away. I was in no mood for giving up. The forest was pitch-dark and dead silent. The hunt continued. Following them, we reached a small hamlet along the border. They had taken shelter in one of the houses. The chase had me fuming. We frantically searched every hut. Hiding behind a cattle shed, they fired at us. We took cover behind a cart to retaliate. Sharma attacked one of the terrorists, and hand-to-hand combat ensued while another escaped. I joined in to finish off the captor. The escapee disappeared into the forest again. I looked into Sharma's eyes. He was livid.

'Sahib, Yadav aur mein 8 saal se saath mein duty kar rahe hain. Mein uske murderer ko nahi chhodunga.' (Sir, Yadav and I have worked together for eight years. I won't let his murderer escape.)

And he disappeared into the woods. We were already on Pak soil, had slaughtered two of them. I was reluctant but Sharma had disappeared, with no option but to trail him. Not far away from the village was a Pak army bunker. We quickly transformed into the stealth mode. I was unwilling to attack an army camp, since that would mean a direct attack and dishonoring the ceasefire. I restrained Sharma and, being a responsible officer, made him realize his duty towards the country. He got back his composure to understand the complications. We decided to head back. But by then it was too late. The Pak army had discovered that some infiltrators had infringed upon their land. We could see them grouping around, hearing the officers' instructions. Suddenly we were on the wrong side of the law and hunted. We had to get back. We decided to lie low and move back to our side, hiding. But the Pakis gathered fast with their search parties everywhere. We had to do something. We couldn't wait to get hounded. I closed my eyes for a moment, took a deep breath, and contemplated. There were more than 100 Pak soldiers on a lookout in the woods. My country was at least two miles away. The sniffer dogs were closing in. We could risk hiding and sneaking. But if caught, we had a bleak chance of making it back alive. The awkward queries for the superiors, the media bashing of the army was an added deterrent. Sharma had fear in his eyes but was hard like a soldier.

'Sahab aap boliye kyaa karna hai? Aap kahe toh surrender ho jaate hai. Lekin inkaa bharosaa nahi. Zinda rakhenge yaa nahi.' (Sahib, you instruct what next? If you command, we can also surrender. But we can't be sure if they would put us to trial or kill us.)

I was nervous but could not afford to be timid. I ventured a few meters towards home but the hunters were fast approaching. We were like fish in the net, waiting to be pulled out. And in the next moment, I started walking towards the army bunker.

Sharma exclaimed, 'Sahab kahan jaa rahe ho sahib? Wahan dushman desh hai.' (Where are you heading, sahib? It's enemy that side.)

I continued marching towards the enemy dugout, determined to find my way home. Sharma trailed me like an obedient soldier. Closing in on the trench, we observed it was almost unoccupied. All the soldiers were out in the forest scouting for us. I decided to seize the opportunity and peeped inside. One soldier was holding guard with an officer inside. An army jeep was standing ready. Pointing towards the jeep, I signaled Sharma that we would overpower the Pakis, take the jeep to make it to the border. We sneaked in closer. From striking distance, Sharma leaped on the guard, taking him down. The soldier was a stalwart, refusing to surrender meekly. He retaliated with full vigor, turning the brawl into a full-fledged no-holds-barred wrestling encounter, the difference being that both the fighters were pursuing the other's death. Ruthless, brutal, merciless, they both were hitting each other with anything they could lay their hands upon. Blood-spattering, hard-hitting, it was a bloodbath. I kept a watch on the officer inside; since he was armed, he could have shot Sharma. Hearing chaos, he emerged from the bunker, looking for noises. I pounced upon him. While all of us were involved in the fistfights, within moments there was a gunshot, and all four of us stood still. Sharma grabbed a gun and killed his opponent. The Pak soldier collapsed lifeless. The officer I was battling froze like a statue.

He exclaimed, 'Tumne hamare sar zameen par iskaa khoon kiyaa hai. Hum tumko nahi chhodenge.' (You have killed a soldier on our soil. We won't let you go.)

Sharma shot and bored a hole right in the middle of the officer's eyes. I was petrified. This was my first encounter on a war front. I wanted to avenge Yadav's killers but suddenly we were the criminals. We entered Pak border and killed two of their officers. But this was no time for regret. We had to move on. Hearing gunshots at the bunker, a few search parties started moving towards us. The look in Sharma's eyes was unapologetic. I instructed him to take the jeep. We were mounting the dead bodies into the vehicle when Sharma suggested, 'Sahab hum inke saath kapde change karte hain. Phir inke logo ne humein dekh bhi liyaa toh pehchanenge nahi.' (Sahib, let's exchange clothes with these soldiers. So even if the search parties catch up, they won't identify us in the night.)

I concurred and we quickly exchanged clothes. Loading the bodies in the rear, we set off. Heading towards the border, we encountered one search party. They recognized the jeep and saluted me, mistaking me as their officer. The dark of the night helped us camouflage. Sharma stopped the vehicle.

'Khoj jaari rakho. Yahin kahin hongey saale harami. Dhoondo unko aur khatam kar do.' (Look out for the rascals. Find them and kill them.)

I instructed them to find me and kill me. The soldiers were already in a tizzy; they did not bother much and continued with the pursuit. We sped off towards the border. It was not far. Seeing the shimmering lights relieved us a bit. As we approached the border, we heard voices from the Indian side.

'Aap border area mein hain. Aapki gaadi ghooma lijiye.' (You are approaching Indian border. Turn around.) 'This is a warning.'

The Indians were seeing us as Paki soldiers driving a Paki jeep. They treated this as an attack. They warned us again to stop. But we could not turn back and surrender ourselves to the Pakis. Instructing Sharma to continue, I stood on top of the jeep waving, shouting. The Indian soldiers were clueless. For them, we were an enemy vehicle trying to barge into their country. As we neared the border, they warned us again. We were relentless. They fired some warning shots. We were being fired upon by our own countrymen, and in the last few meters, I saw a soldier aiming a bazooka. He hit his target. All I remember, the jeep exploded with four bodies flung and scattered in the air.

Since I was alive, I observed the officer whose clothes I donned that night was Mazhar. He was a major in the Pak army. He was a responsible officer, a doting father, and a loving husband. And to my good fate, our blood groups matched.

CHAPTER 10

December 2009

My life was a satire: nursed back to life by the family of an officer whom I killed cold-bloodedly, blown away in an enemy vehicle by my own countrymen, resurrected in an enemy country. I was helpless, weak, injured. My face was bandaged and I didn't know how I looked.

With the passing days, I was regaining my strength and fitness. Though incapable to see or speak, my other functions were operating over capacity. All day long, I used to scheme in my head various options to go back home.

Winters were pleasant in Islamabad. The cold weather made it comfortable in these bandages. Now I could get up, move around, hear people talking, and understand their life and activities. I was learning and training myself for the days to come. I graduated to small quantities of liquid food, juices; daal paani, from straws in between the bandages was my diet. Feeling stronger by the day, my brain was working twice as efficiently. One of such days, Dr Taufiq, on his daily morning visits informed me, 'Major Sahab, you are doing exceedingly well and your recovery has been exceptional, I believe we can remove the bandages in the first week of January. So you will have a new year with a new life. Have a good New Year's Eve, and Allah hafiz.'

The excitement was palpable. I made sure to hear news daily to be updated for the new life. It would be ridiculous to run back to my country screaming and explaining who I am. Nobody believed it the night I was blown away; they wouldn't even consider it this time. This family who had helped me survive, got me back on my feet was like my own. I held a moral responsibility towards them and could not just leave them in the middle of nowhere. It would shatter them and their belief in God. Moreover, the Pak government would add fuel to this fire, questioning them about me. No, I was not built this way. I would go back to my motherland but would not abscond. I resolved to deliver and then leave with grace. The New Year calls for the life of Major Mazhar Qureshi, Pakistan Army. Capt. Rajeev Suri, Indian Army, takes a break. He will arrive when he will succeed.

This was the first New Year's Eve spent on a hospital bed. My foster family was along for this novel celebration. Owing to a speedy recovery, I had started consuming semisolid foods. My new loving wife prepared one of the finest paaya soups for the celebrations. The kids were around to add joy to the occasion. Many of my subordinates visited for the New Year greetings, a happy event in these times helped me train for days to come. I was memorizing names, ranks, learning the language, lifestyle all under the pretense.

One sunny cold morning, after my daily chores, Dr Taufiq came in for routine check-up accompanied by a senior doctor. After discussing for a while, Dr Taufiq revealed today was the penultimate day of these confinements. The docs were going to release me from bandages after months of captivity. I was anxious to see the world and, above all, desperate to see myself after this life-changing experience. The delight and the scare were of equal proportions. What if these Pakis discovered my true identity? Was I Rajeev Suri or was Mazhar my new face? I was dying in anticipation. The doctors gathered around while a nurse started undressing the bandages. My heart was pounding as the knots loosened. The family was standing beside, awaiting the big moment. The noose slackened. Dr Taufiq instructed me to keep the eyes closed. Since they were devoid of light for months, too much brightness could damage them. My wife's sobbing was audible. I was unsure whether they were crying of joy or fear. There was no immediate fright or shock. The doctors sounded pleased with their efforts. They directed the nurse to close windows and pull the curtains to keep the sharp sun out. Dr Taufiq called for a mirror. The nurse removed cotton placed on top of my eyes, asking me to open them slowly. I preferred to look around before looking at myself. A beautiful woman was crying, holding two angelic kids, a team of doctors watching cautiously. I looked at them and smiled. It was difficult to smile since all the muscles were reconstructed; I was not smiling like always. The sneer was stretched on the left. I blinked but couldn't shut my eyes completely. Tried frowning from the nose but it did not respond easily. Then I gathered courage to look at myself. The nurse was holding the mirror for me; I was staring at a complete stranger. Who was this fella? My reflection was a sham and fake. I was disturbed but the world around me was happy. They were congratulating each other on this success. Though I was happy to be alive, this was not me. The new me had a broader, broken nose, injured left eye, and a deep gash running all across the face. There were stitch marks all through the jaw line, and the hair line had receded deep. It was scary to look at this face which was not mine, to live a life of a Pak major, which was not mine. But this was the fact of life; I had to consent and continue. Taufiq held the pic of Mazhar beside my face and bragged, 'We've done a good job, right, ma'am? We tried to reconstruct the new face as close as possible to the original one. And I suppose we have accomplished our goal. What say?'

My wife concurred with tears in her eyes and a smile on her lips. I hugged the kids, not sure whether I was happy or sad.

CHAPTER 11

January 2010

I deliberately constrained my conversations. The dialect was completely novel for me. Luckily the language was not. Barring a few words here and there, India Pakistan speak similar language. But I was picking it up, learning it gradually. Initially, I conversed only with my family. They readily accepted that injuries had changed my voice tone. The kids were wonderful and the family was charming. In the last few days of my hospital stay, I was informed that some senior officers would be visiting me. I was looking forward to this meet. Interacting with Pak army officers on a different perspective would be exciting. One of my early morning walks, the military hospital was being cleaned and polished beyond usual. Lieutenant General Khalid Mahmood and Major General Iqbal Khan along with some senior officers were expected to visit the hospital. I immediately realized they were coming to see me. Instead of making me nervous and awkward, this new life excited me. I had to be cautious to tread this track. This was my first test of being Major Mazhar Qureshi. I was ready to mould myself into the character. We all always want to become something we are not, an actor, a spy, a sportsperson, all in real life. Destiny bestowed upon me this opportunity to enact everything in one go.

An Indian army captain at heart was mistaken as a Pak major in person. Now the real game began.

The officers arrived in full vigor along with their entourage. My wife and the kids were present to welcome them. The officers enquired about my condition and recovery. Dr Taufiq updated them while I nodded my head in agreement. Lieutenant General Mahmood thundered, 'The army and the country are very proud of you, Mazzi. You have demonstrated to the world what this great Pakistan army stands for. You not only managed to finish the Indian infiltrators, you also send them a strong signal not to mess with us again. Look at the Indian doublespeak. Now they are accusing us of breaching the border first that night. There were a lot of diplomatic accusations and counter-allegations after your incident, but the international media upheld our version. You were the only survivor from that jeep explosion. All other occupants of the vehicle were charred beyond recognition. Yes, we lost a soldier but we won a moral fight. We proved Indians also violate the ceasefire and infringe the LOC. Nobody knows what transpired that night but we are proud of you for slaying two of them. The Indians are felicitating the captain whom you killed in the encounter. This is ridiculous. An irresponsible officer who ventured onto our soil is being honored. I recently heard he is going to be decorated with some peacetime award. Outrageous! To defy these Indians we are also considering you for a high gallantry award, we will confer upon you a wartime award. They believe it was an encounter during peacetime but they should understand that stepping on Pakistan soil is no peacetime. We will show them what we are. Take care, Mazzi. You are done with your hard work. Now it's time to reap the benefits. Have a wonderful recovery and I will see you when you resume office.'

I didn't display too many emotions after his enlightening speech. Somehow, I managed a weak smile as they marched off. I had to interpret the information he shared. Firstly, it was very distressing to hear that I was the lone survivor. So Havaldar Sharma was dead for sure. Secondly, the Indian government had conferred an award for the captain slain in the attacks. And thirdly, I was being considered for an award here in Pakistan.

CHAPTER 12

Homecoming

The hospital deemed me fit for discharge in the next few days. After I had spent months in this place, it had become my abode. Dr Taufiq and the staff were more than family. I was very comfortable in these environs, skeptical moving into Mazhar's home. It sent jitters down my spine. Like the past few months, all I could do was follow instructions that this world and this life drafted for me. But the real quest had arrived, asking for a makeover. All of my family showed up to ferry me home. It was a very emotional farewell and finally the journey to my new existence with a new identity commenced. A Paki army soldier was driving a Paki army car transferring an Indian army officer to the home of a Paki army officer. Paradox!

The drive astonished me. Islamabad was surprisingly a very well-planned place. Contrary to the belief that most Indians have, this metropolis was way beyond my expectations. The roads were neat and clean, no hawkers on the roadside, no beggars at the signals, and a much disciplined traffic. The streets were lined with trees along both the sides and shockingly were free of potholes. This could not be Pakistan. The Indians are raised with a belief that Pakistan trails India in all aspects, but this was a major disconnect. Passing in between large government buildings was like driving in New Delhi, very similar surroundings but better drivers. We did not drive long. On a right turn, a huge board proclaimed 'E8, Army Housing Quarters'. Through the by-lanes of a neatly planned locale stood army houses very similar to India's, the senior officers with bigger houses at strategic places while trivial officers were pushed to the corners. Oversized iron gates being guarded by fit, strong army soldiers, large nameplates displaying even larger names written in brass, polished to a sparkle every day. A huge red tent was visible at some distance, with the car making headway towards it. This resembled some marriage ceremony back home. As we neared the place, a band started playing, creating an excitement amongst the crowd. I was dumbstruck, unable to respond. The doors opened up, some elderly people came rushing and hugged me, pouring their love and blessings. A few young men came forward to embrace me. Many kids who were running helter-skelter until now, came closer, kissed me, going back to their naughty ways. So similar is the Indian way of life. We have our elders who bless us, mischievous kids who continue their impish nature no matter what the occasion is, friends who always stick by, and family, who love you unconditionally. I was missing mine. This new family was nothing short of a miracle.

I was carried to my home on the first floor. My army home was full with unknown people. I played it smart, conversed very little, and lodged myself in the bedroom. Sign language with gestures let me sail through this strenuous day. Later in the evening, when crowds receded, I came out to have a look at the occupants of the house: so, Adaah, my present wife, Inshaa, my daughter, Afaaz, my son, along with an army servant. Soon we assembled at the dinner table. The family recited some prayers while I bowed my head in solidarity. It was a great homecoming, a larger-than-life experience, considering who I am. Post–dinner, I was alone, gazing at the stars, thinking about my family, Saakshi, my friends, my country. Adaah sensed the disconnect. She didn't speak much, cozied up beside me, held my hand, and rested her head on my shoulder. Deprived of this love for long, I cuddled up with Adaah to sleep like a log of wood. I purposely avoided this in the hospital, but being aloof and indifferent in the bedroom would have made things worse. It was preferable to inhabit a normal family life to diminish any suspicions.

Keen on getting fit at the earliest, I started early morning walks in the vicinity. The army colony was full of health enthusiasts. Currently the headlines flashed me. Everybody greeted to make my acquaintance. The men gazed proudly and shared a smile; the women glanced shyly and passed by with a giggle. The children were too skeptical to come forward and peeped from a distance. They seemed to be afraid of my scary scars. Many officers shook hands and confessed their appreciation of my fight and valor. They were keen to hear recitals of the incident. Every day, I was congratulated for killing myself.

The morning walks were followed by with intense physiotherapy sessions and some workouts at the gym. Suhail visited me daily. He worked with the admin department of the army stores and was hardly interested in posting at areas of conflict. He was happy leading a civilian life in the luxuries of defense services. One evening, he arrived carrying a bottle of single malt, Glenmorangie eighteen years old. I was surprised to see alcohol in these army quarters, Pakistan being an Islamic country. I was under the impression that drinking alcohol was prohibited under religious laws. But the ease with which he walked in that evening and how comfortably my family accepted it convinced me Mazhar was a regular drinker, with Suhail as his partner. Suhail requested Adaah to prepare kebabs. I was always a hungry demon in India. My mother's biryani and my wife's continental delicacies were to die for. But this was exciting: a new friend, a new life, a wonderful drink, and delicious food.

Suhail announced, 'Aaj do dost party karenge. Lets us celebrate the return of my brave friend who has shown the world the grit of the Pak army.'

Surprisingly, Adaah grabbed a small bottle of wine she had hidden in her wardrobe. I was glad this evening occurred. It was a much needed relaxant in my jumbled life. That evening we drank like a fish. Soon, Suhail's better half joined in and the women were engrossed in their wine and talks. The accompanying food was extraordinary; along with the wonderful cool breeze, it made the first happy evening in this country. I refrained from active participation, but this evening helped me gain a lot of insight into Mazhar's life. He and Suhail went to the same academy for services training. Mazhar belonged to a middle-class family and his parents were no more. He loved his family and was very possessive about his wife. He was always keen to fight on the battlefront, win wars for his country. Then Adaah pulled out the album of old photographs which helped me bridge memories. This was one of the most enlightening evenings. The conversation went on till wee hours of the morning and suddenly Suhail shot up from his seat.

'Oye tu chutti pe hai, par mujhe toh office jaana padega.' (Buddy you are on a holiday but I've a office to catch tomorrow.)

'I am going, bhai. Will see you over the weekend.'

CHAPTER 13

The Discovery of Pakistan, January 2010

I started accompanying Adaah to local markets around for grocery shopping. The traders in the vicinity acknowledged me and smiled. The vegetable vendors used to put in that extra onion or potato beyond the expected measure and boasted, 'Hammare janaab ne iss mulk kaa sar uuncha kiya hai.' (Our janaab has made this country proud.)

Adaah was loving this extra attention showered on us by the populace. The kids were heroes in their school, with teachers reciting my stories for other students. They were enjoying the limelight. We had a string of visitors every day who used to come, just linger around for no reason, ask me questions about the war, and leave. I never entertained too many of such unknown patrons, so I just communicated in gestures. But all this love and affection was completely unexpected. We Indians always had a narrow point of view about the Pakis. We imagined them to be ruthless, cruel, and brutal. But humans are humans. They love, care, feel happy, feel proud, feel hate or doubt, express anger all the same in any part of the world.

One of the evenings, an invitation card proclaimed, 'Saluting the return of the tiger from the jaws of death'.

The local council of Islamabad was celebrating an evening of song and dance, along with dinner to honor my arrival. This civilian felicitation made me nervous. It was an invitation from the city mayor, with many high-flying dignitaries expected to attend. The location said Daman-e-Koh. The family was excited with this appreciation. Everybody was eager to enjoy this grand evening and decided to buy new clothes for the gala event. Keen to discover the city, I consented to this shopping excursion. The kids and I shared equal excitement while Adaah was blooming with contentment. It was the first family outing. The car drove through the city, which made me admire it in amazement. Islamabad was one of the most beautiful cities. It offered a healthy climate, pollution-free atmosphere, plenty of water and lush green area. It was carefully planned, with wide tree-lined streets, large houses, elegant public buildings, well-organized markets / shopping centers, and isolated traffic jams. Roses, jasmine, and bougainvillea filled the parks. The car made its headway towards F7. The perfect layout of the city was genuinely appreciable and the local administration's ability to maintain it deserved applause. On the way, Adaah mentioned we were going to my favorite shopping destination.

The signboards proclaimed Jinnah Super Market, very similar to Sector 17 market of the Indian city of Chandigarh. Short three-storey buildings were neatly placed, surrounded by traffic chaos. The brands of the world graciously displayed their best. Being in the official car, we were treated respectfully by the parking attendant, but people around were howling and shouting to find a parking slot. We got down to be escorted by a soldier. The kids wandered as if the place was their backyard. I was concerned but Adaah seemed confident. 'Don't worry, they are headed to the Munchies to have their usual. Come, let's go there.' The kids were confident, roaming around freely. On the contrary, I was insecure like a baby so I preferred to stick closer to Adaah. A mesmerizing barbeque aroma attracted us. Inshaa and Afaaz were conversing with the waiters like friends, exhibiting that the family was a regular to this place. We had our snack and moved around the regular shopping places. All of the family bought clothes; Adaah pampered herself with some cosmetics and jewelry as well. In between all this, an electronics store pulled me towards it. I had been longing for a laptop of my own. Though my home had a desktop, it would be risky using it for my intentions and purposes. While I examined a few pieces, Adaah came over, admired the gadget, and took it straight over to the purchase counter. Saakshi definitely would have argued the purpose and cribbed about the cost, but Adaah interpreted me inside out and purchased the device in a moment. I was overwhelmed. Shopping trips usually end up being walking drills, thorough cardio workouts, wandering a mile and ending up buying a meter. I assumed Adaah would be a mature woman, understanding me, accepting me, but when it came to shopping, all women under the sun are the same. Though it was a very pleasant evening, it was tiring for no reason. This family loves me, I care for them, but they are not my family. It was pointless to squander energy on such trips. I had to be focused. We wrapped up the evening with a dinner at Kabul Restaurant, a simple place with mind-boggling food. The treat was summed up with a dash to the ice cream parlor, a fruit filled ice cream and a fruitful evening. Today I was armed with my first weapon to attain freedom.

CHAPTER 14

Irony of Life
(26 January 2010)

The next morning, I woke up eager to start fidgeting with the laptop. I was always a gadget freak; this was my first indulgence in the new life. Configuring the passwords and studying other settings was the first task. After the early morning routine, I spend time on Google, doing research, trying to learn things. Suddenly it struck me; the lieutenant general had mentioned that the Indian captain was being felicitated. As I was desperate to know more, Google prompted, 'Capt. Rajeev Suri awarded second highest peacetime gallantry award, the *Kirti Chakra*, posthumously.'

I drowned in grief with tears rolling from my eyes, happy, glad, and ecstatic with the fact that Saakshi and my parents would now enjoy all the benefits of a *Kirti Chakra* awardee, but also sad, gloomy, and poignant. What could be worse for an individual than being honored posthumously for his achievements and being alive reading the news, alive in an enemy country and honored for killing the officer whose life he is living? With head in my hands, I was sulking. Adaah sensed the distress and tried to console me. She was not sure of the reason but she stood by me.

The twenty-sixth of January is a day of pride for every Indian. This day the country became a republic. I remember being confused as a student whether the Independence Day on 15 August was significant or 26 January was prominent. After joining the army, the importance of a country being republic became clear. Though we were independent on 15 August 1947, the final authority came to the people of India on 26 January 1950. It was the last day of the governing ties with Britain, bringing an end to the king's reign. The authority was transferred to a representative of India. The king was replaced by the president, a quasi-emperor under whose powers the country is run by elected representatives. The president can dissolve the Lok Sabha, can declare emergencies, gives consent to money bills, can pardon a convict, apart from a lot of other authorities. And most importantly for all the defense services personnel, he/she is the supreme commander of the armed forces. Though the president has all the powers of a dictator, the only difference is that he is indirectly elected by the people. The post is the pride of every Indian. Everyone in the armed forces is excited about this day of the year. It's a day when the country displays its might, prowess, capability, potential to the world.

This was the first year, since army days, of my absence at the ceremony. I spent time searching and reading about the death of Capt. Rajeev Suri. There were many articles and a lot of skirmishes between the governments of the two countries. Both sides came forward claiming innocence, blaming the other. The Indians made it an act of valor, capturing Havaldar Trivedi's assailants and bringing them to justice. The Pakistanis made it an act of bravery where Major Mazhar stood his ground to foil an attack from the Indians. They claimed that the major was chasing a group of Indian Army intruders when the incident occurred. The major killed the infiltrators and was injured in the act. Both versions carried the fact that there were no other survivors. All other corpses were unrecognizable. Since the jeep was a Pak army jeep driven by a person in Pak army fatigues, the international media stood by Pakistan claiming there was no need for an Indian officer to wander around on Pak soil. But nonetheless, who else knew the truth other than me? I was proud of my motherland and the fact that it always propagated truth. Finally the news emerged: 'Wife of Capt. Rajeev Suri to receive the *Kirti Chakra* on this Republic Day.'

Saakshi, wife of daredevil Captain Rajeev Suri, will receive his posthumous award, the second highest gallantry award during peacetime. The captain was killed fighting with infiltrators who invaded Indian soil. The heroic captain chased the murderers and was killed when an Indian rocket was launched to stop the adventing Pakistani vehicle. Capt. Suri was an officer trained at the NDA who had served at several vital locations. He was posted in J&K only a month before his demise and was on his night vigil when the incident occurred. In the exchange of fire along with a few explosives from both the sides, three persons were killed. Two soldiers of the 58th Punjab regiment lost their lives while one Pakistani soldier was killed and one officer was grievously hurt. The body of the martyr was handed over to the army and he was cremated with full military honors. His is the only gallantry award for this year's event at the Red Fort.

I was numb, staring at my own obituary, reading about my own death, trying to let the feeling sink in. Thoughts of Saakshi and my family and the agony they must have been through invaded my mind. I was broken inside but bound to put up a brave face. Adaah recognized my uneasiness over the days. I spent most of the time on the laptop with my headphones on, listening to music, reading articles about the politics of Pakistan, the situation in various regions of the place, the army rulers, and the democracy thrashed by autocratic army commanders. I didn't want project an image like the usual dim-witted Pak army officer.

The Indian Republic Day parade was not telecast on any Paki channels. I preferred watching Indian news channels on television, to catch a glimpse of Saakshi if possible. Some Pak channels covered the news of the Indian R-Day but briefly. Surfing through the channels, I suddenly discovered an Indian news channel airing the event live. Adaah frequented the television room and was surprised to see me watching this broadcast.

She came closer and suggested, 'You have to move on and leave your past behind. You have suffered a lot, now don't trouble yourself more. You have served your country to the fullest. Mighty Allah will always be with you.'

And she switched off the television. I was infuriated, leading to the first tussle between us. Snatching the television remote from her, I put on the event, yelling at her to mind her own business. Sobbing inconsolably, she ran out of the room. I bolted the door to prevent further disturbance. The ceremony unfolded. The R-Day dignitaries arrived with the usual salutations. Finally the moment arrived; the commentator announced the gallantry award distribution. My story was recited in a few minutes. Saakshi was there, head hanging down, wiping her tears. As the narration was over, she walked to the dais. The president handed over the memento; within a few seconds, she walked back. The cameras covering the event were placed far away. I couldn't get a glimpse of her face, but my Saakshi was up there and her sorrow was conveyed. I shed tears that morning, staring at a mockery of my life. I am going back to my love, my country, I resolved.

CHAPTER 15

An Evening in Pakistan

The felicitation by the city council was scheduled on the twenty-eighth of January. After the disagreement over watching television, I purposely maintained distance from Adaah, wanting to see her reactions under difficult, strained times. But she was a wonderful lady. With people around, she behaved as if there was never any trouble between us; she smiled, cared, performed her duties diligently, but when the doors of the bedroom were bolted, she changed her colors. Though she never raised her voice or misbehaved, she communicated her displeasure. She was stone-cold, not even exchanging a glance. I was purposely being adamant and stubborn in order to gauge and understand her behavior. This was my wife, and it was evident I had to spend considerable time with the lady, win her confidence if I wanted to go back home with no regrets.

On the day of felicitation, the house was buzzing with activity. The kids were doubly excited about the event and dressed up in a flash. Since it was a civilian ceremony, the organizers had requested me to dress in civilian attire. More than happy to oblige, I decided the new Pathani suit was apt for the occasion; teaming it with a waistcoat completed the look. Adaah was also back to her routine manners, being thrilled about the evening. She took her sweet time to dress up. Every moment that she spent was worth the effort. She was always a beautiful woman, but today she was looking well-dressed, gorgeous, stunning. As she walked out of the doorway, I was staring at her in disbelief with my mouth wide open. This lovely woman had been my partner for the last few months.

The family was loaded into the official car. Traveling through the beautiful planned city of Islamabad, I tried to recollect the name of the venue. The name was a little strange, not something very common. I deliberately kept mum trying to hide my unawareness. Leaving behind city lights, we started to climb a hill. The roads were winding but well maintained. Just then Adaah tried to remind me of the times we spent on the Margalla Hills. I nodded in agreement. She reminded me: 'You remember, Mazzi, when we started dating, the place was under construction. We used to trek to reach Daman-e-Koh.'

Alas, I was aware where we were headed to. This place seemed quite endearing. The temperatures dropped as we started ascending and the sights around became pleasing. Within a short span of time we reached a stunning, picturesque location called Daman-e-Koh. There was a huge reception awaiting our arrival. The local media and organizers rushed to our car, escorting us to the stage. It was a packed event. Such attendance was not expected. I engaged with the greeting formalities but couldn't take my eyes off this scenic place.

The program began with the local politicians rendering speeches, making sure to recite my ordeal. They spoke about the India–Pakistan relations, the border tension, and the future of their country. None of these politicians had any idea of what they were trying to educate the attendees about, reminding me of mindless uneducated Indian politicians. Nonetheless, the speeches were followed by performances of school students. I was overwhelmed with the effort and profusely thanked the city council. But it constantly nagged me that all this celebration was actually meant for Mazhar. As the evening progressed, the ambiance turned enchanting. While the performances came to an end, I requested one of the organizers to take me for a guided tour around this mesmerizing place. He gladly obliged. While the snacks were flowing amongst the guests, Afaaz and I, along with an organizer, took a stroll around the park. My guide informed us: 'Janaab, this place is around 500 feet above the city of Islamabad. Apart from the usual mosques and buildings, this wide road running through the city, lined with trees on both the sides is Seventh Avenue.'

It reminded me of the Rajpath of New Delhi, India. Afaaz enthusiastically shared this was his favorite spot to watch the grandeur of Seventh Avenue. My escort continued, 'The name of this place is a combination of Urdu and Persian words: Daman, which means center, and Koh, which means hill. Daman-e-Koh, therefore, means center of the hill. It has telescopes installed to take a closer look at the city. The other side of Daman-e-Koh is a beautiful lake. Rawal Lake was an artificially built water reservoir to supply water to the twin cities of Islamabad and Rawalpindi.'

I was aware about Rawalpindi city but never knew it was very close to this place and in fact was the original city. Islamabad was built after the formation of Pakistan, when they decided to build a capital city. Seventh Avenue, the beautiful lake, and the well-equipped hilltop, the whole setting was thoroughly impressive. Adaah was busy chatting with the ladies at the event. Her face was glowing with pride and her eyes followed me anywhere I went. The kids were running around with a new bunch of friends. Everybody present for the event wanted to interact with me or the family. The men gathered around and enquired about the whole experience. I befriended some of them.

In the middle of all this chaos, a beautiful woman was constantly staring at me. She did this right from the onset of the evening. I found her gazing at me whenever we exchanged glances. She was hiding the pleasure of meeting my eyes in her sweet smile. Dressed in a traditional salwar kurta, her voluptuous body could not be contained. The assets were oozing out from the low-necked kurta and the curvaceous rear was striking. She was definitely the most gorgeous woman at the event. She too had her share of admirers. People were walking up to her, asking for autographs and clicking pictures. The vicious man in me was shaken up after a long time, desperate to know who the woman was. Passing through the crowd, some children rushed to ask for an autograph. I was baffled. My autograph was still the one of my Indian identity. This was a new life with a new character. But luckily this was not a place where the autograph had substantial significance; I scribbled my new name on the piece of paper. The lady in red grabbed this opportunity.

'Hi, I am Aafreen, I am an actress in movies. I would like to meet you sometime and know more about your whole experience. The whole country is proud of you, officer.'

She was quick to give me her contact number. My sharp memory helped me memorize it in a split second. The adrenaline was overflowing, but Adaah was watching all this interaction from a distance, keeping me in check. Nonetheless, I had the lady's contact number. In the meanwhile, a Sufi singer enthralled the audience. The beautiful evening came to a close, teaching me a few lessons. The first thing was my study of the geography of Pakistan, to know its major cities, places; secondly, I had to get used to the signature Mazhar used to operate with. With this public appearance, I knew my slumber days were over and time had arrived for real action.

CHAPTER 16

First Day at Office, February 2010

All of the country was aware of my story after the event; the newspapers were overflowing with my pictures, making me a celebrity. I was being mobbed everywhere, like a national hero. The politicians started to include me and my stories in their speeches. Some of them demanded a gallantry award for me to cash in on my popularity. My life was the talk of the town. The family was enjoying every moment, but words could hardly describe the fear in my head. Any mistake from my side would mean definite death. There was no margin for error in this land of extremists. Today they hailed me as a hero, but one error and these people wouldn't blink an eye to gouge out my eyes, feed me to their vultures.

The limelight was exciting but it made my life difficult and complicated. I had to win hearts along with my freedom to tread this high life. A regular mediocre life would make me rot in this hell. Not that this family was an agony or the life was a torture, but every moment away from my mother, my motherland, and my beloved Saakshi was a nightmare.

The officers' club in the residential area was apt for my recovery. Suhail was my constant companion. The club offered me priority treatment and care. Resurgence was firm and fast. Daily exercises along with love and care made me a healthy man within months. The day was arriving for me to don my new uniform. I informed the army about my fitness and my keenness to rejoin. I had worn a Pak army uniform on the fateful night which changed my life, though I never wanted to, but had to. Never had I imagined a day would come to flaunt a Pak army uniform. But all such materialistic attachments had to be conquered to achieve my goal. This uniform or that, I had to live a life I was destined to.

I was nervous like a kid on the first day of school, standing in front of the mirror, gazing at the uniform which was hanging neatly at its usual place. Adaah was excited about me resuming work. Suhail joined me for breakfast and accompanied me to the army headquarters. My hands and feet went cold as we neared the place. Suhail noticed this fidgety behavior. He tried to calm me with some comforting words, but was he aware of my dilemma? The vehicle parked inside the grand porch, I alighted slowly and kept low. A majestic entrance lobby had huge posters of ex–army commanders gracing the walls. The place was not very different from army offices of India. Magnificent arrival hall, long corridor, huge portraits, long lists of brave soldiers—it was very similar to what I had seen in my country. As the word spread of my arrival, there was excitement around. Many officers greeted Suhail with a desire to interact with me. But I had one simple plan: minimum interaction, minimum trouble. We walked straight into the office of Lt. Gen. Khalid Mahmood, the officer who visited me in the hospital. I fairly remembered him and as soon as we stepped inside his cabin, he sprung onto his feet and greeted me with enthusiasm.

'Welcome, my boy, welcome to the place you belong to. I am very glad to see you back on your feet and ready for action.'

I matched his energy in action displaying my eagerness to join again. We had a hearty conversation for a while. After all the formal queries, he arrived at the point.

'If you remember, Mazzi, I informed you at the hospital that your bravery has to be felicitated to set an example for the fellow officers. All of us have strongly recommended your name for a gallantry award, and we firmly believe that the committee is seriously considering this proposal. So I would suggest you hold on for a little while. It's February, wait for the award to be announced before Republic Day. If you get the honor, you will be promoted automatically. Then you can expect a plump posting of your choice. So don't rush into things. Let's wait and watch.'

Suhail concurred and I had no choice but nod in agreement. The rest of the day was spent sipping lots of coffee in Suhail's office, chatting with other officers. The past three months helped me master the language, making me confident to converse. I was gaining faith and getting comfortable in Mazhar's skin. Amongst the many officers, Yusuf was notable and very excited to see me. He walked into Suhail's chamber with a wicked smile on his face, pounced, hugged me tight. I had to respond with equal zest. As he loosened the grip, his watery eyes surprised me. Suhail also sprung up from his seat and it was a threesome hug. Such bonding stunned me. I held back my emotions to mute for the next few minutes. I was trying to place him, struggling to recollect if I had met him earlier, and failed thoroughly. He took a few moments to get back his composure and started on a very emotional note, 'Hum toh tere ko kho gaye the yaar. (We had lost you my brother.)

'The Almighty Allah has bestowed his grace on us to return you back. I had come to the hospital when you were in coma, called twice at your place to talk, but either you were resting or were out. I spoke to Adaah and the kids as well but couldn't connect with you. As you are aware, my posting with ISI doesn't provide me with enough personal space but thanks to Allah's mercy, my friend is back, and back with a bang.'

Well, he's somebody really close. He knows my family, speaks to my children, sheds a tear on seeing me and Suhail is also friends with him. I am cynical of such people who were familiar with Mazhar. They have a better chance to spot an anomaly if any exists.

The subsequent discussion informed me that he, Suhail, and I had been to the same army training school and spent a gala time together. Refraining from participation in this discussion, I learned that Yusuf, like me was always in the middle of action; he had been working with the ISI. He was also restless during peacetime and preferred to be posted at troubled assignments. He was a sharp and intelligent individual. He reminded me so much of AD. After hours of chatting, we decided to head home. The three of us were on our way out when Yusuf dropped a bomb.

'Mazzi, you've changed, yaar. You are not the same person I knew and had fun with. Not everything is right. I am sure the injury has transformed you. I don't like this somber, dull, lifeless person. I want my life-loving, enthusiastic friend.'

His words scared the shit out of me. I regained my composure and left in a jiffy. We got into the car when

Suhail invited Yusuf home for dinner. He responded negatively, saying he was in Islamabad for an official visit and had to return to base immediately. So with an assurance of a dinner next time he visited, we left the premises.

CHAPTER 17

The Pakistan Felicitation, March 2010

The next few days were spent getting fit to regain much of the lost physical strength. With continuous and rigorous training, I could now run around three miles, lift weights, and stretch to my fullest. My inner strength and composure was reclaimed. It was a quiet family time, a sort of vacation. The family revisited Daman-e-Koh to experience its beauty from close quarters and was mesmerized again. And then in the following days, there a news broadcast: 'Maj. Mazhar Qureshi has been conferred the second highest gallantry award of the country, the *Hilal-i-Jur'at*.'

The second highest military award of Pakistan, given for acts of valor, courage, or devotion to duties performed on land, at sea, or in the air in the face of the enemy, holds significant benefits for the recipient, including social, political, and financial benefits. Land and pensions are awarded as recompense for serving in the army of Pakistan on behalf of the state, for acts of valor and courage during battle against the enemy.

The announcement of this news caused pandemonium all around. Earlier, it was regular morning, the kids were off to school, and I was enjoying my breakfast with Adaah, when the newsreader declared it. Adaah jumped from her seat, straight into my lap and squeezed me till I choked. We shared a full-blown passionate kiss before the servant came rushing in. Within seconds, the phone rang and it was Suhail shouting at the top of his voice in excitement. He hung up, rushing to the door within minutes. Still wearing his nightclothes, he came running all the way to greet me. I was ecstatic, but then again it was not my honor. It was Mazhar's. I responded enthusiastically but was gloomy inside. The award came with many varied benefits which made me happy for the family. But I did not deserve it. All this was not mine. The Almighty had different plans. He made me miss my felicitation so he gifted me with another, an honor from an enemy country.

The whole day was full of activity. The telephone couldn't stop ringing. After the first few calls, I stopped answering them; Adaah was more than happy to receive the greetings on my behalf. The kids came rushing after school and Inshaa climbed onto me. Afaaz hugged me tight and I embraced them in bliss. Visitors started pouring in to greet and congratulate. The honest officer in me was restless. I was weary of all this attention, wanting to run away to solace. Suhail, watching this uneasiness, invited me to his home, away from the chaos. I gladly accepted the invitation and, informing Adaah, slipped away to his home. Handing me a pint of beer, he enquired, 'Mazzi, you don't seem to be happy. You don't even seem to be the same Mazzi we all knew before. Is there something biting you inside? Come on, you can share it with me.'

I had a thousand topics to be discussed. I blamed the uneasiness on the injury and the time away from home.

'You have served all your life in administrative position, Suhail, so you would never know how it feels for a soldier coming back from a battleground. What we experience is an extended absence of comfort, family, or leisure. On the war front, we deal with the same set of people day in and day out. We don't have a choice. We work, eat, wash, live with them. If we cannot stand them, we can't complain. If the boss is a jerk, it's icing on the cake. The interactions are not very comforting. There are constant abuses, insults to deal with. There is no break or an escape for a weekend, 24/7 we are under constant threat of an attack, every step we take can explode into a landmine. The people whom we look at apart from our company are angry with our presence and stare us to death. In a best-case scenario, we actually have a conflict, we kill people, we lose some friends, a few get impaired for life. We carry them on our shoulders to safety and might see them breathe their last. It's not easy to see death every day. Then we come home. After a long absence, there is a considerable difference in the family as well. The individual is the same, but they too move on in life. So your wife might have a new haircut, look different, she goes from slim to fat or vice versa from the last time you had seen her. Our kids grow from toddlers to boys to teenagers in our absence. We are unaware of their likes, dislikes, their friends, habits, and lifestyle. We come back home for a brief period, and as we are about to enjoy these finer nuances of life, we are recalled to duty and subjected to the same strenuous environments. In my case, coming back from near death with such a scary face to stare at, though I am enjoying the spotlight, it takes a toll on me internally. The sight of the rocket from the bazooka hitting the vehicle still splashes in front of me in the middle of the night, waking me up with a shock. I can't crib about it, present a weak picture, not after I've been conferred an award for bravery, but on a personal front, it dents me inside.'

I gasped a breath. Suahil heard the tirade with composure, opened another pint for me, and we stared into the setting sun silently.

The Pakistan Republic Day is celebrated on the twenty-third of March. This day is observed to mark and recall 23 March 1940, when the historic Pakistan Resolution was adopted in Lahore, which led to the creation of a separate homeland for the Muslims of the Indian subcontinent. Though Pakistan gained freedom on 14 August and was a breakaway faction from India, on 23 March 1956, it became the first Islamic republic of the world. I had studied about the same in my Indian high school from a different perspective. Here, Google educated me on the outlook of an independent Islamic republic. As Mohammed Ali Jinnah, the founder of Pakistan, aka Quaid-i-Azam, stated his ideology for the formation of Pakistan:

> Hindus and the Muslims belong to two different religions, philosophies, social customs, and literature. They neither inter-marry nor inter-dine and, indeed, they belong to two different civilizations that are based mainly on conflicting ideas and conceptions. Their concepts on life and of life are different. It is quite clear that Hindus and Muslims derive their inspiration from different sources of history. They

have different epics, different heroes, and different episodes. Very often the hero of one is a foe of the other, and likewise, their victories and defeats overlap. To yoke together two such nations under a single state, one as a numerical minority and the other as a majority, must lead to growing discontent and final destruction of any fabric that may be so built up for the government of such a state.

The felicitations were scheduled at the official residence of the president. It was an event where heavyweight dignitaries from all spheres of the society were honored. Civilian awards and military decorations were presented by the president, witnessed by the PM, political leaders, army commanders, with every important person of the country. For the first time, I was going to formally don a Pakistan Army officer's uniform displaying full honors, dressed up feeling awkward but ironically the whole country was proud of me. An array of vehicles arrived to pick up me and the family for the event. The official residence of the Sadr-e-Mumlikat is called the Aiwan-e-Sadr. Just like the residences of the head of the country, this place was decked out with all that is needed for a luxurious life of a de-facto head of a country. The convocation hall was packed to the brim. As I walked down the place, there was a murmur about my arrival; everybody greeted me with a smile. I was seated in the front row along with the prime minister and other dignitaries. The president, Mr Asif Ali Zardari, occupied his chair and the ceremony began. I was shivering with anxiety when my name was called. I marched to the dais in complete army parade. He smiled and heaped praises on me. I was still like a statuette, keeping my composure. The thunderous applause came to a halt as I descended from the dais. In between all these happenings, an announcement declared I was promoted to the rank of a brigadier. Adaah shared a proud smile. The rest of the ceremony passed smoothly where I was glued to my seat. During dinner, I had a chance to interact with the power brokers of the country. Pakistan had always been an army controlled country so a gallantry-award-winning army man is definitely a crowd-puller. I conversed with politicians, businessmen, artists, cricketers, and representatives of different countries at the event. They all were aware of me and my story and were vocal about their appreciation. Adaah was enjoying her limelight, busy talking to the lovely ladies present at the event. The evening came to a close with many new acquaintances who might be of help in the future. I had to strategize to make the best use of these influential men to attain my goals.

I was overwhelmed with the appreciation. I decided to transform myself into a Paki citizen from this day. In my heart, in my head, my first priority was to go back to my motherland, but during my time here, I decided to live to the fullest. My scarred face became the symbol of a defiant country which waged war for what they called the freedom of Kashmir. I was a national hero.

CHAPTER 18

The Job, April 2010

After the government decoration, many civilian organizations followed suit, conferring various titles on me. Somewhere I was Babbar Sher-e-Pakistan, Khudaa kaa Bandaa, and a lot of other titles. All the admiration was obliged but the soldier in me was itching to get back on the field, eager to get back in the middle of action.

Suhail and I visited Lt. Gen. Khalid Mahmood again. He welcomed us and asked me to name the position of choice. He informed me the position of the head of the purchase department was lying vacant and recommended that after a death-defying experience should be time to spend with family and friends. Suhail was working in the same department and would be directly reporting to me.

The job profile did not include any conflict-driven tensions or confrontations. It was an office job to select vendors, place orders, and oversee delivery. As Lt. Gen. Mahmood suggested the post, Suhail's face lit up and he was brimming with excitement. He wanted me to agree immediately but this was not something on my mind. I sought a day from Gen. Mahmood to notify him of my decision. On my way back home, Suhail tried convincing me to take up the assignment. He explained me the advantages and the perks that were attached with the same. The memories of heading the purchase department of NDA where I met Saakshi flashed in front of my eyes.

At home, I discussed the proposition with Adaah, and she, like any other woman, was more than happy. She reacted positively, saying it would give me the opportunity to recover completely along with a chance to spend time with the kids and friends. The lovely wife said she would support any decision I make. So even if I opted to get back in the field, she would be proud. I gave it long hard thought. This was a time to keep my enthusiasm in check and learn the tricks of the trade. I was new to this person and should not overestimate my capabilities. If anything went awry, it would result in a catastrophe. Not only the families or friends would be hurt but it would be an issue where the warring governments would find another subject for mud-slinging, causing international uproar. I decided to learn the conduct, the mannerisms, the behavior of the organization to actually penetrate and then find a way out of this maze. This post offered the security of being with the family, and with the support of Suhail, who had already spent long years in the same department, a cautious approach was the need of the hour. A long discussion with Suhail helped me arrive at the verdict of accepting the position. The following morning Suhail accompanied me to Lt. Gen Mahmood's office and conveyed him the decision. He instructed to get necessary documentation ready and wished me luck. I gladly accepted the offer and was keen to join immediately. So many months under wraps, the hibernation made me rusty inside. I needed to get blood flowing in my brains and adrenaline rushing through my veins.

The army headquarters were located in the city of Rawalpindi. Interestingly, all the operations and administration were run from Islamabad, the twin city, where my office was located. After being promoted as a brigadier, I was spearheading the department, being the supreme authority in negotiating prices, finalizing vendors, ordering equipment, along with a lot of other things. The army not only fights battles but also has to keep up and maintain the forces in top-notch condition to be battle ready any moment. The provisions are to be made for their rations, hygiene, attire, and everything needed to keep them in peak form. This involves great deal of hard work.

I reported for duty the following day. The department organized a greeting event to welcome their new head with an introduction session with a pack of army officers. There was a queue of vendors lined up even before I occupied my chair. A plethora of floral bouquets was waiting my arrival. Meeting and interacting with so many civilians was unusual for an army officer. However, Adaah was happy to decorate the house with flowers on reaching home after a long day at office. I was always a sincere and earnest employee. The time had arrived to discharge the duties diligently and make a difference.

CHAPTER 19

National Storekeeper

A dynamic battle-ready soldier was transformed into a static desk worker. I had a huge cabin all for myself with a battery of staff reporting. I headed the army stores for all of the country's defense forces, a post of national importance. With my name inscribed on the list of department heads, I was the youngest to hold a position of utmost importance. The residence shifted from a mediocre building to a sprawling bungalow in an elite neighborhood. The place was enormous, closer to some of the most prominent power brokers of the country. And now I was one of them. Subsidiary offices under my command were strewn through the length and breadth of the country. Inexperienced to shoulder such responsibility, I decided to study the functioning of such a large organization. Where were the funds generated from, the way they traversed through the establishment, and how were they utilized? A few of these statistics and the figures were astonishing.

The present financial year had Rs. 495.2 billion allocated for the defense services. The spend on purchase and maintenance of military hardware was over and above this. Considering the above figure, the government was planning to spend around Rs. 1.3 billion on the armed forces every day. A further breakdown revealed more shocking numbers. The army utilized Rs. 642 million per day for meeting its salaries and operating expenses. Contrastingly, Rs. 640 million was the amount allocated to the basic utilities, like education, across Pakistan for the whole year. The vital health ministry's annual spend was a little less than daily spend of the Pakistani air force. The Health Ministry operated on a miniscule budget of Rs. 270 million for the whole year, whereas the air force managed to splurge Rs. 290 million in a single day. The Pakistan navy spent around Rs. 141 million every day. The country spent Rs 8.60 million daily on the president and the prime minister and Rs 7.8 million per day on the Senate and the National Assembly but a paltry amount of Rs. 3 lakhs per day on human rights. No wonder this country was in shambles. I was heading funds worth Rs. 2.1 billion for the year 2010/2011. The number of zeroes in the figure left me baffled. I was authorized to make this spend for the whole Territorial Army and their families.

I organized meetings with the regional heads to get a pulse of the situation. The Pakistani fiscal year begins on the first of July, so it was time for me to plan for the upcoming year. With Suhail alongside, we spent time assessing ground facts. Pakistan is a small country but with varied climatic conditions. We had to take into consideration all the details and the specifics of the various regions before we proposed the expense. My inquisitive nature and enthusiastic character kept me involved beyond measure. I was an honest soldier who had performed all duties meticulously. Though Suhail was aiding me, he was not serious about the whole effort. In fact, he joked about it whenever I questioned his negligent approach. This dereliction of duty disappointed me. One of such evenings, Suhail visited me for our usual evening session of Glenfiddich. After a few drinks, when poked about his laid-back approach, he gave me a stare, then a grin and then burst out laughing. His response was disturbing. But then he suggested, 'Mazzi, keep calm and take a break. You have been appointed to this position to relax and take a sort of vacation from your heroics. This organization has been running efficiently for more than fifty years. Now that you are my superior, I request you not to meddle too much. There is more than what meets the eye. If you inquire into every small detail, there might be larger interests that you might hurt. You are a high-ranking officer but concerns here are beyond officers and their positions. I've spent more than a decade in this muck, I understand the underlying layers.

There are many personal vendettas that neophytes like you and me can't understand. I suggest you let the things function the way they have been for so many years. You are at the top of the pyramid and there are many experienced officers who are going to aid you in the functioning of the department. Every proposal that reaches you has already been scrutinized several times by your staff, so just ride the flow and reap the benefits. Your overenthusiasm might offend somebody. Don't be a roadblock. Chalo bhai, It's getting really late. I think I need to make a move, will see you tomorrow morning.'

Such a piece of advice was disheartening. All I wanted to do was to work sincerely and deliver the best for the country that had given me a new life, to hell with the country and its people. If any good intentions lead to skirmishes, why should it bother me? I will be more than happy to enjoy my time.

CHAPTER 20

Thrilling Times

In the next few days, I enjoyed the benefits of being myself. Living so close to the civilian life had its own advantages: an absolutely conventional life, fixed working hours, proper housing facility, leisure times, holidays, everything my civilian friends used to brag about. We used to enjoy movie evenings, short picnics, dinners out. Being a decorated Pakistani army officer was awesome. The army supply business was one big trade. The revenues and the magnitude of orders and the scale of operations were humungous. There were traders who had been suppliers to the army for decades together. Many of these countless merchants who visited me were extremely generous. I was not used to being pampered at work. But these wealthy men took pride in gifting me with the most expensive gifts available. I vehemently refused them early on but Suhail happily represented me and also was my courier. Such wonderful gifts obviously made the family happy. A vendor presented a Visconti limited-edition pen to begin with, another trader followed it up with a state-of-the-art Vertu mobile, while some other personnel bought me a Piaget wristwatch and almost all accessories required to flaunt big money. Such indulgence was uncalled for. But the gifts just kept pouring in.

One evening, Suhail said some vendor had invited us for dinner. He enlightened me that Islamabad had a secretive but beautiful nightlife. Tonight we planned to rediscover the nights of Islamabad. I informed Adaah about his escapade and she was perfectly fine with it. Her non-reaction helped me conclude that such overnight exploits must have been usual with Mazhar. Suhail picked me up in his private car. Both of us were dressed casually in T-shirt and denims. We traveled for a distance then Suhail parked his car at a discreet location. I kept mum in anticipation. Within minutes a huge Hummer arrived. A person alighted from the monstrous car and invited us for a ride. This mean machine was a full-on party place. The accomplice introduced himself as relative of some vendor I was supposed to know. I had a blank look on my face. As the car glided around the streets, booze flowed along with music, coming to a halt at a basement of some hotel. Suhail seemed to be comfortable, walking ahead confidently. The doors opened to screeching music with a whole new world.

Disco lights, blazing sounds, people swinging—it was a thumping party scene. I followed Suhail into the mayhem and settled in a corner. The person accompanying us made sure we were treated royally. Two beautiful young girls joined us shortly. They introduced themselves and started chatting. I was puzzled but Suhail was at ease. He recognized my anxiety, leaned over to whisper in my ear, 'They are ours for the night. Enjoy them. I give you the right to choose. I will spend time with the other. Release you inhibitions, enjoy, brave heart.'

I was a courageous man but women made me go weak in my knees, never experienced this revelry back home. Rajeev Suri was averse to this act but Mazhar needed it. I had to pick one of the girls. Both the girls were young and attractive. I was consorting with the one next to me; Suhail interpreted he was to cuddle up with the other lady. Not wasting any time, they both hit the dance floor and were all over each other. My partner, having finished her drink, was raring to go, pulling me along. It was awkward but it was fun exploring this new exuberance. I started caressing the woman and in no time she was fondling me all over. All four of us headed to the bar, Suhail ordered for some shots, and we gulped them in moments. The girls went berserk after this. In the middle of all this chaos, I recognized a face in the darkness, staring at me. The woman marched, came real close, pulled me from my partner's arms, and said, 'Remember me, handsome? I met you at your Daman-e-Koh felicitation, I am Aafreen.'

She was the same lady in red. Suddenly two beautiful women were vying for me. I never had such an opportunity in my life. The actress was definitely more exciting so I naturally drifted. She walked me to the other corner. In no time she owned me. The darkness around made me desperate to see more of her. The person who drove us to this place was keeping a vigil all this while. He realized I was searching for something as he enquired, 'Sir, are you tired? Do you want to rest for a while? The rooms in this hotel have excellent view of the city. I can book one for you right away.'

I nodded in agreement. The lady was smiling and consented to the proceeding. Suhail, who was enjoying his time, gave me a thumbs-up. He gestured that he would wait for me. I winked and left with the lady.

We occupied a large palatial room on the top floor of the hotel. It was one of the tallest buildings in Islamabad. As we settled in the room, we spoke for a while to get acquainted and comfortable. It was difficult to hold back. I grazed her soft hair to arouse her immediately. Without waiting any further, we stuck our lips while she sucked me ferociously. It was an intense, passionate, no-holds-barred kiss. We got wedged to each other. I took a few steps behind, getting cozy on a recliner. She was watching me with fire in her eyes. What followed was an outburst of infatuation. With all her clothes on, she sat on my lap to undress me. She ran her fingers through my hair; pulling back my head, she planted her tongue in my ear, wetting it completely. I gripped the chair to let her exploit me. Starting with my face, she licked me from head to toe. As she lifted my T-shirt, the injury marks on my body aroused her further.

'This is for the first time I have a chance to adore a true hero. Just sit back and let me explore. I assure you a ride to Jannat.'

She was in no hurry and took her sweet time to caress me. Her fingers continued to explore my scars. The nerve endings on the injury marks were extra sensitive; she was gently fondling them. I made a move to strip her but she resisted, gently shrugged, asking me to hold on. Starting with my upper body, she slowly moved down to unzip my denim. My cock was rock solid, desperate to pounce. She was calm and patient, took a few steps back to undress. Her assets bounced as she pulled off the tight top, while I couldn't stop admiring the flawless skin and her perfect hourglass shape. She was definitely the most beautiful woman I had ever seen in my life. I reached for her outstretched hand; she led me to the king-size bed. When she climbed on top of me, her body was scorching. I embraced her tight, sandwiching my leg in between hers. We rubbed our naked bodies against each other for a heavenly feeling. Now it was my chance to make a move. I pushed her down gently to take control. My hands explored her curves as I engaged her in a passionate smooch. Her big round mounds were delicious to suck and I began my journey downwards. I licked her navel, while my fingers were massaging her inner thighs. I could feel she was already wet. She spread her legs, inviting me to probe inside. Desperate to feel the heat, my hot tip entered her searing moist opening. Hard all the way in, I put my arms around her, squeezing her to death, pulled out, and slammed back in, and she leaned back her head; I continued to thrust into her ferociously. The thump of my body hitting hers was getting louder and harsher. As the forces multiplied, she dug her nails on my back. Within minutes, the spasm made her bite my arm. I continued thrusting hard into her till the last stroke and spilled all over her body. We looked at each other, getting together for another steamy kiss. I was desperate to carry on this adventure, but commitments compelled me to consider reality. I dressed up quickly and engaged playing with her body as she was dressing up.

After such an incredible time she noted down my number urging me to stay in touch. She disclosed, 'I am an actress of repute here and in India as well. Pakistan is a conservative market so I didn't have ample opportunities for skin show. I started my career in Pakistan but later moved to India for better prospects.'

My watch suggested no time to indulge in her career talks so I wished her good luck and hurried downstairs to Suhail. But her India story stuck to my mind. I had to meet this woman again. You never know who can be a help in such a situation. Downstairs, Suhail and I made a dash to our car, back to our families.

CHAPTER 21

A Nation Ruled by Army

I shortlisted some vendors based on their past performances with transparent functioning. A high-level committee meeting was called for planning and execution. The meeting was chaired by the defense minister, attended by the army chief, the defense secretary, the finance secretary, and all the important officials. I headed the team which made a presentation that would streamline the supply system, plug the loopholes, and make optimum utilization of the funds to build a dominant army. We suggested change of vendors, alterations in order patterns, amendments in the tendering system, along with many other modifications. The officials present were impressed with our job, applauding our efforts. In the next few days, the orders were to be placed and I was awaiting confirmation on my suggestions. The defense ministry appreciated my effort and instructed me to issue the orders as directed. Surprised to know that the directives were already issued, I was supposed to merely sign them and approve. None of my suggestions were implemented; all the traditional, age-old, obsolete, incompetent vendors were back in business. All our effort was down the drain. Disheartened, I learnt my lessons. Higher budgets meant higher interference. Suhail studied the proposals and gave me a long stare.

'I told you earlier, don't try to wash this sewage. This dirt is deep-rooted in the system and runs in politicians' blood. You cannot get up one morning to make a change. I would still suggest you to enjoy your time, let the proceedings happen the way they always have been. Enjoy being a husband, a father, and a friend. Leave all these worries.'

Imagine being told by a Pak officer to let corruption run through the system. Miles away from my country, I was doing this as a favor to improve the present dilapidated system of a foe. Instead, I was being requested to let it rot. I was more than happy to let it decay, corrode, and decompose. It was better for my country.

The political situation in Pakistan has always been chaos. The sixty-odd years of existence are scarred by rampant interference of armed forces in politics and administration. The military had unceremoniously uprooted the elected governments making a mockery of democracy. With an army ruling a country, the citizens are expected to follow the infamous obedience. Though these military rulers never called themselves dictators, they have justified their actions by appointing rubber-stamp judiciary and choked politicians who don't have the courage to resist any atrocities. These army commanders have thrived in their own imaginary world of bringing peace and prosperity to the region. So in almost sixty years of existence, the four military authoritarian dictators have ruled for more than thirty-two years and the nineteen democratically elected governments have had a paltry twenty-eight years run at the office. None of the democratically elected governments have completed their tenure. The populace has been a mute spectator in the running of the state and is forcefully subjected to policies framed by a certain section of the armed forces that have always focused on displaying their strength to the world rather than pondering over basic necessities of life.

The military is run more like enterprise in this part of the world. And once the military was at the helm, they ensured maximum profits for their enterprises. This military is involved in manufacturing cement, in banking services, act as landlords on expansive tracts of land, collect revenue in the form of rent, and own an oil terminal and a number of delivery stations. Cross-country trucking and logistics to rural inaccessible places is their monopoly. They also run an airline to ferry passengers and own almost one-third of heavy engineering of the country. The military and its subsidiaries own almost 12 per cent of land in the most fertile locations and run sugar factories. The US estimates this organization to be worth $20 billion. The net worth of 100 top-ranking military officers is estimated to be around $70 million. All these numbers were mind-boggling. The military was introduced in these trades and businesses because of the fact of their discipline in implementations, but over the years, these have turned into individual profit-churning entities. Apart from running business affairs in the country, the military also has a commanding voice in the foreign and financial affairs of the country. They draft the foreign policies and make budgetary allowances. So definitely they make sure their organization is the biggest beneficiary. A retired army soldier earns almost Rs. 32,000 per month whereas a government employee makes a mere Rs. 2,800. When strategies are drafted with only defense into consideration, it beats the whole purpose of being a republic. It seems like Pakistan is not a country with an army to manage; it is an army with a country to manage.

The Hilal-i-Jur'at came with many benefits apart from just recognition and medal I was allotted five marlas of land in the outskirts of Islamabad. It was a beautiful location with many decorated defense personnel as neighbors. With the present posting, many vendors were keen to lend me a helping hand to build my dream home. I, Adaah, and the kids visited the site with some contractors to initiate the process. Not sure of being in this country for long, I decided to let Adaah take charge and build the bungalow as she wanted to. Suahil made all the necessary arrangements for the payments required to raise a bungalow. I was a mere spectator and didn't spend a single penny from my pocket. In a month's time, construction started. I was beginning to settle down in this new life—lovable family, supportive friends, good quality of life, everything any person could hope for. In these few months, enough money arrived for the family to live a comfortable life. I obediently signed all the directives from the ministry and was happy to reap the benefits, rewarded not only in kind but also cash. So big cars, modern electronics, jewelry for the ladies, everything under the sun was being delivered without any hassle. Aafreen and her antics kept the fire burning inside once in a fortnight. Nobody bothered to raise a suspicion. It was an unsaid, implicit rule every army colleague consented to and made me wonder, does the Indian army function like this? High-ranking officers were opulent, but was it because of corruption? I was a battle-loving soldier there. These things hardly crossed my mind.

But this person was not me. The life that I was living was not mine. All the decorations and appreciations didn't belong to me. This troubled me inside, made me restless and agitated. Saakshi's social media updates informed me of her and the family. My parents were growing old. I longed for my mother's daal rice, my wife's pasta in white sauce, my friends' non-stop nonsense discussions. I was trapped in this body, in this person, helpless. Now that nobody doubted my credentials and my identity, I had to plan my next move, opting for some posting of significance where I might get a chance to interact with the Indians or with international army officers. I had to find my way out of this maze to get back to my life. I would not let my wife sulk all her life, my parents yearn for me. It was time to take action on the ideas.

I disclosed my unhappiness and discussed a possibility of a different posting with Suhail. Giggling, he was sure I would not hang on to such dull, lifeless, comfortable post for long. Mazhar and I had a lot of behavioral similarities. I didn't want to go to a place directly in the line of fire. I wanted to explore Pakistan and its tribal land fascinated me. Suhail informed me of the various regions in which the army operated. In this conversation, he divulged to me a very exciting place called the FATA.

FATA—Federally Administered Tribal Area—the name was exciting. Researching this interesting place, I discovered this place always fascinated me. I was an ardent fan of the Bollywood superstar Amitabh Bachchan, watched all his movies many times over. One of his movie characters that imprinted on my mind was Badshah Khan from the movie *Khuda*

Gawah. I was blown away by the place where he hailed from, his dress, his hair, his grit in the movie. The Pathans were always a respected community in the Hindi film industry. They were physically well-built and were portrayed as the men who would give their life but won't give up on their word and promises. I was mesmerized by such commitment always wanting to be a man of my word like the great Badshah Khan. This forbidden land was land of the great Pathans, the Pashtun tribe, the valiant and fearless Pathans. So FATA it was. The Pakistani army was dormant in the region but it was a hotbed of the Taliban and Islamic fundamentalist. The US drones were more active in this area. With an opportunity to study the working of the jihadis up close and personal, I could help my country back home. I expressed my dilemma to Gen. Mahmood.

'Sir, though I am happy being so close to the family and leading a comfortable life, I am a soldier and want to sweat it out for the country. These months of placated life and secure environs are rusting my indomitable spirit. I am restless to feel the dust on my face and to get the adrenaline rushing through my veins again.' Gen. Mahmood was more than elated to hear my enthusiasm and went gung-ho about it to the whole office. He enquired about my preferences when I suggested FATA.

'FATA? Mazzi boy, really? Wow, I am glad you have chosen FATA as your next assignment. This is one unique place on this planet. Let me talk to the department and find a position which will justify your capabilities. I won't promise you what and when as of yet, but I will not disappoint you. I will definitely find a posting worthy of you.'

I reached home, revealed my intentions to Adaah. She was disappointed to hear my place of choice but being the understanding woman that she always was, she nodded in agreement.

CHAPTER 22

The Next Move, September 2010

The Ministry of Defence communicated in a week's time. They conceded to my request and granted me the honor of leading a brigade in the famous Khyber agency, posting me in Landi Kotal, the HQ for the Khyber Rifles.

Before proceeding to FATA, I spent time with Aafreen. The five months of mischief addicted us to each other and I had a sexciting send-off, with promises to stay in touch and help each other if need arose.

Then was the most difficult part of this effort. When informed about the transfer, the kids were distraught. They were getting used to the fact of their father being with them, staying along and then suddenly this news broke their heart. Inshaa in particular was hurt and she cried the whole night. It was a difficult decision for me as well; this family had bestowed upon me this life. But I had to go back to my country and my home. I could not just sit back to enjoy the perks of a decorated army officer; I had to relocate. It was tough to let the kids go. I might come back to them sparingly, but if an opportunity arrives, I might disappear and never see them again. I spent a week with the kids, taking them out shopping and to movies and places they loved. It was a very emotional goodbye, but time had arrived to move on.

I arrived in Landi Kotal to very pleasant weather. More than 1,000 feet above sea level, it is the highest point on the Khyber Pass. The Khyber Pass always had historical significance. It was the gateway of the Indian subcontinent. Many invaders came through this Silk Route to explore and exploit opulent India. Raiders such as Alexander, Genghis Khan, Muhammad Ghori used these passes. Landi Kotal is an important city on the Peshawar–Kabul trade route. Present day, it was of prime importance to the NATO forces that are stationed in Pakistan. Around 80 per cent of arms and ammo that travelled by road went through this route. This place was a hotbed for NATO activities.

FATA is a unique administrative place in the world. Here the local tribes are the supreme authority. These tribes have been fiercely independent since historical times. They have been able to maintain their identity and sovereignty for centuries. FATA was created sometime in 1890 to draw a boundary between Afghanistan and British India. This border known as the Durand Line was created to divide the local tribesmen in an attempt to control them. But soon the British had foregone their aspiration to wrestle control on this part of the world. So they suggested this unique form of administrative set-up. The British administration signed treaties with local tribal leaders. These treaties consisted of commitments from the tribal's not to commit crimes in the British territories or on the trade routes, or give refuge to an outlaw. In exchange for these services, the tribal leaders were paid an annual fee and had the freedom to govern their land with minimal interference. The place has a gun-loving culture and is still ruled by local jirgas to dispense justice.

At Landi Kotal, the local army commanding unit was a regular military set-up with administrative offices, ammunition depots, canteens, etc. I was one of the youngest commanders of this region. After joining, I proceeded the next day to meet my senior officer Maj. Gen. Anwar. He was a very popular officer with vast experience in various positions. His stint in Azad Kashmir won him many awards. He was also involved in pacifying the anti-army sentiment amongst the people of Pakistan. Maj. Gen. Anwar was a man of honor with infinite knowledge and was consulted regularly by the central administration on matters of internal and external importance. Suhail heaped praises on this gentleman, so obviously his advice was of utmost importance. The army HQ for this region was located in Peshawar, which was not far off from my town of Landi Kotal. I was welcomed by Gen. Anwar.

'Meet the bravest man in Pakistan. Here is a person who faced an explosive to chase two Indian intruders,' he proudly introduced me to his staff.

Maj. Gen. Anwar was a very learned man and was fluent in numerous languages. This was one of the reasons he was popular among local tribesmen. He always heard them patiently to resolve their disputes amicably. Maj. Gen. Anwar was an unbiased officer who genuinely strived for peace in his region. After the long day of introductions, he invited me for dinner. He revealed to me that his family was very proud of my achievements and they often discussed my story. I gladly accepted the invitation.

Maj. Gen. Anwar was the commander-in-chief for the whole Khyber agency, who resided in a palatial army bungalow. The sight of his magnificent residence was mesmerizing, and even more enchanting was his family. He had a very pretty wife, a chirpy young daughter, and a handsome son. It was a proud army family. In Pakistan there exist these rich, very well-learned families who have been serving the army through generations. So the wife was the daughter of some legendary Pakistani army officer, the boy was already on his way to an army school, and the girl was inspired to become an army doctor. I was surprised to see their love towards the nation but my last posting taught me that this was the most profit-making entity in the country. Love for country or not, everybody knew in Pakistan, the route to power and big money resides in the army. Nonetheless it was a sweet family, who treated me well.

Over the dinner, the major general explained to me the complications of working in this part of the world. He clarified, 'This is one of the most dangerous places on the planet. We are the authority of the Pakistan army here, but the army itself has limited influence in this area. Since 9/11, the NATO forces command this region more than we do. A US drone will attack and kill people under your jurisdiction almost every day. We don't know where they attack; we don't know whom they will kill. We are like mute dummies made to stand in the corner to observe this mockery of administration. In the internal matters, the local tribal leaders are supreme. You cannot question their intent or decision. The literacy rate here is less than 20 per cent. The women have no access to any education. They are still ruled by old sharia laws. These can be disturbing and dangerous.

'Since you are controlling the trade route, be cautious about whom you impede or obstruct. The traders have well-oiled networks that go right up to Islamabad and Washington. So don't act on impulse. Take suggestions from experienced elderly junior officers who have spent more time in this area. They will introduce you to the tribal leaders and help you get acquainted with their functioning. I would suggest you keep busy with official administrative work. You hardly know their language so it will be difficult for you to communicate. I won't ask you to be lenient but don't have an iron fist while dealing with these tribes. They are very sociable to officers whom they are secure with but they can be equally intimidating towards non-cooperative officers. So play your game with caution and ease.'

I was baffled.

CHAPTER 23

Exploring FATA

The soothing climate, the mesmerizing backdrop of Landi Kotal, the love of the populace was a pleasurable experience. A deputy political agent governed the Landi Kotal area for civilian activities, reporting to the political agent of the Khyber agency. But the powers of justice and day-to-day governance rested with the tribal leader. In addition to this, the Khyber Pass was the most important transit route for the NATO forces to conduct their attacks in Afghanistan. We did not have any right to interfere in their operations. So as Anwar sir advised, I decided to lie back and observe. Captain Raza was my subordinate and a veteran. I had a slew of visitors in the first few weeks. My story and my titles preceded me. Many civilians came in to express their gratitude. Capt. Raza pleasantly informed me this had never happened before. After the Twin Towers bombing, the Khyber agency had become more of an army base for the NATO forces, which carried out most of their operations through this Khyber Pass. So any commanding officer of this post was not a very popular figure amongst the masses. He was looked upon as a spineless puppet of the Americans and the British. This place had been a live battlefield since then. Raza explained I was one of the first officers whom the locals had a glimpse of hope and expected me to bring a change.

One fine morning, as I settled in my office, there was commotion outside. Herds of horses and cars with a mob of tribals were heading towards the office. At first, my soldiers thought of it as a security threat, but as the tribals neared, they got chatting with the guards while many of them had already entered the campus, making me nervous. Capt. Raza came storming inside my chamber and exclaimed, 'Sir, Maulana Asad Gul is here. He's come all the way to meet and greet you.'

Maulana Gul, the famous preacher of the Pakistan Taliban? I wondered.

'Whoever it is, Capt. Raza, don't just let him in. Make him wait, send me a message. I will call him when I can spare some time,' I instructed the captain.

He looked astonished and worried. Being a true soldier, he saluted and left. After a few minutes, my secretary informed me of a visitor called Maulana Gul. I granted audience to the visitor after a while. A huge, towering person entered the room while many followed him. All bearded individuals were dressed in the traditional tribal attire. The sheer size of these people and their Pathani suits and long beards intimidated me. But I was the authority here.

Looking up at this gang, I asked, 'Who is Maulana Gul?'

An elderly person replied.

'Phir aap sab kaun hain? Maulana sahib ko hum milenge baaki log tashreef le jaa sakte hain.' (Then who are the others? I will meet Maulana sahib, the rest can leave.)

The crowd was furious but the maulana urged them to leave.

'Pharmaaiye janaab, mein appki kyaa khidmat kar saktaa hoon?' (Tell me, janaab, what can I do for you?)

The maulana was very impressed with my work culture and discipline. He did not say much but insisted that I visit his tribal village.

'Brigadier sahib, kai arsaa beet gaya lekin humne kisi army waale afsar ko daawat par nahi bulaaya. Humne aapki taarifo kii kahaaniyaan suni issliye chale aaye. Hum aap ke liye duaa karenge aur aap humein khafaa naa karein. Yahan ke Jirga ke Sardar hein hum.

Aap iss baat kaa leehaj karenge aisi umeed karte hain.' (It has been long since we invited an army officer to our village. We have heard a lot of your valor so we thought of meeting you. We request you not to disappoint us. I am the chief of the jirga here so I appeal you to accept our invitation.)

Gauging the aggression in his voice, I summoned my secretary.

'What are the activities for the week?'

He informed me Thursday (the coming Jumme Raat) was relatively unoccupied.

'The visit to Kabilla would be on the coming Jumme Raat,' I confirmed with the maulana.

'Brigadier sahib, iss jumme raat jashn hoga. Poori Jirga aapki khidmat mein haazr hogi. Hum bhi iss mulk kee sarkaar ke mullajim hai. Aap dekhiye hum aapki kaisi khidmat karte hain.' (It will be a celebration this Thursday night. The whole jirga will be present. You are a decorated officer. Wait and watch how we pamper you.) The maulana departed.

Capt. Raza came rushing as the mob left the premises.

'Sir, this is very rare opportunity. These tribes have been very aloof from the army officials for a very long time. We could visit their locations only if they wanted us to. It was more for official trips or foreign human rights activists. But this is very uncommon. An invitation from a tribal leader with him gathering all the jirga leaders is a privilege. I hope we can start new reformed relations with the locals.'

The reactions to this invitation were worrying. I was an outsider to this world but my heroics made me a celebrity. I did not ask or seek this attention but had no choice. My life and this journey was a saga in itself and every day was a challenge. That very evening, I called Gen. Anwar.

'Sir, Maulana Gul was here today and invited me to the jirga. Please advise.'

He was delighted and heaped praises on me.

'I've rarely seen a dedicated soldier like you. On the battlefront you have already proven your worth; now with these relations you are developing with the tribes, I am sure you will become a popular figure with the locals and a favorite with the top brass. Just don't be overenthusiastic. Please tread with caution. All the best, Mazzi, and definitely update me about what happens.'

It was a routine Thursday; having completed the office work, I assembled a few officers to take along. Capt. Raza was obviously one of them. We took a caravan of vehicles to the designated location. Landi Kotal being situated on a hill top, we descended to reach the village. Swirling our way through mountains, I could see small hutments resembling rural Rajasthan. We approached a place where hundreds of Pathans were awaiting my arrival. Pajeros, Prados, Land Rovers, horses, and camels were abundant. Their cheering was nerve-wracking. My soldiers descended fast to form a security ring around my car. I stepped out; Maulana Gul greeted me with a hug, along with some elderly people. I happily obliged him; so did my staff exchange pleasantries. We proceeded inside. The center of the village was more like a place where the panchayats of Indian villages assemble. The makeshift pandals erected had a cloth spread on the ground, with large hookahs. We settled on the ground and were served sherbet while the hookahs were lit. A special hookah was ignited and placed in front of me. I was a non-smoker, hence apprehensive. But Gul sahib insisted me that I try. I was averse to acting rude on the first day, so I tried to smoke the hookah and discovered it was relatively easy, a flavored smoke with a pleasant odour. The elders from other tribes introduced themselves along with some young lads, not shy to express how honored they were with my presence. As the evening progressed, some men came forward with dhols and a wind instrument. The rhythmic beating of drums made a very pleasurable atmosphere. I was engrossed discussing with the leaders about the situation of the region. They conveyed their dissatisfaction with the administration. In between these discussions, the whiff of roasted meat was alluring. The inviting aroma awakened the beast in me. Suddenly a few men encircled the dhols and started an impromptu dance.

Many others joined in. The setting became a little informal with laughter and mirth as the men danced around. Gul sahib came closer and whispered in my ear, 'Sahib kucch naya karenge. Kucch mukhtalif.' (Sir, will you try something new?)

Having already learned my lesson not to refute these people, I nodded in agreement. Gul sahib made some gestures and immediately the first hookah was replaced by another. I repeated the procedure of smoking the new offering. The dancing men were joined by many others, and there was a big ring of Pathani-clad people making merry. Gul sahib proudly informed,

'Yeh nazaakat Khattak hain. Humare illaake mein isse jashn kehte hai.' (This dance form is the Khattak. We celebrate every occasion with this.)

Smoking the new hookah made me dizzy. Gul sahib disclosed this new hookah was made from their finest quality produce which they exported around the world. It was difficult to understand what this desert could yield that was exported. But smoking this stuff made me high. Capt. Raza was smiling at me from a distance. I smiled back but he still kept the grin on his face. This response was uncalled for. In the meanwhile, many leaders joined the dancing crowd; Gul sahib insisted that I join in. The smoke made me flighty; it was not the usual alcohol high. The dance reminded me of Garbhaa. Dhol beats and rhythmic dancing around carried me back to Navratri nights in my NDA times. We used to sneak out from the institute to accompany Saakshi and her friends. But this was for the first time I was dancing with so many men around. These tribals were conservative about their women but not even a glimpse of any female was unexpected. Anyways, I was in my own world having a good time. The food served was exemplary. It was a novel and joyous experience for the team as well. I was so happy and high that I danced my way to the car. Capt. Raza helped me inside and we left.

The following morning was with a heavy headache, no memories of return journey and who put me in my bed. The smoke and its high were worse than alcohol trips. It was hard to recollect the events of the earlier evening. Thank God, it was Jumma, an official holiday in this region. I woke up, had a stomach full and crashed back to sleep. Capt. Raza visited me in the evening. And like an elder brother he inquired, 'Mazhar sahib, kyaa aap jaante the uss doosre hookah mein kyaa tha?' (Are you aware of the contents of the second hookah you smoked?)

I obviously wasn't.

'Sahib woh afeem kaa hookah tha. Aur aap toh tafreeh le rahe the.' (It was an opium hookah and you were relishing it!)

Afeem? Did he mean opium? Amazed but still too high to comprehend, I headed back to my room and slumped into the bed.

CHAPTER 24

The Opium Den

With such a fascinating experience, the adventurer in me was roused. I called for Capt. Raza.

'This is an interesting place, captain. I am keen to explore other areas under my jurisdiction. I want to know the people, understand their life, witness the flora and fauna. Tell me, how do we go about it?'

'Sir, this is an excellent idea. This will definitely bridge the gap between the fundamentalists and the administration,' concurred Raza.

He unwrapped a detailed regional map, discussing the various villages under my authority. This was not on my mind.

'No, captain, I don't want a guided tour like a tourist. I want to just reach and watch the locals in their day-to-day life. I don't want the leaders to be informed of my arrival. Let's make it a surprise visit.'

'Sir, this could be dangerous owing to the past relations between us and the tribesmen,' Capt. Raza objected, raising security concerns.

I was adamant and he had little choice. So it was decided to commence the tour in the next two days. We geared up all the necessary security. Though the Pakistan army was the governing and protecting authority, it was not always welcome in many of these places. I decided to keep this expedition to the hinterland under wraps. I purposely did not inform any superiors about the same.

With one jeep leading and a truck full of soldiers trailing my armored vehicle, we embarked on this journey. Through the winding roads our vehicles descended. It was breathtaking terrain with rugged naked mountains as a backdrop and streams carving their route through. Capt. Raza educated me about the geography of the region.

'Sir, the majestic Lacha Ghar, Karagah Ghar, Surghar, and Kalauch mountain ranges congregate here to make this unparalleled hilly topography. Amid these valleys, the tribes have their civilizations scattered. The Bara and the Kabul rivers provide water to this area.'

In the middle of this barren terrain, an appealing stretch of flowers was inescapable. We drove closer to the beautiful flowers of white and pink, with deeper shades of purple and red. The pleasant sight intrigued me enough to visit these stunning and picturesque farmlands. I hinted for the driver to stop.

'Please stop the vehicle, I want to see these beautiful farms.'

Capt. Raza did not approve. 'Sir, let's not stop here.' He was restraining the driver.

This infuriated me and I ordered the car to be halted immediately. The convoy came to a grinding halt. I alighted from the vehicle, striding towards the farm. The pasture of pretty flowers was a mind-blowing scenario. On closer observation, I noticed some gun-toting men guarding the field. Scarecrows guarding farmlands was known; also, men with sticks protecting their crops from the cattle was heard of, but this was one of a kind. What crop needed security with guns? The crop guards sighted army vehicles and fired warning shots in the air. Enraged, my guards formed a security ring around me, also responding with fire in the air. I was here not to escalate tension but to calm the situation.

Capt. Raza cautioned, 'Sahib, this is an opium farm. It is a property of the local tribe. They look at us as enemies who restrain and uproot the plantations. Let's not invoke another issue. Please, let's leave.'

The farm was mesmerizing. Thoroughly unaware of all the beauty that came with the bane, I was determined to know more. Poppy and opium was a part of culture for centuries in this part of the world. Keen to know the reason why tribes preferred growing this dreaded crop to other more valuable yields, I asked for a handheld loudspeaker to make an appeal.

'Janaab hum yahan kucch khojne yaa aapko rokne nahin aaye hain. Hum yahan ke lashkar ke afsar hain aur hum aap se aur aap ke rehnumaa se baat karna chahte hain.' (We are here not to search or destroy your crops. I am the commanding officer of this area and would like to speak to your leader.)

The crop guards disappeared amongst the tall plants and did not respond. We were waiting impatiently. After a while, a turbaned Pathan walked towards us with his gun still pointing. He enquired something in a local language. One of my soldiers responded and he relaxed the gun. I asked the soldier to convey my desire to visit the village. The local was confused but he had no choice. He was in the middle of twenty army men who were not being rude. His suspicious eyes spoke volumes since they were used to arrogant soldiers. He agreed, leading us to a small dusty village not far away.

Watching these many army vehicles advancing, the villagers misunderstood it for an attack. The women rushed to veil themselves, the kids ran to safety, and the men hurried to collect their arms. We headed straight to the leader's house; stopping the cavalry at a distance, I walked to his home. I did not want to offend the chief. Hearing all the noise, he had stepped outside. He sprinted to greet me. Now I was confused. He introduced himself as one of the leaders at Gul sahib's evening. That evening was full of similar people; it was impossible to distinguish him. I reciprocated his enthusiasm, and Capt. Raza had a sigh of relief, relieved with the acquaintance and the fact that there wouldn't be any trouble.

The leader welcomed us to his home and arranged for refreshments. Through my interpreter soldier, I communicated that while we were moving around the village, the farms were my preference. No army officer had visited this village in decades. We took a walk around where poverty and despair was plentiful. At the village border, the poppy farms were unmissable. This plant was the base raw material for drugs, like cocaine or heroin, and this region was the highest producer of these narcotics. With innumerable government and foreign efforts, these locals went back to this infamous wicked crop. I was anxious to know the reason. As we finished our walk around the village, we settled inside the leader's house. He urged us to lunch with them. We discussed about many topics including the troubles of the NATO forces, the drone attacks, and the Pakistan Taliban. In between these discussions, I managed to bring up the topic of poppy plantations.

'Iss fasal mein aisaa kyaa hain jo aap itnaa khatraa lekar iski upaj lete ho. Aap chhod kyun nahi dete isey.' (What is it about these crops that you endanger lives to cultivate it? Why don't you stop this?)

He explained that this crop was not a choice but a need.

'Sir, I was sure you would ask this question. Poppy is one of the few crops that does not require any special care and is cultivated in harsh conditions. It doesn't rot and never is attacked by pests. It matures quickly which helps us reap multiple crops in a year. No fertilizers or special treatments are required. Transportation of the harvest is always a challenge in our country with such pathetic infrastructure. Again storage can be an issue, whereas opium can be stored easily, does not need special packaging or refrigeration. Raising poppy is a labor-intensive activity and requires participation from the whole family. This keeps the young involved in something productive rather than align with religious fundamentalists. And most importantly, it is the only crop which has a guaranteed international market, so definite clientele and better price.

'In our regions, women are restricted from participating in any industrious activity. But they play a central role in many aspects of poppy production, from planting to usage of by-products. The practice of purdah is very stringent, but in the poppy fields, the men and the women work next to each other.

And most importantly, Islam approves of this crop. For the western world, this may be a leisure activity, but this crop is our only lifeline. Many people are illiterate here. How can we adapt and compete with modern agricultural methods? When government agencies come and destroy the crop, they might salvage hundreds of Westerners but they fail to understand that they devastate our lives with the crop. With no other option, the young boys join the fundamentalists and wage a war. This war is fought with the foreigners and the local army as well, leading us to nowhere. We don't have a preference for this crop but we don't have an alternative. We have allowed an army official deep inside our lives after a long time. I hope you will respect and maintain our faith. We don't expect any support from your side but please don't interfere in our life. It is a humble request.'

My soldiers listened to this appeal with composure. We were exposed to a stark point of view. The soldiers walked to their respective vehicles. Some elderly people escorted us and bid farewell. All this while, Capt. Raza was absolutely quiet. Somebody who vehemently opposed the tribes was mum for long. We bid the villagers goodbye to continue on our voyage.

CHAPTER 25

The Dreaded Jirgas

As we travelled further along the mountainous ranges and huge valleys the devastations made a scary picture. Blasted vehicles, empty villages, scattered skeletons were a display of human disparity. The NATO forces uprooted humane verve from this part of the world in the name of protecting the larger cause of world security. Men with firearms were protecting their family, their lands from internal, external armies, elderly people who fought all their lives for life and now were staring at death, children with no future in their eyes. A woman was nothing but a hijab here. I never got to see any lady to gauge her sorrow. But their suffering was enormous behind that veil.

Capt. Raza briefed me about the size and value of the opium trade. He said, 'This place is farmland of 80 per cent of the opium of the world. These areas have is no banking or credit facility. Here drug lords fill in the space and provide the farmers with advance Salaam to procure opium seeds and farming activities. This Salaam is similar to futures trading in stocks, opium has a futures market in the country. A price is paid to the farmer in advance as a loan, to deliver a fixed amount of opium at the end of harvest season. If the farmer fails to deliver this quantity, which more often than not he does fail, owing to the government eradication programs, the poor farmer does not get a reprieve. He still has to pay back the Salaam or take more. If the helpless farmer is trapped in this vicious cycle, a point comes where the drug lords take away the women of the family. These are the *opium brides*.'

Driving through abandoned roads, we came across a village cluttered with NATO vehicles. The cavalry halted to examine the reason for such heavy foreign army deployment. With large walls on the perimeter, the village resembled an old fort. The high walls masked any insidious activity. Word spread like fire of our arrival. Many leaders came rushing forward to welcome us. We responded with equal zeal. Looking at the mob, Capt. Raza whispered in my ear, 'Jirga ho raha hai.' (It's the jirga day.)

The local leaders congregated for jirga. A corner was occupied by some officers of the US army. We exchanged pleasantries after formal introductions. Major Watson was leader of the NATO contingent. The venue was packed to capacity as some important judgements were to be taken. The jirga leaders invited me and Major Watson to join them on the jury. Everybody was seated on the ground in a circle, where the jirga began with a prayer to Allah. The whole gathering joined in the prayers, after which one of the leaders recited in a local language the issues they had to settle in this jirga. He read them out loud and clear for the mob. My interpreter helped me understand the proceedings. Some of the issues were personal while some were communal. The leader called the appellants in, and a young man and elderly person came forward.

One of the cases was of a man who had pestered a few ladies at the *godar*. A *godar* is a place from where women fetch water for their families, and this sex pest used to follow and ogle them, passing lewd comments. The man looked schizophrenic standing there smiling throughout the proceedings, when his ghastly acts were declared. There was no mercy in this land, and the jirga unanimously decided to execute the man immediately. The tribes were fiercely protective about their women and wanted this to set an example to deter any future occurrences. The mental state of the guilty was hardly taken into consideration when they collectively ordered death. It was decided to stone the man to his last breath after the jirga was over.

The other case was of a land dispute between two families. One of the families claimed ownership on a piece of land, while the other family contested, claiming all the males of the owner family had died or were killed in drone attacks so they had sowed the land and they deserved harvest. The second family had also helped the NATO forces in providing some information about the hiding terrorists, so here Maj. Watson took a step ahead and spoke favoring the family. This caused a huge furor amongst the leaders. They vehemently objected to the participation and interference of a foreign delegate. A mute spectator until then, when I saw an US officer meddling with the affairs in my area, I politely requested the officer to leave. He gauged the gravity of the situation and made an exit. Though the contingent did not leave the village, it waited till the jirga was over. This gathering continued for another hour, after which the crowd cheered their way towards the local graveyard. It was time to lynch the psycho abuser of women, and the mob was merrily heading towards it. Having witnessed enough of violence in my life, I stayed back. Village leaders accompanied us for some refreshments.

We moved towards one of the larger houses, a huge place with a big garden in the front and an even bigger backyard. We proceeded to the rear of this massive place which was more like a warehouse. There were large sheds of sacks and cartons lined up. Very few of my confidant officers were allowed to access this backyard. The US army soldiers were roaming around freely, examining the packaged stuff, checking it for quality. They seemed to be at ease and were fluent in their work. On close observation, I discovered that the packaged material was opium and this backyard was an opium depot. Tribals from nearby villages deposited their harvest at this place for safekeeping. This occupied one half of the backyard. I ventured to the other half and was stunned to find an arms and ammunition repository. Modern weaponry, the latest guns, sophisticated gadgets were neatly stacked and labeled. I was shocked, but I was here not to investigate and purposely behaved normally, consenting to the dealings around. The Americans were so comfortable and friendly with these tribals to an extent that it aroused suspicion. As the day progressed, the Americans started loading opium in their vehicles. They were stocking the stuff in their empty missile blocks, gun carriers, and other empty cartons. I was flabbergasted. They took away a major chunk of the produce and thanked the locals. I walked up to Maj. Watson.

'What on earth is going on, major? Where are you taking all this opium?'

'Brig. Mazzi, you know that we have all of the arms needed for modern-day warfare but we are far away from victory. What we lack is local support and logistics. This is where these tribals fill in. The arms and ammunitions that our homeland provides us are not accounted for back home. The guns we carry, the number of magazines, rocket launchers, missiles, equipment, nothing is reported. We have abundance of artillery but we are fools trying to hunt an old bloke in this hell. Then we decided to put this weaponry to better use. We barter our ammunition for opium with these tribes. Back home, nobody values guns but this opium is invaluable. The price for such produce ranges in millions of dollars. It's easy. We supply them with our guns, which strengthen their hold over the region. In turn they furnish us with vital information that no money can buy. How else do you think we spot these terrorists and our drones bomb them? This is a small price for a huge value. We have the safest channel to carry this produce back to our country. It rakes in personal profits as well: revenue for us trading this produce, a victory for the US locating HVTs, and happy tribals with the most sophisticated arms—a win-win situation for everybody. So, brigadier, this dirty little secret is out in the open but I hope you will cooperate and let us operate.'

I smiled and let him proceed. The US army is the largest carrier of narcotics. Wow! This was mind-blowing. But I had better things to worry about and advanced towards the local leaders. The village chief came forward to explain his position. He clarified, 'Mazhar sir, there is lot of risk involved in the opium trade but since this village and the surrounding area are protected by the NATO forces, the local administration maintained distance. The fundamentalists harass us in extracting zakat in various names. But the arms provided by these Americans help us keep the fundamentalists away. The NATO forces also provide a definite buyer for our produce at a good price. We want to live a simple life and keep our family happy but the religious misinterpreters have made a mess. With the American protection, even the local government or administration does not dare to touch our crops.'

This was too much of a revelation for me here. It was almost day's end. We spent the night in the local army camp and headed back to Landi Kotal the next day.

CHAPTER 26

A New Interest, December 2010

Winters were harsh in these areas. Nature showed no mercy. Heavy snowfall lasting for days, soaring prices of commodities coupled with firewood prices shooting up made life miserable. There may be other places on the planet where temperatures fall much lower, but the government and the populace at such places are prepared for the onslaught. Here, in FATA, there is a dearth of everything. The tribals don't heed the government and the government reciprocates by ill-treating them. Many families rush downhill to the city of Peshawar to escape winter woes. But others have no choice but to battle it out. On the other hand, the army is well prepared and stocked to fight the frost. For officers inside the army complex, winters are like holidays. The senior officers assemble in the evenings to enjoy a drink or two and share their stories of valor. This year I was the latest participant in the winter discussions. Sipping single malt by a warm fireside made the evenings charming.

My family visited to experience snowfall. The kids were ecstatic with this European setting. A white blanket covered large mountains and a sheet of snow spread across the valley. The firewood, barbeque kebabs, snow fights made it an apt family holiday. As the year came to an end, there was an interesting observation. These tribal lands had plenty of Christian population. Many Christians resided in army camps but they adapted names very similar to the locals. So Ijaz Riaz, Aiman Mazzah, Fanyas Wazir were a few locals whom I met at social events. But this time of the year, I was astonished to know they were Christians. I was always aware some minorities resided in Pakistan, but this was the last place to expect them. I thought the cities must be home to these minorities.

Inshaa and Afaaz were glad to be a part of the Christmas celebrations. The Landi Kotal Christmas bazaar was an attraction. Clothes, shoes, accessories related to Christmas celebrations were available here. The local Christian community did not consider themselves as a part of tribal society and they had been residing here since pre-Pakistan days, living life on their own terms. Well, accepting local names to escape identification was a paradox to these claims. I instructed that a Christmas tree would be put in the army complex to convey greetings. It was fun for the kids to help soldiers decorate the tree. Hundreds of Christians gathered at local churches to offer collective prayers for solidarity and integrity of Pakistan. The army also organized a tea party at the army garrison to distribute cash and sweets to the Christian families. Children in colorful dresses presented a tableau and sang songs at a stage show. I presided over the cash distribution ceremony while my family was proud standing beside me through the event.

Regular routine work commenced after the year end. The family was back in Islamabad, kids resumed school, and the Americans continued bombing innocent civilians. It was heartbreaking to tag this loss of human life as collateral damage. The plight of people living in fear and being happy to live for another day was agonizing. There was no blink of future in their eyes.

In between such routine days, I received an official communication to host a team of human rights volunteers from the NGO Save the Child, who were visiting the area. I had never been a part of any such initiative earlier. A team of eight American individuals visited in the first week of January. The team was led by a middle-aged man called Tony. Tony and his volunteers arrived by a chopper on a cold morning early January. The ministry asked me to attend to these visitors and make a good impression. With no motivation to serve the Pak army, I found this a welcome break. The arrival of Americans aptly added some zest at work. I received them and led them to the guest house. Hordes of containers accompanied the Americans. My staff made space for this load within the garrison. The team rested for a day.

The following day, they were keen to survey the area, for which I provided security. The harsh winters added to the misery of the local people where these Americans arrived as angels. As we gathered around the bonfire in the evening, they informed me of the humanitarian items they brought along to help the people fight the frost. They had medicines, blankets, clothes, food, and a lot of stuff to help these locals. Though the name suggested they were focused on aiding children, under such harsh circumstances, they were ready to help everybody around. I was impressed with their efforts and assured them full cooperation in delivering these goods. My soldiers helped the Americans unpack their stuff. The next few days were spent in putting the things in order and labeling them for the specific regions. In these times of teamwork, I befriended the visitors. The Americans were unaware of my story; one of the evenings when they enquired about the scars on my face, I narrated to them the entire incident. They listened very attentively and were delighted to know that a decorated soldier was aiding them. I also invited a few prominent medicine professionals from the surrounding areas to discuss further aid and medicine required. Dr Shakil, Dr Hasib, Dr Mrs Husnaa, and many others informed the visitors about the ground realities. They were briefed about the challenges faced and specific ailments of the people.

A beautiful, enthusiastic girl in her early thirties accompanied the American contingent. Sandra was the live wire of the group, jovial, hard-working, sincere, and genuinely committed towards her job. She was tall, blonde with a fulsome body. The soft winter sun reflected on her silky golden tresses, and her deep blue eyes seemed to be made up of pristine crystals. She was busty with the right mounds at the right places and some curvy oomph. Her spotless skin and her striking pink lips were a pleasure to watch. As her lips moved, the dimples on her cheeks spread joy in this sad gloomy place. She was extremely friendly and surprisingly comfortable in these difficult environs. We shared very cozy working relations, where she was never shy of expressing her admiration of my valor.

After all the stuff was segregated, it was time to dispatch them to the surrounding areas. The Americans made two teams of four individuals each to carry out this task. I also set two teams of soldiers for security of these Good Samaritans. I obviously accompanied Sandra. We travelled to a few places with some of the worst of human conditions. Kids chased our vehicles; the women would thank and bless us. The men came chatting with them; the village leaders would host the group for tea and discuss their issues. The visit of the Americans was a very welcome change. After I witnessed their horror face, this was their compassionate side. A whole week passed by, and finally the time arrived for the Americans to depart. I ordered my staff to host a grand dinner for the kind guests before their departure. Elaborate arrangements were made to show our gratitude. I called for a local DJ who played wonderful Bollywood tracks. The amazing food made the Americans lick their fingers. A bonfire on a frozen night, the best quality single malt, and a congregation of some interesting people made it an exciting evening. The next morning, the Americans were lock, stock, and loaded, when I observed Sandra lingering around, not packed. As I arrived, Sandra came running.

'Brigadier Mazzi, I am not going with the team. I've decided to stay behind and study the area so it will improvise the next batch of aid that would come.'

I was delighted inside. Some feelings are better expressed without words. Her enthusiasm revealed a thousand emotions and my never ending smile divulged the joy in my belly.

After the Americans were gone, Sandra went back to her place while I continued with my job. She joined me for dinner where we indulged in a hearty chat. After dinner, I invited her to my quarters for a coffee to which she readily agreed. My heart was pounding and I was sweating in bitter cold. Never did I have an opportunity to host such a beautiful blonde at my house so late in the night. She looked a tad fidgety but she was confident. We walked to my place where I lit the fire. My staff delivered the coffee and I asked him to leave for the day.

'So tell me about yourself, Sandra. I never had the chance to inquire about you with your teammates were around.'

'Brigadier sir, I am a simple girl who is deeply interested in human life. I feel a lot for the underprivileged. Every human on this planet deserves an equal life. Equality to food, shelter, clothing is a basic necessity. But capitalism and self-centered businessmen have spoiled all human values. Today everybody works for a personal agenda. Never anything is enough. About my personal life, I've lived all my life in the US, did my master's in humanitarian sciences from Colombia University, and right now I am pursuing my doctorate on "Life in Af-Pak after US intrusion" from Stanford University. I am here to study how this war has affected the life of a commoner and suggest ways to make it better.'

She was a rare combination of beauty with brains. Time glided fast in between such interesting discussion. I decided to walk her to the guest house in the cold dark night. She was confident to go alone but the gentleman in me could not let a lady go without an escort. We strolled to her place, enjoying the snow, where she disappeared not without landing a peck on my cheek and arousing the man from his winter hibernation. Over the next few days, our friendship grew stronger. My brave story was a definite lure for any woman, and her beauty was too good to resist. I accompanied her on field trips where her interactions with the tribals were lovable and caring. She was fluent in local languages which eased her way with the locals. The evening coffee sessions soon upgraded to a few single malts to help fight the frost.

One of such whisky evenings, we got into an argument over her favorite topics. I debated, 'This war on terror has encouraged terrorism and terrorists. The drone war which started way back in 2004 is responsible for more than 300 attacks killing in excess of 2,000 people. Many of these were innocent civilians, women, and children. These naïve people are aloof of any politics or religion, work hard for a life. Suddenly a random bomb explodes in their vicinity, killing their friends and family. Many have lost their lives; many have lost their vision, hearing, limbs, leaving them impaired for life. The Pakistan government had never openly admitted to helping NATO for these UAV attacks, but the fact that they operated from the Shamsi air base in Balochistan speaks loudly of their duplicity. This is gross violation of human rights and a joke on a country's sovereignty. Your government has made a mockery of our nation.'

She, being a typical scholarly student, defended her country's actions. She disputed and justified the attacks, claiming the higher cause of world security.

'The search for Baitullah Mehsud and the destruction of his training camps has made the terrorists run for cover. Your government has been responsible for these incessant attacks. Had Pakistan not airlifted them from Kunduz in November 2001, we had every chance to catch the whole network and terrorist organization in one place. This Airlift of Evil in which thousands of top commanders of al-Qaeda, Taliban, jihadi volunteers and sympathizers had congregated were evacuated from Kunduz in Pak air force cargo planes and moved to Pak air force base in Chitral and Gilgit in Pakistan Occupied Kashmir. We captured Kunduz within days of this airlift. If they were holed up there, we would have captured them, thus saving troubles for your populace. But your country wanted the best of both worlds, presenting a picture of ally to the NATO forces and joining hands with the fundamentalists. Why do all of the world terrorists hide in these areas? Why do they kidnap people who come here to help these poor countries? These terrorists have no country and no religion. They are selfish individuals who sell death in the name of the Almighty. It's your government's apathy that they let such fundamentalists dwell in these mountains. If your government drives them out of here, we have nothing against your country.'

Our glasses were refilled, our argument extended, our voices were raised. At one point in time, I was staring right into her eyes and she was screaming at my face. We were so close to each other, I could hear her breathing and unknowingly grabbed her waist, pulled her closer to smooch her with all my might. She shoved me away lividly. I was embarrassed but instantaneously she came running and leaped. She retaliated with a kiss of equal passion. She cut my upper lip but continued to suck and held on. We were like two animals hungry for each other. Desperate, I carried her to the bedroom. Tearing apart my shirt, she went crazy from the ugly scars. She pushed me to the bed, taking a few steps back. My heart was pounding; I wanted to hump her. She removed her sweater along with her top. In my first experience to watch a blonde strip, I was going berserk. I started undressing myself, and within moments, we were nude. Asian women are usually uncomfortable being naked, but this American babe was at ease. She was rosy red on the inside, with pink nipples. The golden tresses on her pastel skin were too good to resist. Her rear was a perfect round and tight, the well-toned body of an athlete. As she came closer, the demon inside me seized her and brought her down. I spend the next few minutes exploring her nimble frame and spotless body. Starting with her well-rounded bosom, I licked her all around. The flavor was unparalleled. As I was making my next move, she resisted. It was the time for reversal. She climbed on top of me, positioned herself, made me slither in, and then started with her acrobatics. She was agile, svelte, and stretchy. I had the most amazing feeling to see a gorgeous woman, not shy, giving me the pleasure of a lifetime. She changed numerous positions and every variation was better than the previous. The postures she attained along with the strength in her grip made me howl in enjoyable pain. She was equally tough with a great stamina. I squeezed her close, fighting to get on top. She relented and now it was my turn. I stretched her legs and entered the wet hole with all my might. The fair skin changed its shade to red with all this exuberance. But the excitement did not stop. One session was not enough. We got together for another round of madness. With equal fervor and craze, we continued till the wee hours of the morning. This was the wildest session of physical intimacy and what a fulfilling experience!

CHAPTER 27

Special Assignment

Sandra and I bonded intimately over the next few days. Every evening she spent at my place got us together for the night. We were addicted. She was an intelligent woman; spending time with her made me understand a different viewpoint about the war on terror, its global impact, among other things. We used to have long conversations about the past, present, and future of the country. Seldom did we agree but that did not take away the passion of togetherness. Every night, the rush of blood was soaring and the fondness was growing. She used to complete her studies, dine with me, and sleep in my warm embrace. In between some of the best times of my life, one fine day, a communication arrived from the headquarters instructing me to a special assignment. I was in a beautiful epoch, forgetting about all of my past, lost in the pleasures of life. But this assignment was a wake-up call to grab my prospects on the way back home. The government wanted me for a month-long posting in Balochistan. A Baloch leader was demanding severance of ties with the government, and the administration was keen to cash in on my popularity to suppress this revolution. After Gen. Anwar appraised my job of strengthening ties with local FATA tribes, they wanted me to open channels of dialogues to restrain the discontent in Balochistan. The call of duty was unexpected and I expressed my displeasure to Sandra, who was also equally disappointed. Since it was a short assignment, she decided to holiday in Dubai with her friends. She promised me her return whenever I did. I made a dash to Islamabad to spend a couple of days with Adaah and the kids before taking up this new assignment. The army headquarters called me in for a briefing attended by the army chief which elevated the significance of my visit.

The chopper took me to Quetta, the capital town of Balochistan. Located 5,000 feet above sea level, this beautiful high-altitude city surrounded by majestic mountains is a major trade center between Afghanistan and Pakistan. It hosts the highest railway and airport of Pakistan. With a rousing welcome at the army recruitment center, I checked in at the senior officers' guest house. The first few days were spent meeting new recruits and spreading the word of bravery amongst them. The local officers arranged a presentation which enlightened me about the present political turmoil, the issues for the deadlock and the government stance. The army chief had concurred with my decision for necessary action to be taken to improvise the situation. Requesting an audience with the local leader of the mutiny, I studied the factors that led to this uprising.

Balochistan was the most backward province of Pakistan. With an area covering around 44 per cent of the country, it was home to only 5 per cent of the population. Since the formation of Pakistan, it had been facing separatist insurgency by rebels belonging to the Baloch tribe. Baloch nationalists have complained for decades of ethnic discrimination and exploitation by the Pakistani state. But the recent sequence of events had turned the complaint of discontent into a movement for outright secession. I asked for an audience with the local leader Sardar Raisani. I was informed the supreme leader of the region, Shahjahan Bugti, had been underground for more than six months, fearing for his life, from the Pak military. The local leader was averse to meeting an army officer, but my reputation made things easier. The media praised me for bridging gaps with the local FATA leaders and they had already been writing about my arrival to normalize the situation. These Baloch leaders had rejected meeting any of the government representatives, leaving the situation in a deadlock. With my name proposed, they agreed to table their demands. So I was permitted to visit with my special task force at their designated location. This was a challenging proposition. I, along with Capt. Raza, a few of my trusted soldiers, and local translators, agreed on a mutual location for the meeting. It was a high-profile event with the whole of the local media and international media awaiting and anticipating the outcome.

Balochistan has long been on a boil. Its infinite, empty deserts and long borders lure every act of vandalism. It is the homeland for misdirected terrorists. Taliban fighters make a freeway of the 800-mile Afghan border; Iranian rebels hide inside the 570-mile frontier. Like most of tribal areas, drug trade is the primary source of earnings here. The drug cartel crosses the border from Helmand, the world's largest source of heroin, on their way to Iran. Wealthy Arab sheikhs fly into secret airstrips on hunting expeditions for the houbara bustard, a bird they believe is an aphrodisiac. At Shamsi, a secretive airbase in a remote valley in the centre of the province, CIA operatives launch drones that attack Islamists in the tribal belt. Pakistanis, Afghans, Iranians, Americans, British all work in tandem to make this place a living hell.

The Baloch are spread between Afghanistan, Pakistan, and Iran with several militants' groups claiming to be fighting for a Greater Balochistan uniting the community living in all three countries. The first Baloch revolt erupted way back in 1948; since then, they have always been reluctant Pakistanis. They use guerrilla tactics like bombing gas pipelines, bombing government agency offices, ambushing military convoys. For the past few years, these acts have grown manifold, and the participation is not restricted to men and fighters. In this male-dominated province, even women have been vocal about their dissent from Pakistan; Baloch schools and the students refuse to fly the Pak flag or sing the national anthem. The Baloch rage is deep-rooted in poverty. The region is one of the most underdeveloped regions in the world. With literacy rates as low as 20 per cent, only 6 per cent of the people have access to tap water. And this is only the tip of the iceberg.

Sardar Raisani arrived with his panel of negotiators at the administrator's office in Khurzid district headquarters. I arrived a day prior to overlook preparations, was eager to make a mark here since it would lead to my elevation in international ranks.

Behaving like a novice, I said, 'Raisani sahib, I was born in Islamabad and spent all of my career in Kashmir. The media has been my only informant of Balochistan. I am unaware of the ground realities, and it is imperative to discuss them to find a solution. Today I am here to hear you. Please feel free to say whatever you want to. I assure you complete confidentiality.'

He appeared a little skeptical.

Raisani explained, 'I am sure you must be aware of the conflict of Baloch people. This is basically a war between races. We are Baloch and they are the Punjabis. These Punjabis comprise 45 per cent of the Pak population and the rest is divided among a lot of factions. We Baloch occupy the largest area of the country, still our population is diminished to a mere 5 per cent. If the administration continues their evil barbaric means, our people will either vanish or will be pushed out of the Pak boundary to Iran or Afghanistan. This is our land; our ancestors have ruled these mountains for centuries. Even the Westerners recognized our independence and never enforced themselves. All these ideological arguments can continue forever, but of late, the barbaric behavior of the government is unbelievable. Around January 2010, the Balochistan student organization Azaad called for a peaceful march to draw government's attention towards the plight of this region. It was a perfectly silent protest by young students when the Pak army, showing its true colors, sprayed the protesters with bullets, mercilessly slaughtered young lives. After this incident, there have been innumerable cases of disappearances. This time, when the Baloch raised their voice, the Pak army adopted a new strategy of forced disappearances, kill and dump. Students, lawyers, farmers, laborers, drivers, teachers have been kidnapped, and their bodies surface two or three days later. These corpses are dumped in isolated hills or deserted roads. These lively people are butchered in broad daylight and the carnage is unforgiving. The limbs are ripped off, faces are swollen, indicating marks of torture, and skin is peeled off private parts. The hands and legs are found at a different location from the torso, it becomes impossible to identify the body from these parts. Many times scavengers bite off the mutilated bodies and all that is left is a stinking mass of rotting flesh. One thing common in all these dead is they have a gunshot through the head. The martyrs don't even receive a *shahadat*. These atrocities are carried out with flagrant impunity. The forces of justice seem forgotten in these cases. Not a single person is accused or arrested. In fact, the local police openly admit there is not even a single case registered for such violence. This lack of interest in investigating this mass genocide speaks in itself of the involvement of the ever-powerful military. The Baloch people's rights are under assault from all directions. The military blatantly kill the commoners, the state-sponsored fundamentalists hunt the Baloch, peaceful protesters are shot at, political leaders are indefinitely detained, and there is an absolute impeachment of freedom of speech and assembly. We Baloch are the most secular tribe of the country who happily dwell with people of all caste and religion. We have a huge source of minerals and are home to the deep-sea port of Gwadar. Many cross-country fuel pipelines run through our region. We are here not to garner any sympathy from the government, but if the regime has failed to deliver in sixty years, we are cynical about the future. So if you cannot deliver us our right to livelihood, at least renounce us to form our own space and identity.'

His recitation left me dumbstruck. I looked at my peers; many of them hung their heads in agreement and shame. Lost for words to make a point, gathering some courage, I convinced them that their issues were noted, and a talk with the superiors would find a solution. Spending the night at the army garrison, we made our way back to Quetta the next day. The media was awaiting my arrival for a briefing, but I chose to avoid them and presented a case to the bosses. They listened carefully and reacted nonchalantly. It was evident these officers were well aware of the realities. In fact, it seemed as if they were hand in glove for such atrocities. I was perturbed by this reaction. The Baloch had so much of faith but I was helpless.

CHAPTER 28

A Ray of Hope

After visiting a few areas in the vicinity of Quetta, I was convinced of atrocities by the local army. The Pak government kept the world engaged with stories of Kashmir, but they failed miserably to recognize the plight of the poor Baloch. This reminded me of the carnage of the Pak army in East Pakistan. They raped and murdered thousands of Bengali women before their defeat in the war of 1969. They were nothing better than Hitler's Germany, or Stalin's Russia. In fact, this army harked back to the nightmares of the Khmer Rouge of Cambodia. With another fortnight to go of this special assignment, I was not keen to visit any more villages and make a mockery of myself. I chose to be happy in my own army world, attending felicitation and seminars and delivering lectures to recruits. The experience was disturbing but the world was always aware of this two-faced Pakistan army. All my life being an Indian, I hated this country; as destiny made me live this life, this assignment made me abhor it more. I wanted to go back to my Khyber hills to spend time with Sandra or make my way back home.

Bolan medical college was the only academy of medicine in this area. Balochistan had the worst medical care ratio in the world, 1 doctor to 10,000 people. I was invited as chief guest to the annual cultural festival of the college. This was a welcome break from the depressing surroundings, so I readily agreed to be a part of the celebrations. At the institute, the boys were wearing the trademark Pathani and the girls were covered in a hijab. Very unlikely for medical professionals but I guessed they didn't want to upset the locals. The girls entered the campus in hijabs and on campus wore the traditional salwar kameez. It was heartbreaking to see innocent hard-working students undergoing such difficulties, but this is Pakistan. What you wear is what you are. The pleasant song-and-dance routine reminded me of good old days with Saakshi. Our National Defence Academy rarely had such celebrations, but I attended a few in Saakshi's college. The enthusiasm of the students, the zest in their performances was appreciable. One of the highlights of the evening was a play presented by the students. It was intelligent satire, taking potshots at the government. The students apologized for their daring to take up the issue, but I was mighty impressed and personally lauded their efforts. The entire evening was like a breath of fresh air in these troubled years of my life.

I joined the students for dinner. Many of them enquired about my near-death experience and life after that. The zeal in their eyes made me recite the incident with equal fervor. After the students, it was the time for professors, lecturers, and the support staff. They surrounded me and came in their barrage of medical queries. How did I feel when I was in the blast, during the blast, after the blast, during coma, after coma? Did these doctors realize that pain does not have a parameter to measure it? Pain is pain. But I had to be cooperative since I owed my life to these professionals. Amongst the support staff was a very interesting gentleman. He shied away from eye contact with me and was reluctant to interact. After initial introduction, he kept himself occupied in a corner. It was a very novel experience for me. Since I awoke in this country, people always flocked to me, were keen to hear me. But this gentleman was an exception which invoked curiosity. As the crowd moved away for dinner, I went to him and got chatting. He introduced himself as Mr Shaikh. There was a very evident apprehension in his approach. He was not an employee of the institution but was a vendor for medicine supply. He used to source surgical equipment, medicines, other equipment from around the world. This invoked my interest and I summoned him to my workplace the next day.

The scared look on his face excited me. He escaped immediately as I diverted my attention. But I called him from behind, reminding him of the appointment next day.

Next morning, before I reached the garrison, Mr Shaikh was eagerly awaiting my arrival. Fumbling and fidgety, he greeted me. I put an arm across his shoulders, taking him out for a walk, wanted him to be comfortable to open up.

'Mr. Shaikh, being a Pakistan army officer is a huge responsibility. There are thousands of expectations to shoulder.'

I spoke to him about my last stint as the head of the purchase department for the army.

'I am eager to understand methods for cost-cutting in procuring medicines. Since I was heading stores a few months back, can you educate me from where are these medicines and medical equipments procured?'

I disclosed my encounters in FATA, the tribes, opium, and experiences at the battlefront. As I unlocked some of my stories to him, he eased up with me. We shared a few laughs before I started to probe him.

He informed me, 'Brigadier sir, the sourcing of medical equipment and pharmaceuticals is from locations such as India, China, and other nations. Pakistan has a sparse pharma industry so India was the preferred country to source low-cost drugs and equipments.'

This made me jump for joy. After a long time, I encountered somebody who had India connections.

'You must be aware that the army is the largest consumer of medicines in this country, I am sure you can help us here.'

I was trying to ease him, entice him with a business opportunity to extract information. The lunch together got us talking about our families. By evening, we were like pals when I invited him to dinner, but he excused himself. He informed me about the exporter from India; a Gujarati gentleman called Mr Patel was travelling to Quetta and he would be glad to introduce me to Mr Patel for further prospects. This is exactly what I wanted.

The morning after, Shaikh came with his Indian partner, Mr Aslam Patel, a well-stocked gentleman. I was aware of these Gujarati Muslims who traded with Pakistan. Projecting to be busy, my staff informed them to meet me at the guest house in the evening. I wanted to present a different picture to this Indian. In the evening after formal introductions we had a long chat about business in Pakistan. Mr Patel was an experienced person with thorough knowledge of exports. He was apprehensive in the beginning. For him, I was a decorated Pak army officer, very patriotic and loyal to the country. He assumed divulging too many facts might turn the tables. But I needed to know more than Mr Patel's business experiences. I urged both of them to stay back for dinner. Mr Patel, being a typical Gujju anticipating huge business, agreed immediately.

As I opened up a bottle of single malt, the Gujju was excited and then flowed hours of narrations of business—India, Pakistan, export, import, religion, life, and every topic under the sun. Patel boasted of his connections in India and Pakistan, how he managed to make a multimillion-rupee business in such a sensitive corridor under these edgy times, the way he greased palms of influential people in both countries. He revealed about Pakistani artists moving to India to make money and he helped many Pak actors, actresses, musicians, singers to find the right connection in Bollywood. Once these artists were established in their careers, they would return him favors, helping expand business in Pakistan by finding the right contacts. He divulged to me there was a large syndicate and it was not just medicines or art that was being exchanged between the two countries. There were dirty dark secrets. I listened to him patiently and tried not to offend in any way, to elevate his confidence in me. After a sumptuous dinner, the duo left. By now, I was certain of an Indian connection.

I was raring to learn about the Indian indulgence in this part of the world. Mr Patel was a seed to my ambition. Our friendship grew stronger in the next few days. Mr Patel used to drop by every evening for tea and sometimes stay back for dinner. We had long conversations over politics and the way ahead for the two countries. It was a very weird conversation for me since he was the one who was on India's side while I was defending Pakistan. I had to depict a Paki image since this Mr Patel had loyalties on both sides, and for his personal benefits, he could swing either way. As we became thick friends, I discussed with him how the injury and the subsequent life had changed my personality.

'This close encounter with death has changed my approach towards war. Though the Indians bombed me, I don't hold any grudges against them. The soldier at the border is unaware of whom he is shooting. They are mere puppets, innocent laborers who are made to follow a master's orders. They are not allowed to think. What transpired that night, nobody knows except me, but whatever happened has changed me completely. Today, my family takes precedence over everything. I need to take care of them and fulfill their needs. Luck won't be on my side to escape alive every time. So I have to make the most with this little time in hand and gather all for the family. My son should be foreign-educated and in a corporate, daughter should study medicine in the US, wife to have all the luxuries of life. I want to indulge in every pleasure and regret nothing. Life can bring many twists. My country matters to me but what is more important today is me, my family, and my personal gains.'

This confession made Mr Patel's eyes sparkle. He anticipated another high-ranking officer falling to his decoy and expected business coming his way. I was purposely projecting a corrupt image for my reward of a way back home. My intent was to identify a person who could believe in my story and set me en route. These were last the few days in Quetta, and I was scheduled to go back to my workplace, Landi Kotal. After the army pampering the vendor, it was time for him to oblige. I didn't hesitate to share the wicked nights in Islamabad. Patel was an astute businessman and immediately picked the path. Subsequently he invited me to a dinner out in Quetta town.

'Sir, this will be a private dinner attended by close friends and no government official will be present. I assure you an unforgettable night.'

A car picked me up and drove straight to a hotel where Patel was waiting for me. Walking through the narrow corridors, we entered a dimly lighted foyer. The lights inside were so diffused, it was difficult to see even a few meters away. A huge bar at the other end of the room was raided by people trying hard to grab a bottle or a glass. There was some peppy music playing softly, but loud enough to make the already high-spirited dance. It was like a hiding nightclub and trying hard to be the hot spot.

But nonetheless I was amazed to see such a place in this ultra-conservative town. Patel grabbed my hand like a friend and helped me through the chaos to my table. He made me comfortable and posted an attendant at my service. He came back in a few minutes with some of his friends. Their introductions were hardly audible and their faces were barely visible. I got chatting to these new acquaintances about the weather, current affairs, and other topics. I conversed with one Mr Tuli seated next to me. Mr Tuli was from India but settled in Malaysia. He also was a trader of some equipment to this part of the world. He educated me this was the only place where people from different nationalities met once in a week to have a drink, socialize, and have a party. Otherwise consumption of alcohol was thoroughly banned in this area. The others with us at the table were all Asians. They were here for some professional commitments. After a few hours of mindless chatter, it was time for the place to down shutters. The hotel staff urged the guests to leave and it was an end of a dull, uninspiring evening. I was expecting more out of Patel but he disappointed me. As we were about to leave, Patel and Tuli held me back.

'Sir, this is the end of the party for the world. We deserve a celebration that is out of this world. This, what you experienced, was just a trailer. Wait until you see the complete picture.'

Now this was exciting. Not much for the revelry, but to find me a window of opportunity. This was the best chance I encountered in the past year to connect with somebody from India. And when the individual is a businessman trading across borders, he surely has the right connections with the right people at the right places. After much of the crowd exited, Patel and Tuli and me drove to hotel Quetta Serena, a spacious property with some lovely architecture, beautiful manicured gardens, lovely furniture, a glorious building, and stunning interiors—a very rare estate in the middle of this desert. The staff was very cordial and acknowledged Patel and Tuli. I was surprised with the opulence of the place and conveyed to the gentlemen there was no need of such lavish expense. Patel ignored me and said that some of his friends would be joining. The two strode down the lobby through the corridors to the top floor. I followed them diligently, walking swiftly, avoiding eye contact with the people around. I was a public figure and didn't want to make a scam out of this venture but was willing to take the risk for a brighter prospect. The splendid view overlooking the city surrounded by Chiltan and the Murdar ranges in the night was breathtaking. The suite was the Sultan Suite. A three-roomed all-amenities-loaded party place welcomed us. The men asked me to freshen up until they would make arrangements. Patel walked me into a spacious bedroom with a closet full of stylish clothes and offered me everything.

'Sir, pick what you like. It's all for you. We will set up the evening.'

I had already breached a barrier and ventured far with these people but somehow I trusted them. My Indian sensibilities trained me to interpret how a Gujarati responds when he sees a business prospect. If these people cannot find me the road home, I will at least make some money for my family and in turn help my countrymen earn. So I decided to make the most of the opportunity, one way or the other. I bolted the door, had a long bath, and dressed up smart for the after-party. The mood was set right in the drawing room and Tuli announced my arrival to the guests. The men were busy filling their glasses, with many women to be drooling over. I was introduced to some individuals whom Tuli claimed were prominent figures in the Indo-Pak trade links. The glasses were raised and the ladies took charge of the evening. Swaying to Bollywood beats, they enthralled the men to join in the salsa. Patel was nowhere to be seen, and when I enquired, Tuli informed me Patel went to fetch a gift, while handing me a tequila shot. Someone knocked on the door at 2 a.m.; I was a little perturbed but Tuli was perfectly confident it was Patel. Patel walked in with a beautiful woman in his arms. They walked up to me and before Patel could introduce us, the lady sprinted and gave me a tight hug. Four pegs of single malt, some tequila shots, and the dimly lit room didn't help much in identifying her, but both Patel and Tuli were surprised. As the woman loosened her grip, I held her close to look at the pretty face. And boy oh boy! She was Aafreen, my love, my indulgence. I immediately gave her a long hard smooch, and before anybody could question our acquaintance, we bid farewell to the party. These three months of parting were long enough to keep our hands off each other.

The next morning, I opened my eyes to see pretty Aafreen dressing herself. Though glad to spend the night with her, as the morning arrived, sensibilities set in. I was curious to know her story with Patel or Tuli, and how did she land up in Quetta? She looked a tad embarrassed. I held her close to my chest; she started sobbing. There was a brief moment of silence to let her calm down. With a heavy voice, she disclosed, 'After a fleeting stint of stardom and glamour in Mumbai, I was out of work. The very people who praised me, hailed me as the next superstar started rejecting my calls and avoided me. My resources drained, I was broke and lived off credit for some time. But the creditors piled up and then one of my friends in Mumbai suggested to me this vicious route to make a quick buck. Mumbai is an expensive city. To maintain a life, I was unknowingly trapped in this muck. I was never this kind of a girl and it hurt my conscience. One such occasion I met a gentleman who was an Indo-Pak trader. He sought my help to find the right contacts in this country. I was always a Pakistan citizen so I travelled back to my country and helped him set up the business. This earned me enough repute amongst the trader community and they lined up for my help. I realized that my star power could not get me any movies but helped me in some way. As a Paki, I always knew the army is the strongest force in the country, and to actually make a mark, I had to entrap some officers at prominent positions to help build business for my Indian friends. That was precisely the reason I met you and enjoyed those naughty nights. But you were different from the usual breed of officers. You were caring and compassionate. I really liked you. When you informed me about the transfer to Khyber, I was heartbroken, but that's life. I continued with my consultancy services which help in linking the two warring countries, building positive business. I have various means to build bridges, and if nothing works, my charm is the final bait. I am sorry to have concealed some information, but I did it all in good faith. I had no intention to harm you but was trying to build a mutually beneficial relationship. I never expected you in this part of the country. This is Balochistan.'

This revelation was disturbing but exciting, not Aafreen's plight, but I was confident that with her help I would find somebody of help. I embraced her tight and she reciprocated the warmth. We stepped out of the bedroom to find Patel and Tuli eagerly awaiting our arrival; rising from their seats, they greeted me. They were beaming with happiness of having one more officer in their kitty. But I was the happiest, sure to work my way home.

CHAPTER 29

February 2011, Embarking on the Journey

It was the last week of this Balochistan stint, little time in hand and an enormous task to accomplish. After the night of exploits, Tuli dropped me off at my guest house and promised to catch up for evening tea. I crashed asleep after the long, tiring, fun-filled night. After the high tea, I left with Patel and Tuli for the outskirts of the city. Driving towards the hills, Patel stopped the vehicle at a cliff from where we could see the entire town. I preferred to be seated in the car, not wanting to attract unwanted attention. Patel, being a typical businessman, didn't waste any time and straight made his point.

'Mazzi sir, we understand that every man has desires in life. Everybody wants to make money for himself and his family, earn respect, and garner recognition. Anybody would be lying if he says that all these things don't excite him. An individual's growth is stunted if he stops aspiring. A few lucky people have their families to thank for fulfilling these desires, but for self-made entities like us, it is a long tiring journey. In this journey there are a thousands of covets yet to be fulfilled. We would be glad to help you and your family accomplish such dreams if you give us an opportunity to serve you. We guarantee you these words will never leak out of these windows. You can rest assured of complete secrecy.'

Skeptical to overestimate their capabilities, I decided to dig into their intentions.

'So what is it that you guys want? With the businesses you built over the years, you have all the right contacts at strategic locations. How can an officer like me help international businessmen like you?'

Tuli jumped into the conversation.

'Sir, you are a legend today, an icon of Pakistan's bravery, and our experience teaches that you have every opportunity to hold some very important positions in the country. Army cover is always sought while dealing in Pakistan. We traders would like a long-standing relationship with every officer in the country. Not expecting anything today but we are pleased to be friends with a brave Pakistan army officer. Though your story involves my country as a foe, still it does not take away your achievement and valor. We are more than happy to befriend you.'

They sounded like any typical middlemen trying to make me feel secure for being corrupt. I was short on time, not looking for a monthly retainer from these businesses to help me live a comfortable life. I wanted to escape from this life and realized that these two were not much help.

'Mr Patel, Mr Tuli, I genuinely thank you for your kind hospitality. You have been generous in pampering me and I can't thank you enough for helping me reconnect with Aafreen. Speaking frankly without prejudice, I am aware of what you bring to the table in this association and confident you have every resource in the world that will help me make my future very happy and exciting. But to remind you, I am a person who's back from the dead. I was in a coma for almost a month, and it took me six months for complete recovery. I have garnered all the recognition in the world, the government has rewarded me enough for a smooth sail for the rest of my life. The country loves me and my story. But such a close encounter with death also made me realize how vulnerable and unpredictable life can be. This country, its relationships with the neighboring countries, or international alliances, I am afraid to say it's difficult to foresee a promising future. Honestly speaking, I am not very keen to continue living in this country for long and want to send my family to the West to lead a better life. Small inlets to fill my coffers are not to my liking; I want to play that one master stroke after which I can retire for the rest of my life. As the old saying goes, "Sau sonar kii aur ek lohar kii". (A hundred strokes of a goldsmith and one stroke of a blacksmith)

'Short of time and patience to occupy a position of importance and then expect you to make my life comfortable. I am in Quetta for the next few days and you know where to find me. Thank you for your hospitality, and please, let's head back now.'

I planted a seed in their head. Now it was their turn to interpret the message. I was on shaky ground, and it would be difficult for these businessmen to understand my story. My target was somebody whose interest was beyond monetary gains, and this somebody with enough influence would help me head back home.

I was a proud Indian soldier and a decorated Pakistani soldier; I was dead in my early life, where I wanted to go back and live, and I was alive in this life where I wanted to be dead.

Tuli arrived the following evening. Sipping tea, Tuli informed me, 'Sir, we are simple businessmen and are unaware of any such routes of monetizing, but I can introduce you to some people who would definitely be interested.'

'Why don't we meet at someplace else to discuss further?' I enquired.

'Sir, it will be difficult to find these people or arrange this meeting at such short notice. These are highly reclusive individuals. If you move towards the Af-Pak border, I'll arrange for somebody to see you in a few days.'

I had only two days left in Quetta, and there were number on programs lined up for my farewell. A press briefing was organized to inform the media about my stint in Balochistan. But this was an exciting opportunity and couldn't let it pass. I informed Tuli the next day about my itinerary and asked him to locate these people. I was a serving soldier and couldn't disappear without a reason. So I applied for a week-long leave before joining back in Khyber, reasoning that I would explore this beautiful region. The leave was immediately granted.

CHAPTER 30

A Positive Lead

After my official work days, I informed Adaah about this backpacking trip. She was surprised but worried since the Pak army was not exactly welcome in this region. I convinced her of my experience and influence to ensure safety, spoke with the kids as well. To make this look like a tourist outing, I asked Aafreen to join me. She, being a sport, agreed immediately. She was also a known face so it dispersed the fact of any shady intent. We hired a large SUV, engaged a driver cum guide, packed our bags and set off on the adventure. This was the first holiday in my Pakistani life. With Aafreen by my side, I was sure of an amazing journey. Finding somebody who could help me go back home was dubious, but nonetheless, it was a holiday with a very pretty woman. Aafreen was aware of some grey intentions for this journey;

she was unaware of the gravity. Tuli was constantly in touch with me, assuring me that he would find some positive lead. He asked us to drive towards the town of Chaman on the Af-Pak border.

The dusty border town of Chaman was the last post of Pakistan on the Durand Line, just like any other Pakistan tribal town, surrounded by mountains, with small congested roads, burqa-clad women, and Pathani-flaunting men. What surprised me was the density of population in this tiny place. It had an overcrowded market with traders lined up. The insider lanes were narrower and cramped. The number of high-end cars in this bustling town was mind-boggling. Land Cruisers, Pajeros, Prados, Toyotas, Hondas occupied the roads in abundance. The activity on this frontier was impressive. Our driver, being well versed with the place, drove us around for a while until we reached a decent place. Not very luxurious, it had all the amenities for a comfortable stay. The hotel manager immediately recognized Aafreen, with closer observation, acknowledged me as well. I informed Tuli of my arrival and the place of stay. Weary after a three-hour journey through tumbling roads, we opted for a naughty nap. As we descended from our room in the evening, the lobby was packed. We hurried towards the exit; some of the guests identified Aafreen but by then our car arrived, we hopped in, and sped away.

While we moved around the town, our driver educated us about the town and its businesses.

'Sir, as any frontier town, this place is a hotbed for smuggling activities. All goods smuggled through Afghanistan are routed through this town into Pakistan. This is exactly the reason for profusion of business.'

We came back to the hotel after a tour of the city. Happy spending time with Afreen, I was anticipating some message from Tuli. There were better locations in Pakistan to visit and admire. My mission and intention here was to find a lead. Every passing hour made me anxious. Aafreen kept me entertained with her seductive, impish moves but my mind was occupied with something more important. Just as we ordered dinner, the reception called to inform me of a visitor. I jumped out from the bed to rush downstairs. A restless elderly gentleman handed me an envelope and left in a jiffy. Not impressed, I was expecting more. The envelope revealed two tickets for a football game. Unaware of the operations in secret services, I concluded this must be a lead towards something more concrete. The night was pleasurable as usual. Next morning, I informed Aafreen, 'I've a surprise for you, baby doll. We are going to watch a football match today.'

'What on earth! A football match on Afghanistan border. You army officers have unique ways for amusement. Since you have planned it, I am sure it is going to be fun,' concurred Aafreen.

A game was the last thing she expected to see on the Af-Pak border. After the NDA days, this was the first time that I had an opportunity to experience live football.

The excitement was palpable as we drove towards the Chaman high school stadium. The usually conservative populace had a spring in their feet and were enjoying themselves en route to the stadium. Though their attire didn't change, definitely their mood did. I wondered, what clothes did the players don? Pathani suits? Well, that was ambitious. But nonetheless, there was enthusiasm in the air. The driver informed us, 'Football is a huge sport in Afghanistan. Many Afghan refugees crossed the border and settled in this town during the 1979 Soviet-Afghan war. Despite their orthodox mindset and religious lifestyle, these locals are very much in love with this game. When the Afghans arrived, this sport played a major role for normalizing relations between the immigrants and the natives. Football has helped these people ease tensions and vent their furies. Pakistan's most famous football club, Afghan FC, belongs to this town and we are on our way to watch the match between Afghan FC and Muslim FC. This is one of the high-profile encounters, so many people are expected from across the border as well. They enter the borders illegally since the police are busy making preparations for the matches. So let's enjoy the match, sir.'

The school campus transformed into a funfair. Thousands of people flocked the grounds and were hustling to find seats for themselves. As we approached, security personnel checked our passes, directing us to the far corner. After parking the vehicle, the driver escorted us to our enclosure. We passed smoothly, escaping identification, occupying a chamber with the best view of the ground. There were a few more of such chambers, which were already occupied with dignitaries. The ground was almost packed to capacity. I was doubly excited. Apart from the delight of watching the game, a further lead was expected. As the match started, a couple of people joined us in our box. We were busy watching the game, but their arrival diverted my attention. I greeted them and they responded. Making Aafreen comfortable, I occupied a seat behind the strangers. One of them joined and exchanged a smile.

He introduced himself, 'Hi, I am Iftaar. You like football? Our association with football goes back years. The Britishers, after conquering all of the Indian subcontinent, came to Afghanistan but couldn't find a footing here. They introduced football to garner some local support. The Afghans were fiercely protective of their freedom, they kicked away the British but retained their game. This part of the world has been playing football for decades. Chaman was an Afghan town until these British formed the new country of Pakistan.'

After a few minutes, the other person, Husain, also joined and soon all three of us got talking. Their command of English was startling, a rare attribute.

Husain chipped in, 'Sir, we recognize you and the woman. It is difficult to believe renowned personalities like you have come all the way to watch this match.'

I nodded in agreement. After almost half an hour of aimless chatter, Iftaar enquired, 'Can you disclose the real purpose of such well-known people visiting this miniscule town?'

I replied, 'Holiday.'

With stares at each other, we roared in laughter. Aafreen, at a distance, was worried to see us growling but she looked delighted as for her it sounded that a deal was sealed.

Husain took the lead.

'Let's not beat around the bush, and come straight to the point. Our sources tell us that you have arrived here with a definite purpose. You are not interested in helping our friends grow business but are keen to aid in some other prospects. Can you please elaborate how can we be of mutual benefit?'

To find a solid lead, it was impossible to hide and fake for long. I had to open up and let a few little secrets out, start trusting people, and make them trust me.

'You must be aware of my saga, a middle-aged man, but only a few months old. I just had a fresh lease on life. Let's not get into those details, but frankly speaking, I am not very keen on continuing this job for long. I need to collect all I can, as fast as I can, and disappear.'

Right at this moment, Afghan FC scored a goal and the stadium erupted. Hussain and Iftaar joined the celebration. After the chaos settled, Hussain replied, 'Brigadier Mazhar, we completely sympathize for all the hardships you had to face. Trust me, this country does not deserve sacrifice. This is a country of selfish populace. The politicians are hungry for power, the military is corrupt for money, the cricketers are selfish, the tribals are self-centered for dominance, and lastly the farmer is only interested to grow his weed and kill the next generation. This country does not deserve martyrs. But as I understand, you don't want to stay back in this country and want to make a fortune before you depart. Now that's a difficult proposition. What is that you can offer which will excite anybody to pay you enough to suffice for a lifetime? A supply contract or an assurance for a huge order will definitely pull in some money but I doubt if will last for a lifetime. I will have to talk to people to find an amicable way where you can achieve your goals.'

I intervened. 'Mr Husain, I am Hilal-i-Jur'at of the Pakistan army, a jewel in their crown, their blue-eyed boy. I have access to every department, every office, every agency, all information, however discreet. Your businessmen friends might find this futile but I am sure there are many seekers for such services. I need not elaborate. You are a wise man who understands the value of this association.'

They were hustled. Rising up from their seats, asked for permission to leave. The football match lost its sheen. I could spot giggles in their eyes and enthusiasm in their walk. They bid goodbye to Aafreen. I accompanied them to the door. With a handshake, Husain whispered, 'What do you think about India?'

My heart skipped a beat; I regained my composure and replied like an honest-to-goodness corrupt officer, 'Payments are accepted only in US dollars. It doesn't matter to me which country provides them.'

Hussain's face lit up and he rushed away. Sitting beside the lady, I felt my heart pounding. Was this for real? Would he actually introduce me to an Indian here? Would I be able to go to my motherland again? Would I see my parents and Saakshi again?

CHAPTER 31

Friends or Foes

The exciting football match ended with the home team taking the victory lap. Aafreen and I quickly slipped into our vehicle and sped away. On our way through the market was a Hindu temple. This was the first time I noticed a temple in this country and it was impossible to hold back. I didn't have the chance to thank my deity after resurrection; the divine place charmed me. Aafreen and the driver were shocked but I didn't care. They were pawns in my game but this was the Almighty. The place was a broken structure with a pandit praying inside. I bowed, prayed for a while, sipped the holy water, and came back to the car. Aafreen was stunned but she did not dare question my faith. The driver was scandalized but chose to stay mum. Suddenly this town seemed interesting. With closer observation, I discovered there were numerous shops with Hindu names. This was surprising. As we arrived at our hotel, I enquired with the manager about the Hindus in the area and was pleasantly surprised to see that he was a Hindu himself—Jeetu Wadhwani. He explained that because this was a border town, there was a lot of trading activity. Most of the Hindus in this town were Sindhi-speaking Hindu businessmen. We struck up a friendship and he offered me a visit to his home. Skeptical to go overboard and raise suspicion, I requested a homemade meal from him. He immediately obliged, and within an hour, I enjoyed a hearty homemade Hindu meal. Good old days were reminiscent.

Next day, a person arrived.

'Good morning, sir. I am Zuben, a car trader. Iftaar tells me that you need to purchase a car. Don't worry about the costs. The bills will be settled in subsequent dealings.'

I concluded businessmen are narrow-minded people who can think only about their personal profits. Tuli must have instigated some local trader to make me purchase a car for some commission. I refused.

But this man insisted, 'Sir, please don't be stingy. This is an exciting opportunity and you might get a chance to travel to the other side of the border into Afghanistan.'

Now this interested me. He invited me to cross over in the evening to broker the deal. Owing to my reputation, one of the biggest car dealers of this region was coming to attend me personally. I had an intuition that things were definitely moving in the right direction. Aafreen preferred to stay back.

Zuben arrived in the evening to pick me up. After a short drive, we lined up in a long queue. Zuben enlightened me, 'Sir, this is the Chaman Gate, border between Afghanistan and Pakistan.'

Suddenly our car swerved left and, cutting across lanes, came straight to a magnificent gate. It was almost 100 feet tall with PROUD PAKISTAN and PAKISTAN FIRST inscribed, Pakistan flags fluttering, and Jinnah staring from above. Zuben asked me keep mum and act normal. As we neared the checkpoint, my heart was palpitating. But surprisingly nobody verified anything. The driver just rolled down his window a few inches, handed the guard a 5,000 Pakistani rupee note and we were sailing on the other side. I was in Afghanistan, a smooth passage without any hindrances. Since we were travelling in the car which belonged to the biggest car trader of the region, nobody bothered to check us. I was confused about the importance of cars and car trade in the region. Zuben educated me.

'Sir, all the used cars that come into ports of Afghanistan are primarily from Japan. Afghanistan is a country with no import duties and a left-hand-drive country so these Japanese cars are of no use here. The cars are refurbished and smuggled into Pakistan, which is right-hand drive. Along with the cars, there are other articles which cross borders and trade hands.'

We arrived at a unique place. Thousands of containers were strewn all over. Some of them were used as offices; some were homes to people. Clothes were drying on container doors, kids running from one container to another, women grinding their spices inside a container. It was a container hamlet. We halted in front of one of the very few buildings in this town: Al-Hadaad car trading. The huge parking lot had all the cars in the world, mostly SUVs.

Zuben requested me to identify a high-end car. The expense of this car was to be reimbursed later, but to display my solidarity, I was expected to buy one for confirmation. Disinterested in the whole activity, I asked him to find me anything suitable. He suggested a swanky Land Cruiser. We climbed to the second floor, where two people joined us. I handed a token cheque to the cashier. The other person kept mum, observing all activities. The cashier left, leaving the two of us behind. The person went over to the door, peeped outside to check, and bolted the door from inside. His move alerted me.

'Major Mazhar, it is a pleasure meeting you. You are a true legend in army circles.'

Army circles? I was astonished and decided to keep a straight face.

He continued, 'After all that you have done for your country, you definitely deserve more, sir. I've seen Pakistani army officers who have made millions of dollars without even seeing a battlefield in their entire life. You definitely deserve better.'

I was still doubtful and cynical about this person. It had been only a few minutes of seeing him and he was commenting about my whole life. I had to be cautious since this trap would finish my career, reputation in this new life. I didn't entertain him.

'I am not interested in small talk. If you can help me in any way, please let me know, or else I am going back.'

He sensed my discomfort.

'Sir, we are sorry to put you through this ordeal. It would have been a privilege to come over to your place, but we were meeting on very short notice. So we had to gauge your commitment. We had to comprehend whether you were ready to take risks for this our association. Now that you have taken all the pain, don't worry, sir, we are at your service. We will make sure you have all you want. I am sorry, I didn't introduce myself yet. I am Capt. Hamid of RAAM.'

RAAM? I had never heard of such an organization. I acted ignorant and continued the blank stare. Hamid was an intelligent chap; he immediately interpreted I was unaware of RAAM.

'RAAM, Riyast-i-Amoor-o-Amanat-i-Milliyah, is the premier intelligence agency of Afghanistan. CIA to the US, MI7 to the British, R&AW to the Indians, and RAAM to the Afghans.'

Now things were really serious.

I paused for a moment, ecstatic but equally nervous. Was this game going to take such enormous proportions? I had to be prepared for this. This was a story of a slain decorated Indian army officer trying to escape from his highly established, comfortable life as a Pakistani army officer. All the planning, beliefs, ideations, thoughts—it was time to deploy them.

'OK, I believe in you. Now tell me, Hamid, how can we help to each other?'

'Sir, I am a small bunny of this larger-than-life circus. I am the fast, agile hands and feet of this well-oiled machine. I scout, identify, notify, and disappear in my rabbit hole again. I am not aware of what happens after my job is done. So I won't be able to help you much with the details at this point of time, but let me go back. I am sure we can take this lead ahead. I am completely aware of you, your achievements, and your reach. So I will do my best. You have a safe journey back to Chaman.'

Before probing any further, he disappeared amongst the containers.

Zuben was waiting to drop me off at the hotel; he informed me the car would be delivered next day. Well, the car was the last thing on my mind. I was mute for the rest of the journey.

Emotions are abstract. They cannot be measured, because I am sure if there was an instrument to quantify them, all my emotions would be breaching the safety mark now. Happy, scared, anxious, nervous, ecstatic—my head was a mixed bag of feelings.

Aafreen was like a goddess in the morning: the strides as she was balancing the tea tray, her flowing hair, and her heavenly body gleaming in the morning light. This woman was responsible for all these proceedings. She was happy keeping me happy. I just couldn't thank her enough.

Around midday, the reception informed me that a new car had arrived. Aafreen was equally excited and rushed downstairs with me. She was busy admiring the car, while I spoke to the delivery man. I enquired about Hamid, and invited him for a tea inside. In the restaurant, he introduced himself as Zulfikar.

'Sir, this region is a desert. Not many animals survive in these harsh conditions. Some very few birds have been trusted messengers over centuries for the people of this area. I am a modern-day messenger hawk, sir. I carry gossip and rumors across the borders. I will be your local contact and will make arrangements of the logistics whenever you have anything to share, anything critical. I know everything about you so feel free to head back to your home in Islamabad or posting in Landi Kotal. We will stay in touch with you. In such cases, remuneration works on the information, its criticality and urgency. We have a foolproof channel working, so if we require any specific info, we will get in touch as and when the time arrives. If you take the initiative to provide us with anything of importance we would be glad to oblige. Payments in cash and kind, in currency of any country, in a bank account of any country can be made. So rest assured.'

I was flatly disappointed. Yes, making some money was on my mind but not this way. I was expecting an Indian headway, upset, but I had to be patient. I signed the car documents and escorted Zulfikar to the door. Suddenly it struck me: my Pak family was completely unaware about this purchase. In between thoughts, the driver handed me the keys, asking me to take a test drive. Least interested in the drive, but to project myself as a genuine buyer, I relented, took it for a short spin. On one of the crowded streets, the driver had to alight to instruct me for a safe reverse; when I glanced at his face. He looked familiar. A heavily built Pathani-clad, turbaned Pashtun with a long beard and no moustache was suddenly identifiable. As he climbed back in the vehicle, he took precedence in my thoughts. He was shying away from eye contact but I was adamant, scanning through my memories, trying to place him over the years. I was unable to trace him but those eyes, that face behind the beard, that grin was seen somewhere. As we came back to the hotel premises, I asked,

'Zulfikar, who is this driver you have brought along?'

He was reluctant and informed me, 'Sir, he is a local Afghan, a languages teacher coach in a local school who doubled as a driver to earn some extra bucks.'

'Zulfikar, I need some practice to get used to the new car so ask the driver to stay behind for today.'

Both of them vehemently refused.

'Sir, this person is an Afghan citizen, if caught, he will be detained for illegally entering into Pakistan.'

This repulsive behavior charged me; I insisted, 'I am not asking you, Zulfikar, I am commanding you to let the driver stay. You know me and my influence. Don't worry if anything untoward happens, I am capable of handling it.'

The driver was taken aback but he had no choice. He could not deny an officer of my stature. Zulfikar walked to him, made him understand the situation convincing him to stay behind. Zulfikar confirmed that the driver would stay to coach me. I was scheduled to go back to Khyber the next day so it was only a matter of twenty-four hours. The driver was suddenly looking confident and stared back at me with equal fanaticism. Zulfikar left, Aafreen went upstairs to rest when I instructed the driver to accompany me on a drive. We hit the street and I initiated a dialogue with him, generally inquiring about his village, conditions after the NATO intervention, local politics, etc. I probed his job profile, his line of work. He was not entirely honest with his replies. I immediately concluded that he was deceitful on this facet. As we drove away from the town, driving towards Quetta highway, I started humming some Bollywood number, which he identified. Now my suspicions grew stronger, and suddenly in the middle of the drive, I mumbled, 'PBeyakistanrele Beyisrele grBeyeatrele cBeyountryrele.' (Pakistan is a great country.)

The driver was ogling me and replied, 'YBeyesrele, Beyitrele Beyisrele!' (Yes, it is.)

With tears streaming down, he refused to accept it or believe his eyes, but his heart knew it was me. On the face of this planet, this dialect was unique between only the two of us. He was gaping as if he had seen a ghost. I was thrilled to hear the golden words. I got down enthusiastically; he got down cautiously. I shrieked, 'JAY AMBE, AMBE BHAWANI MAA, HEE HAA HOO . . . JAY DURGE, DURGE BHAWANI MAA, HEE HAA HOO!'

Yes, it was AD, my friend, my buddy, my partner in crime, my companion in good and bad. He alighted and we shared the signature chest bump. We hugged each other so tight that it almost choked us. Tears were rolling down from my eyes and he was weeping like a kid. We simply couldn't get over the joy of discovering each other in the middle of one of the most hostile places on the planet. For him, I was dead. So his joy was out of bounds. For me, he was the last person to expect but was definitely my jaunt back home. The deserts were glowing in happiness. He was staring into the face of a decorated Pakistan army officer who sounded like his best buddy and closest friend.

CHAPTER 32

Indo-Af, Af-Pak, Indo-Pak

After a long period of overflowing emotions, both of us realized that we were at a very treacherous place, two Indian army officers driving on the Af-Pak border. Before we could resume our journey, AD asked me to take the passenger seat and he took the wheel. He bent down under the car and came back with a small electronic instrument in his hand. As he sat in the driver's place, he dismantled the music system. I was wondering, what was he up to? Using some clippers, he chopped off another electronic instrument from inside the music system panel. He crushed both the devices with his feet and trampled them beyond recognition. He informed me, 'The intelligence agencies usually rig officers' cars. This was a very delicate situation and I don't trust anybody out there.'

He destroyed the devices and was desperate to hear my saga. I narrated him the entire chain of events on the way back. He was somber, gloomy, confused but ecstatic at the same time. Back at the hotel, we were the usual officer and driver to avoid suspicion. I went to my room and he refreshed himself in the drivers' cabins. I was more than eager to hear his side of the story. Up in my room, I realized that Hindu gods in Pakistan were more powerful than gods in India. The Almighty answered my prayers without any delay. I smiled at the fact there were very few Hindus here, so definitely the Almighty was burdened with less workload.

Without wasting any time, we hurried for another spin in the car. I was keen to know AD's journey from the NDA to the Afghanistan.

'After NDA, as you are aware, I was selected to the elite services of R&AW. In the initial days, I was a desk worker in the administrative office, filing, documenting, reporting, and all the donkey work that was never expected. I was feeling suffocated but I worked diligently. We had already chosen our path so there was no turning back. I was an honest officer who followed every word of senior's advice. Life in a secret agency appears very rosy. But participating in daily activities and executing the duties is a huge task. An ambiguity prevails in these agencies; there are no specific rankings to officers. A junior recruit can be your senior if he has more hands-on knowledge of the mission or situation. Nobody is aware of the agency's complete staff. So anybody can be your colleague, superior, or an influential contact. There can be multiple teams working on the same mission but they are seldom aware of each other. Contacts, connections used on the same task also differ. The information transferred from one place to another has different routes and codes. So this may look like a large organization, but internally there are thousands of smaller entities who are working together. All this information is assembled at a central repository and analyzed to take necessary actions.

'After spending almost eight to ten months on a single chair, the agency recognized my dedication and selected me for an on-field post. I was posted in the Afghan embassy in New Delhi, again for a desk job. Here I was the travel coordinator for all the embassy delegates, booked tickets, made travel arrangements, and was basically aware of the complete itinerary of anybody going to Afghanistan. Though I was officially being paid by the government of Afghanistan, I was reporting back to R&AW. Impressed with my work, they moved me to the visa filing department. So now R&AW had eyes and ears on anybody coming in and going out of Afghanistan from India. With the intensive NATO strikes and dilapidating conditions in Afghanistan, the government of India decided to ramp up their team at the Indira Gandhi Children's Hospital in Kabul. I was selected to head the team of administrative staff for better cooperation. The years spent at the embassy helped me pick up the language. For R&AW, I was a proven resource who could speak fluent Pashto. The embassy approved my posting and I was transferred to Kabul. On reaching Kabul, I was not assigned to any special task for the first few months. They let me blend in and establish my credentials. I also eased my way into these Afghans where my hard-working nature was quickly appreciated. With the experience of embassy work, I helped the Indian embassy as and when required. In the meanwhile, I also started dressing like a Pathan. After a brief period, I was called back to India to be sent back to training. This time I was a trainer with the Indian Military Academy. I trained the new recruits for handling guns, laying mines, and other army activities. I also spent time with family for a short while before the duty came calling again. Back home I enquired with your mother and was informed that you were posted in the north-east corridor. I wanted to connect with you but it is an unsaid law of our organization not to publicize our postings. So I decided to keep mum and returned to Afghanistan. But this time R&AW sent me with a delegation of Indian teachers who were coming as a part of goodwill exchange program between the two countries. I was inducted as a languages master supposed to coach Afghan schoolkids. Coming to Kabul, our delegation was immediately transferred to Spin Boldak. We commenced duty in a school set up by the Indian embassy. Spin Boldak had always been a war-torn place since the Soviet invasion in the '80s.

These Baloch refugees who crossed over to Pakistan to escape war came back to a dispersed life. Every day is a struggle for these Baloch since then. The Soviets, the Americans, the British, the Pakis have made a mockery of their lives. Anyways, I was inducted as a languages instructor to the schoolkids, enjoyed the first few days of training the kids in Pashto, after which came the real calling. In the evenings, I used to travel to an abandoned school on the outskirts of the town. Here a few newbies joined and I had an official communication to get them trained for the battlefield. Here the short stint at the IMA made sense. I never bothered to enquire whether the recruits were Afghans or Pakistanis or Baloch. This is a very porous border and the same tribe exists on both sides. They speak the same language and follow the same lifestyle. So it's impossible to identify their nationalities. But knowing R&AW and their activities, these were mostly Baloch rebels from Pakistan who were getting ready to fight the Pak army. This school was slowly developed into a complete training centre. I was handed the task to develop it into a world-class preparation centre. R&AW promptly delivered different kinds of training equipment. I was spending mornings with the kids at the school and evenings with young recruits getting them war ready. Maj. Singh was my inspiration, who made us what we are today. I am a tough but dedicated coach. Fresh batches kept pouring in every two months and also two more trainers have joined in. Today I am an Afghan specialist. Anybody can mistake me as a

Pathan as you did. But real friends are hard to fool. With this spare time in hand, I was asked to mingle around with the locals to understand the trade that happens across the border. As you have seen, car dealing is the most prevalent trade. These locals have high regard for teachers so it was easy for me to penetrate into the biggest dealer and mingle with their staff. I have been friends with them for a few months now and can easily pass things to either side of the border.

'When Zulfikar informed us about some prominent Pak army officer getting lured, I was keen to know more about the individual. So I volunteered to deliver the car. Never in my wildest imagination did I imagine this: a dead Suri, alive and kicking. I wept inconsolably the day we learnt about your death, had a word with your parents and Saakshi to share the grief. We had lost you, the world had lost you, but this is the ugliest twist of destiny. I cannot imagine I am talking to you, Kirti Chakra Shaheed Captain Rajeev Suri. This is simply unbelievable.'

We shared a warm hug and then came the big question: 'What next?' I asked and he returned the same question.

I was always honest with AD about every small little secret of my life.

'OK, you know how much I love my country, my family, and my wife. I am trapped in this body. This is a corpse lying over a dead soul. I am alive because these doctors could get back life in me. I never wanted to be in this situation. Nobody does. Since I was resurrected, I want to rush back to my family, want to serve my country again. This country has treated me well. I have a good family, a good posting, all the appreciation and recognition a man could ever dream of, but this is not me. I am suffocating every day to fake an identity. It is not easy inside. AD, you can do this. I have always believed in you. Please, I plead with you to help me get back home. I will do everything you ask me to. Please help me get back to my parents, my wife, and my motherland.' Unknowingly, tears rolled down my face.

AD was dumbstruck.

'Suri, you have to understand this is a very delicate situation. You are a decorated dead Indian officer, dead for more than a year now. On the other hand, you are a highly recognized face of the Pakistan army here and also internationally. You have a family back in India and you also have a family here in Pakistan. You cannot ditch one of them to find solace in another. This is not just a matter of personal agendas but there are two nuclear-powered enemy nations here. The Indian government would find it very hard to believe this, and the Pakistani counterpart will be furious. You cannot disappear into thin air. If you escape like a coward, the Pakis won't hesitate to harm your present family. I have already lost my best friend once and cannot afford to risk your life again, just being honest with you. I am not saying I won't help any further but you should be aware of all the ground realities before we make a decision. I will have to talk it out with my superiors before committing you anything. As for a R&AW officer, you are a very precious asset. You are a gold mine of information. We are thoroughly aware of how the Pakistani army functions and the information an officer of your stature can possess and will have access to. We definitely have a strong case to plead, but this is something that has never happened on this planet ever before. So please head back to your workplace, I have contacts to stay in touch with you. As a friend, I will make sure that you come back, and as an officer, I will inform you of everything that will be needed to make this happen. It won't be an easy transition but I will put my heart and soul into it.'

We reached the hotel premises; AD bowed to me like a servant and made an exit. I came rushing upstairs to my room to share a passionate hour with Aafreen to celebrate this completely unexpected event.

CHAPTER 33

First Steps to Way Back

I dropped off Aafreen at the Quetta airport, hugged her with an assurance to stay in touch. I was greatly indebted to this person in my life. She did sow a seed to my journey back home.

Before joining back in Khyber, I visited Islamabad to my new bungalow, which was under construction when I left the city. The family was lovely as always. With summer was setting in, the temperatures were on the rise. School examinations were approaching; Adaah was glad to have me around. She handed me the toughest task of my life: tutor the kids for good grades. I was out of ideas for this unexpected duty, waiting desperately for AD's response when suddenly I was handed this. Spending time with kids with science, maths, history, geography, languages was not just difficult, it was impossible. I didn't have the patience to teach them. I was a student of a military school where any mistake was followed by a punishment; obviously I couldn't do any of that with my kids. Inshaa was too young. Afaaz was a little mature to learn fast. But both posed similar problems to me. I was not prepared for this stint. These times that we spent together bonded us. We had times of annoyance, disagreements, punishments, fun, and frolic. The kids were inseparable. The new car was an added attraction. Every evening, we used to head out for a drive on Seventh Avenue, with the kids feeling the wind in their hair from the sunroof and Adaah also joining them once in a while. The car was a pride for the family and I often dropped off the kids at the school, went shopping with family, dinner dates with Adaah. The kids were a part of my life now and Adaah was always a loveable, dedicated wife. There was no reason for me to leave this place. One of such dinner nights, I joked, 'I am going to disappear again. You will never find me.'

All three started crying. Inshaa was weeping at the top of her voice, Afaaz had tears rolling down his eyes, and Adaah was sobbing inconsolably. I passed the comment on a lighter note but it broke the whole family. They couldn't foresee a future without me now. Adaah convinced me, 'If you ever leave us again, we will follow me to wherever, Jannat or Jahannam.'

I laughed, but it made her miserable. Hearing all the gloomy talk, the kids were depressed and walked out of the restaurant. We abandoned the dinner midway. I was greatly disturbed by this reaction. It was impossible to reveal to them the truth at this point of time. Even a discussion of me leaving spoiled our beautiful evening. I was distraught. As we reached home that evening, the kids hugged me goodnight and made me swear to never leave them. I embraced and comforted them.

During one of such days, the service station called to inform me that my new car needed some attention. This was definitely some news from my discreet friend. The technician at the service center asked me to talk to the supervisor. The supervisor shared an exorbitant price for repairs. I was astonished. My car was working fine so why such costs? He ignored my query, and handed me a long list.

'Sir, This is the list of parts that need to be replaced from your vehicle. Please arrange for the same. You can contact our local service station for further queries.'

The list had names in Urdu. It didn't make any sense. No car spare parts were mentioned so it took a little time to decipher. I drove back home, picked up my laptop and searched for these names. Almost all of them were Pak citizens; some were respected individuals in this country like Riyaasat Ali. On studying the Indian perspective over the Internet,

I found out all of them were branded terrorists. Riyaasat Ali was in fact Abu Jundal, a 26/11 handler. Abdul Karim Tunda, Riyaz Bhatkal, Ibrahim Memon, Syed Salahuddin, Shadab Beg, and others were on the list. This was definitely AD's note. He wanted me to get the addresses, contacts, bank accounts, family details of these dreaded terrorists. So now things were getting serious. This was definitely working in the right direction.

The following day I received an invite to attend an event at the Pakistan Institute of Medical Sciences. Patel and Tuli were present at this event. I interacted with a few acquaintances and then we slipped away to a corner. Patel and Tuli were not aware of the proceedings but they were glad of the association. As we went to a secluded corner, Tuli whipped out his cell phone, connected a call, and handed it over.

'AD here. I have conveyed about your intentions but I did not reveal any details. It's too complicated to make anybody believe in such short notice. My side is ready to help, provided you can accumulate all the spare parts that you have been requested from you. My team does not want to get into your details but will stand by their commitments only if you can furnish them the said requisite information.'

'AD, I have a query. This family that I have been living with is very precious to me. I cannot leave them alone in the middle of nowhere. They will be devastated if

I disappear. Can you talk it out to your team and let me know how can we help them?'

AD was furious and blasted, 'Are you out of your mind? I had a hard time convincing them about you. There is no way that they will allow a whole family to come in. Besides you should understand that an officer, his wife, and two schoolgoing kids cannot disappear from the face of the planet just overnight. There will be serious repercussions of this. We are already at loggerheads with this country and this will worsen it. And where will you go with them? You cannot go back to your Indian family, inform them about this Pakistani family, and expect everybody to live together. Have you ever thought about Saakshi? How would she react? What would you tell your friends and parents about this newly found family? This cannot be done, my friend. Let's not complicate this further. You are already in a mess. I am trying my best to help you out of it. I will stick to my commitment to ensure you a passage but you alone. We also have to tread with caution of your disappearance. You are a celebrity in here. Lose your present family, collect the information, and call me whenever you are ready. I will need fifteen days and a million Pak rupees to prepare for this event. Please pay the amount cause it's very imperative to get local support. Take care. Bye.'

Tuli and Patel did not enquire much about what transpired on the call. All they cared for was a multi-crore consignment business. The three of us had been hiding for long so we dispersed fast.

At home, Inshaa came running to my arms and caressed me. Adaah had set a pretty table for dinner, and Afaaz came along to clear up some science doubts. We enjoyed the sumptuous meal, laughed about Afaaz's school incident. This was one happy life. As we retired for the day, I put a chair in my magnificent garden and had to recollect the call with AD.

He had spoken to his authorities. They were ready to help me provided I deliver them the information of these rogue folks. A window of fifteen days was needed to make arrangements and a million Pak rupees for this ride back home. But then was the harshest fact of life. I was supposed to dump my present doting family, a loving, respectful, caring, devoted family who breathed new life in me. I was determined not to let this happen. I could not leave them in the hands of these devils. If they could not come with me, they could not stay back here. This country could not be trusted with the life of my beautiful wife, my handsome son, and my most precious daughter. The idea sent shivers down my spine. Mazhar was a loving husband, a responsible father and a good human being. I was unknowingly but responsible for his death. His family does not need to pay the price. I laid back my head in despair and Adaah was there to ease my mind. She offered me a head massage, the only thing needed in this hour of agony. I decided to dig in and investigate these suspicious individuals, would keep my part of the task ready. Subsequently I would put in efforts to find an opportunity for my family to escape this treacherous place, probably find them citizenship in some European country or America, provide them with enough money to sustain and maintain a comfortable life. Then I would walk back home with my head held high.

CHAPTER 34

Back to Work, Back to Khyber

It was March 2011; I was long gone from my workplace. My visit to Balochistan was extensively covered by the media and the government openly acknowledged my suggestions. Governments usually do that without real action. I reported back on duty to a rousing welcome from the staff. General Anwar called to applaud my effort. But all these admirations were last on my mind. My opportunity to go back to India was my priority. It began with gathering the requisite information. My short stint with the purchase department provided me ample opportunity to make abundant wealth, so arranging the amount would not be a problem. I was contemplating my options when suddenly it struck me. My good old friend Yusuf, whom I last met in Suhail's office before resuming active work, had always worked with the ISI. He could definitely help me here. I was not in touch with him since the last meet about a year ago. So I was skeptical about his reaction. Nonetheless, he was supposedly my best buddy from training days. I got his contact coordinates from Suhail, and dialed right away. He was excited to hear me, as we exchanged pleasantries. After the formal chat of family and friends updates, he enquired the real motive to reconnect.

'Bhai, you haven't spoken to me for almost ten months now. I know you very well. You haven't called only to enquire about well-being. Tell me, what can I do for the Hilal-i-Jur'at of the Pak army?'

I had to fabricate my intent, so the strategy was 'Brother, you are aware I work in a very sensitive area of Landi Kotal and recently the government has asked me to travel to Balochistan to settle the uprising there. In these areas there is a prominent presence of foreign forces, US, UK, NATO, India. You know I've served all my life in Kashmir. Seldom did I have a chance to study these tribal areas, the people involved, and other useful info. While interacting with foreign delegates, I am not well informed about many important individuals. You know how I hate to project myself as a novice. And with all the awards and appreciation, it becomes an embarrassment sometimes. You are the ISI, I am sure you have all the information that can make me a scholar in these matters. So can you help me be better informed and not look like a moron?'

Yusuf burst out laughing.

'Such a trivial task. I expected you would ask for something tougher. Tell me, bro, what and whose information you require and I will deliver it to you.'

I was relieved. 'I have a list of people who are discussed a lot amongst officers. But am completely unaware who they are, where they reside, what do they do, and other stuff. So I will mail you this list. If you can send me all the information you have, it will help me a great deal.'

Yusuf was confident. 'You mail me the names and I will send you the information discreetly. Definitely these people you are talking about are individuals who might have dual identities, but don't worry, ISI knows everything about everybody. So just send me the names and your purpose will be served.'

I thanked him profusely; we disconnected after the usual friendly banter. The task was accomplished. A senior ISI officer was on the job. I decided to add some names to AD's list, not wanting to make it look like an Indian surge. Some tribal leaders I was acquainted with in FATA, some leaders of Balochistan were added to provide the list an authentic touch. Yusuf acknowledged the receipt almost immediately.

So one-half of my way back home was sorted. But the most difficult part of this adventure was still dangling in uncertainty. I had a family who could not be abandoned in the middle of nowhere. Sometimes my wicked mind played games to convince me to just let go, forget about these materialistic attachments, and follow my heart. Somehow I failed to obey these immoral incentives and decided to stay put to find a way out for my family.

I was back in Khyber, missing Sandra. I emailed her about my arrival and was delighted to know that she was already in Pakistan. She was in Peshawar, from where she dialed me immediately. To my surprise, she arrived the next day. I sent an escort to pick her up; we were together again. Getting back to our routine, a few drinks, the usual dinner along followed by a passionate lovemaking session. Sandra was fiery hot and she made me go crazy for her all over again. I enquired, 'How come you are back so soon, babes?'

'Mazzi, I don't have opportunities to travel every now and then. I have to collect as much information for my studies in very little time.'

I didn't care much. The next few days were the usual; I was occupied with my office work while Sandra used to visit the villages around. Now we were addicted to each other and couldn't stay away. The best part of this relationship was that we knew all about each other. She was aware of my marriage and the two kids. We had no strings attached. I informed her about my time in Balochistan and the new car. I did not reveal about all that transpired in Quetta but did tell her about the container town, the Chaman border, and other things. She used to spend every night with me. One of these nights, as we were lying next to each other, I expressed my dilemma.

'Sandra, you know I just want to run away from everything. I want to take my family along and disappear from this country, go and hide in a place where nobody knows me, recognizes me, or finds me. I am tired of being brave. I just want to flee and vanish, take some money with me, go into hiding where I and my family can live a quiet, content life away from this world.'

Sandra turned towards me; as she placed her bare thigh on top of mine, I could feel the warmth between her legs. She caressed my chest and asked, 'What can you do to achieve this dream? I mean, how far can you go? What can you compromise?'

I was taken aback; I squeezed her closer and asked, 'What do you mean? Can you help me, babes?'

She chose not to respond but landed an adoring kiss and whispered, 'Just go off to sleep, Mazzi. We will talk tomorrow morning.'

CHAPTER 35

The Pawn

Early morning, Sandra was nowhere to be seen. We usually had breakfast together before continuing with our daily chores. Her comment occupied my mind. As I was ready to depart for the office, Sandra was waiting in the drawing room. She was not the usual sweet, sexy girl I always knew, with her hair tied back, donning formal attire, ready for an official presentation. She was looking sharp and arrogant. I confronted her with a mischievous smile, hoping to understand the transformation, but she looked tough. She requested me to accompany her and I obliged without any uncertainty. She had a car waiting outside. I was amazed since in the past so many days, she never used a vehicle of her own. She always used the army transportation. This was a little disturbing but I was amused instead of angered, eager to know the other side of my love doll. My security team was trailing which she asked me to shrug off. This unruly behavior shocked me. It made me inquisitive. Confident that she would not hurt me for no reason, I instructed my security to proceed to the office. We drove around Landi Kotal for a while, through the narrow lanes, in the same vicinity for more than an hour. I deciphered that they were purposely doing this to confuse me, so I couldn't exactly remember where they had taken me. But why? Why was Sandra doing this? All throughout the journey, Sandra was quiet and didn't interact much. I also made a tough stance. The car halted in front of a two-storey house where Sandra alighted and waited for me to follow. It was a usual home of a local, with kids playing in the compound and women engaged in their household activities. Sandra walked past all of them to climb to the floor above. I trailed her silently without interacting with the house occupants. The residents did not care much, neither surprised to see a foreign lady or an army officer in their house. They were busy with their stuff, ignorant to all other activities. Such reactions from locals heightened my confusion. As I climbed the stairs, a few more Westerners were awaiting my arrival on the floor above. This place was more like a data analysis center with a lot of computers, maps, and pictures. Sandra went on to the other side of the table. There were a few women in the group as well. All this was very strange and I was confused to death. One gentleman rose from his seat to initiate.

'Welcome Brig. Mazhar. I am Brad. We are very glad to see you. Though I will apologize to confess we have been seeing for almost a year now, I am more pleased to meet you. Let me introduce you my team, this is Capt. Susan, the person near the board is Maj. Daniel, this is our IT expert Capt. Lisa, and last but not the least, our brightest star and your companion for more than two months now, Capt. Jenny.'

Capt. Jenny? Sandra? I was slowly but surely understanding this whole set-up.

He continued, 'We are the CIA. An officer of your repute is definitely aware of our organization. We specialize in tracking officers, their movements and intentions. You have been on our radar since you resurrected from that near-fatal injury on the Kashmir border. Our people have also met your pretty wife and the two lovely kids. Our agents were beside you when you resumed a job in the purchase department. Your flourishing income, your exemplary lifestyle invoked interest. We are aware of your exploits with the starlet Aafreen. When you moved out from a comfortable posting from Islamabad, you were looking for something extraordinary. By the time you joined here in Landi Kotal, we knew your likes, dislikes, interests, and all other things. Officer Jenny joined you on that humanitarian mission, after which we have been with you physically. When you were assigned to that special task in Balochistan, we tailed you and we are aware of your visit to Afghanistan followed by the car purchase. This visit was not a leisure outing and it had a definite purpose. We could have and we still can dig in deep and intrude to know the details but we don't want to. We have better things to worry about.

'I and this team are here for a specific purpose. We are not keen on serving in Pakistan for the rest of our lives. We have family back home to whom we wish to go back ASAP. So I request you to cooperate with me and the investigations which will save us a lot of time and embarrassment for you and your country. We do not wish to intimidate you; we are extremely generous and liberal with our friends. We are ready to extend full support, also willing to pay in cash and kind for the services that you render, but we hate a denial. Officer Jenny mentioned that you want to flee from this country to settle in an undisclosed location, with ample money. You must be aware that my organization is perfectly capable to help you fulfill this dream. All we ask for is cooperation from your side. Any mischief will not only hamper your prospects of an isolated, comfortable future but also destroy your present personal and professional life. I am sure your wife will not be pleased to know about Aafreen or Jenny, for that matter. I don't want to sound rude but we will be best friends only if you want us to be. So the decision is yours. You can take a day or two to decide, Officer Jenny will help you take this decision and thank you for your time. Good day!'

The others did not interact with me. A brigadier in this country was being threatened and cornered by some outsider. I was cold and numb, raging with fury. This is FATA, Landi Kotal. Here the NATO forces rule the roost. Shaking hands, I walked back to the car. Sandra—sorry, Capt. Jenny followed me. I was angry and helpless. Sandra joined me on the back seat. I was uncomfortable to sit beside an American agent who made a mockery of my feelings. I was treated like a pawn in this game of international politics. Moreover, these people did not disclose what they wanted from me. What help did they seek? These Americans were the biggest bullies on the planet. They intruded and spied on your personal space, gathered dirty dark secrets, and then they pinned you down to serve them. They unleashed a woman to entrap me. I was feeling dumb and defeated. Nobody spoke on the way back. I was aggravated, instructing the driver to drop me home. A quick shower was the need of the hour to vent the frustration. I desperately needed to spend time with myself to decide the next course of action. Stepping out of the shower, I found Sandra in her luscious best, waiting for me. She changed from her formal clothing to a really sexy body-hugging, revealing outfit. I pretended to be angry and went on to lie beside her but with an uneasy grudge. She started fondling me while I shrugged her away. She was unperturbed and continued with her exploits. I shoved her away a couple of times, but she was too good to resist. Unable to restrain myself, I pounced upon her, tearing her clothes away. I screamed, 'You made a fool of me. You played with me and my emotions. You made me look like a dumb fuck in front of your team. You are a wicked witch. I will rip you apart so hard you will remember me for the rest of your life.'

I was fuming but she preferred to stay calm and let me express my angst. I shredded every piece of cloth from her body and hurled them all over the room. She continued with her smile. This enraged me further; I swooped and took her down. She didn't offer much resistance. I squeezed her in my arms and crammed her feet, continued to exploit her with all my might. I gripped her rear and overturned her. She was equally aroused with this ferocious bout of lovemaking and now even she imitated my actions. She was just as violent with me. I never imagined that such aggression could be so pleasurable. We both were furious with the pain and the only remedy was to inflict more pain. I climbed onto her rear and entered her as she was bellowing. I continued humping her with all my might, spanking her butt blood red. Then it was her turn to make the move. She proceeded downwards and gobbled my genitals. She started sucking me, and so hard was the drag, now I was yelling in pain. But the bliss was unparalleled. It was nothing that I had experienced before.

As we lay naked tangled into each other, Sandra said, 'Mazzi, my task was to lure you and extract information. After spending time, I realized that you are a genuinely nice person. You are not fake or deceptive nor two-faced. My life is spent with people whom their families seldom trust. We are trained to don the mask of trickery and cons. Yes, our work looks like a sham or fraud but we do it under the greater cause of national and world security. I have been on covert missions before, have failed in many and succeeded in a few. When I arrived with my humanitarian team, we all were briefed about this op. We were to decide after meeting you, after interacting with you, after knowing your likes and dislikes, who would stay behind to execute the task. You showed interest in me but you also worked diligently. Your honesty swept me off my feet. I meet too many bogus people on the job but I confess that I sincerely love being with you. You know how to treat a woman. I assure you complete support in the further course of action. I will urge my seniors and the government to deliver everything you want and we will together achieve your dream.'

'But what exactly are you looking for? How can I be of any help?' I enquired.

'I and my team will brief you about this special assignment when you are sure you want to participate. Don't worry. We won't make you do anything stupid that will endanger you or your family. We want access to some strategic information, which I am sure an officer of your stature can definitely deliver. If you really want to hide away from this mad country, this is an opportunity of a lifetime and we are your best chance. We promise you personal safety, monetary security, along with a new identity. Give it a thought and I am sure you won't disappoint me.' She summed it up with a tongue-waggling, lip-sucking, wounding, wet kiss.

Now I realized the secret to the amazing nights with Sandra. Her agile acrobatics and her never-ending stamina was a result of her professional training. She was no doctorate student.

CHAPTER 36

The Mission

My journey back to India was planned. The route was set; my buddy and guide AD was making all the arrangements. I was sure Yusuf was more than capable to deliver the information the Indians were looking for. These Americans were ready to relocate me and my Pak family to a discreet location. They were ready to fill my coffers with enough to suffice for a lifetime. Even if I kept myself out of this American relocation offer, they could definitely secure my Pak family. It would serve my purpose. I could go back to my country and my parents without guilt. All of this looked like a jigsaw puzzle. Life would be drastically different if everything was executed perfectly. I decided to accept the American offer, but wondered, what was the task that these world bullies were handing me? What was it that needed involvement of an officer of my stature? I decided to hear them out.

Sandra prepared the bed tea and solicited my decision.

'I don't mind working with you and your organization provided you don't make me do something preposterous or inhuman. As long as my demands are met, I would love to be by your side, my love doll.'

Sandra's face brightened. After a warm bath together, we set out together to the house again where I was to be briefed about this highly secretive mission. We reached the place; the local kids were playing as usual, the women were busy in their work as we climbed to the floor above. All of the team—Brad, Susan, Daniel, and Lisa—were assembled to welcome me. With smiles on our faces, we shook hands and occupied our places. Sandra was seated beside me. Daniel took the initiative. He wrote large letters on the blackboard.

U B L

Nobody spoke for a while, expecting me to interpret. I gave a long hard thought. I failed. I had a blank look on my face. Then Sandra corrected his words to

O B L

I again stared empty when suddenly lightning struck me.

Osama bin Laden

Stunned, with my eyes wide open, I was staring at Sandra and the team. This was out of nowhere.

As they realized that I had cracked the code, Daniel continued,

'Sorry I didn't realize Asians call him Osama. We mention this murderer as Usama. Anyways, we are one of the many special ops teams that are staying in Pakistan to locate the most wanted man on the planet. I need not brief you about the person we are talking about. This dreaded terrorist has been on the run for more than a decade now. With so much of our technological advancements, we still haven't been able to track or trace him. Technology becomes redundant when you are searching somebody who vehemently lives like a caveman and follows outdated customs. Many like us have squandered years trying to trace him. We finally concluded that nothing works better than human intelligence. So such teams were formed to gather first-hand information on the ground to pinpoint him. This is our and your task. We will get into the details when we have consent of cooperation from your side. So what do you think, Brig. Mazhar? Are you ready to help us trace this criminal and in the meanwhile also help yourself? Are you willing? We are going to find him for sure, with or without your help. With all of us working as a team together, we can find him sooner. We are ready to hear your side of demands and I assure you that we will meet most of them. So tell me, Brig. Mazhar, what is your decision?'

All this was too revealing and was revealing too fast for me to digest. I excused myself to contemplate, walked to the balcony, staring into emptiness. I had nothing to lose in this proposal. They were asking me to help trace Osama, already a declared and self-confessed terrorist. I would table my demands; if they acceded, I would proceed.

'I can definitely consider your offer, under some conditions and a few deliverables.'

'Name them,' said Brad.

'I want American citizenship for me and my family, American passports for everybody. I want pension and all the benefits of a brigadier of the American army. I want a safe house, a new life along with a new identity, all these things to get onboard and take on this mission, irrespective of whether we locate him or not. I don't trust the jihadis here, they are gunning down every army man who helps the Americans. So this part of the deal has to be delivered irrespective of the outcome. And if I deliver to you what you guys are looking for, I want half of the price money on his head. I am aware he is valued at 25 million dollars so I want 10 million and the above said things. So tell me, Brad, can you deliver?'

'Done, I can definitely deliver you all this you are asking for.' Pat came the reply.

'Are you sure? I advise you to have a word with your seniors before you commit. Since this is an out-of-legal-terms agreement, I cannot claim authenticity or ask for a guarantor.'

'As you rightly said, this deal is out of official communication, so you cannot sue me or anybody in a court of law for non-compliance. But trust me, brigadier, in this equation, we are the desperados. We have been hunting this terrorist for almost ten years now and all we have are leads—leads that have kept us confused long enough, leads that have made a mockery of our so-famed intelligence, leads that are just clues without any confirmation. We have a budgetary expense of more than 80 billion dollars for the intelligence operations. Our Afghan surge, in the name of bringing peace to this region, has cost us more than 200 billion dollars. In spite of such staggering amounts, all we achieved is being jokers in front of the world. This capture is not just a matter of financial implications but also pride and honor for the American government. The re-election of our present president is dangling in uncertainty. Only the capture of OBL will help the American citizen resurrect this depleting faith. So I assure you in the name of the president of the United States of America that all your demands would be met. You haven't asked for anything extraordinary. Your demands are extremely justified for the risk you would undertake. My organization has delivered on similar demands earlier and I have complete authority to make this decision. You help us find this man and I assure you a new life altogether.'

We shook hands for confirmation.

'I always knew you would be my knight in shining armor. You will rescue me from this torturous place and help me go back home. Thanks, Mazzi.' And a warm embrace sealed the deal.

With all the consents in place, we settled in our seats. Brad started, 'Jenny will brief you about this particular assignment. This lady has been on the forefront in tracking this HVT. She has spent many years here in Pakistan, she has spent time with the Guantanamo detainees to gather information. Of late she has been very confident and positive about one of her leads. The organization has ignored her request for quite some time now. So she decided to rope in a Pak officer to confirm her belief. So here you are, my friend.'

CHAPTER 37

Tracking OBL

The Pakistani family was courteous enough to accommodate these Americans. They brought us some wonderful home-cooked lunch.

'Money can buy you anything in this part of the world. We pay these locals and they treat us like family. I am glad these people are poor and we have the money to buy their loyalty.'

This unnecessary comment made in the most pitiable manner offended me. Sandra sensed my discomfort.

'Don't enlighten us with your stupid views on poverty, Brad. We are here to discuss something very critical. Let us not disrespect people who have been kind enough to accommodate us. Don't be mean and use your brains when you speak the next time,' thundered Sandra.

Whether in India or Pakistan, I always had this point of view about the Americans. Only because they have the money, they believe they can enslave the world. Anyways it was time to move on, and post-lunch, Sandra took center stage. She went up to the board and started, 'Before I begin with my findings, let me assure all of you that this dreaded leader of the al-Qaeda is very much alive. It has been claimed right from 2001, since the Twin Towers bombing, that Osama is dead. Everybody has their own version but a similar conclusion to proclaim his death. From Pak president Pervez Musharraf and Afghan president Hamid Karzai to popular news channels, everybody is in a hurry to declare him dead in an attempt to satiate their ego. It seems ridiculous to these esteemed gentlemen that with the most progressive tracking systems and proficient intelligence networks deployed in ages, this HVT has managed to evade everybody. So when you don't have the courage to accept defeat, it is easier to deflect it. As my team and organization is aware, I've been working on this mission for almost eight years now. I have wasted some good years of my life tracking this criminal. I derived leads from Guantanamo prisoners, I've followed people from one city to another, I've interrogated local tribesmen and many activities. I will now brief you about some of my leads and why I've come to this conclusion and zeroed in on a location.'

Lead 1

'With the most modern and technologically advanced surveillance support, we are nowhere close to our target. We strongly believe that Osama does not use telephones or Internet or any electronic devices. A man, however reclusive, might get claustrophobic being severed from the world. He is the supreme commander of the most feared organization on the planet and his leadership is imperative for his soldiers to operate. So I managed to convince my superiors that there must be some mode of communication he deploys to guide his terrorist army. With all modern technology being junk, we zeroed in on a human courier. We are sure that there must be some individual who must his port of interaction. Searching through our history of data, we learned that there was one person, Abu Ahmed Al Kuwaiti, whom OBL trusted with his life. This accomplice was his right-hand man even when our own organization trained Osama to fight the Russians. By the way, the US channeled around 5.3 billion dollars into Pakistan during the '80s to keep a check on the USSR's growing influence over the region which indirectly funded the growth of Taliban. So first we spend billions to create a terrorist and then again splurge billions to capture him—American logic.

'Anyways, getting to our man, this particular person was out of our radar. Interrogating one of our captures, Salahi, he claimed that Kuwaiti was injured in the attack at the Tora Bora Mountains and died from the injuries to his arm in 2001. From our other prisoner Hassan Ghul, we learned that Al Kuwaiti was very much alive and should be still close to Osama wherever he may be. When we arrested the feared Khalid Sheikh Mohammed in 2003, he thoroughly denied the existence of such an individual. Our major breakthrough came with the arrest of Abu Faraj Al-Libbi in 2005. The suspected courier was known to be very close this Al-Libbi. The whole organization is known to alter names and modify identities as and when time and situation requires. On rigorous interrogation of Al-Libbi, he incessantly denied knowing Kuwaiti. Two very highly placed Al Qaeda operatives minimized the importance of this Kuwaiti or completely denied his existence. With such strong contradictions, we concluded that this identity must be investigated. This person, like OBL, too dropped off the map and disappeared into thin air. With so many confusing leads, I decided to concentrate only on this one particular individual. All pointers were connecting to the fact that he would be still close and in contact with Osama.

'We tracked down this Abu Ahmed Al Kuwaiti. His name didn't make sense. It simply meant father of Ahmed from Kuwait. But I was intrigued. I wanted to dig into this individual. His real name and credentials were still a mystery for us. One of our detainees, Al Khatani, revealed the real name of Ahmed Kuwaiti was Ibrahim Saeed Ahmed, an ethnic Pashtun Pakistani whose family migrated to Kuwait years ago. His brother was killed in a fight with the Soviets, and ever since, he had foregone his worldly ties and resolved to serve his master and the religion. He was fluent in Arabic and Pashtun languages. Because of his interpersonal skills and ease of conversation in various languages, he quickly rose in ranks. He was never an authoritative person but was more like a messenger. He's suspected to be hiding in a high-walled compound in the city Abbottabad. This is the location I am talking about.'

'A known old accomplice is all you Americans have managed in the last decade? I am sure there are thousands of fanatics who would lay down their life for Osama. Is it worthwhile to risk this huge operation on the basis of a single individual?' I enquired.

'Wait, brigadier sahib, there are other reasons for us to doubt this particular compound and suspect his presence. Being a woman, I particularly trust this lead. Owing to this theory, I convinced our geo-satellite team to keep this house under surveillance.'

Lead 2

'Osama was not always the cruel monster we all know. He had a normal social life before taking up jihad. He lived a regular life in this society before 9/11. As per his personal life goes, he was married five times with the first marriage at seventeen. He fathered around twenty-six children with these women. We pursued these personal bondings, relationships, and family of Osama. Not much is known about his first two wives since they abandoned him in the early years after knowing his vicious ways. But we discovered his third wife Khairiah Saber was in Iranian custody. After 9/11, most of his family crossed over to the Iranian side to evade troubles. But the Iranians, also being wary of them, kept the family under safe custody. Probing further, I learned that this Saber, a PhD scholar, was a teacher of the deaf and dumb and also a child psychologist. She was a perfect bait to open information floodgates, a deterrent being she was in Iran, another old foe. So reaching her was unimaginable. But we had to get her released.

'On November 13, 2008, an Iranian diplomat, Heasmatollah Attarzadeh, was on his way to the Iranian consulate in Peshawar. His car was intercepted, and with a barrage of bullets, he was seized and bundled off to an undisclosed location. This incident made international headlines but later fizzled out. Usually such abductions are followed by some group or organization claiming responsibility for the act. This time there was no ransom demand, no particular ultimatum, nothing. There was a mysterious silence. Iran was ready to pay any amount or meet any demand to seek release of their diplomat. But the apathy was frustrating. We deliberately wanted this.

We convinced one of our tribal groups to carry out this abduction. We kept it low and away from the media glare for another two years. The diplomat was held hostage but was tended in top-notch condition. Regular video footage was being sent to the Iranian consulate and his family. To make this abduction appear indisputable and the work of Pakistani Taliban, we convinced our tribal leader to urge Sirajuddin Haqqani, a Pakistani Taliban rebel and our sworn enemy, to lead the negotiations. He agreed when our tribals lured him with enough publicity of his dominance over the region. He navigated the discussions as we steered him. We asked for the release of several al-Qaeda leaders that were being held in Iran. We remotely managed the complete chain of events.

'As a goodwill gesture and confirmation of their intent, the Iranians released Iman bin Laden, the young eighteen-year-old daughter of Osama who was holed up for five months in the Saudi Arabian embassy in Tehran. She made a quick escape to join Osama's first wife Najwa Ghanhem, in Syria. As the negotiations proceeded, we put forth a demand to release Osama's trusted spokesperson Sulaiman Abu Gaith, who had been under loose house arrest since 2003 in Iran, and another Saif Al Aden, who was a high-profile al-Qaeda operative, along with other family members of Osama. This time we pushed for the release of his wife Khairiah Saber as well. With such high-profile releases, the Iranians demanded the release of their diplomat. We were never interested in keeping their man so the deal was struck and both sides delivered. We stalked all three of them, Sulaiman, Saif, and Khairiah. We were aware all of them were very close to the supremo.

'Osama took a lot of care to make sure his elderly wife reached him safe. He personally supervised her transit and took every precaution to evade being followed. This process took around two months. In the meanwhile, our Pakistani moles had a chance to meet her. She was not very cooperative, in fact, was arrogant and aggressive. Our people felt that she should not be provoked or intimidated, or else she might spoil our prospects. But our smarties managed to make her feel superlative to Osama's present wives. And you go to any part of the world, in any religion or region, a wife is a wife. She gets jealous when she is made to share her husband. Our people managed to poison her thoughts to make her feel inferior. So not much is expected of her, but we convinced her not to bog down meekly, not to live a life under house arrest. She was a learned woman and so definitely an independent thinker. Our sources tell us she also travelled to Abbottabad. So maybe to this very same compound. If she has, then I am definitely sure she must be interacting with some villagers around and making her authority known. The in-house discontent cannot be hidden for long. If you can get around the town, I am sure we can pinpoint and verify our suspicions.'

'Is this a joke or what? The American intelligence has stooped down to this level that they rely on some household skirmish to locate the most feared face of the planet. A woman lost in a big country like Pakistan expected to quarrel with the wives of her polygamous husband. Should I risk my whole life, career, reputation, my family for such claims?' I enquired.

'No, there's more.'

Lead 3

'Recently with the help of some Pak officers, we traced an individual identical to Al Kuwaiti in Peshawar frequenting a medical store in a span of every couple of months, purchasing the same set of medications. This intrigued me to track Osama's health condition. The entire world is aware of Osama's kidney ailments. He was in a hospital in Dubai between July 4 and July 14, 2001, just two months before the September 11 bombings, for treatment. I interacted with Dr Terry Callaway, who is known to have treated Osama in this Dubai hospital.

'I unearthed the list of medicines treating Osama's diseases and tracked all the suppliers and the purchasers here in Pakistan. We traced most of the patients and found nothing suspicious until this one medical store in Peshawar. One Pashtun money changer named Arshad Khan was regularly buying prescription drugs for kidney illness. It was mysterious to see a trader from the tribal Waziristan area, as he claimed to be, buying medicines from Peshawar. We probed to discover he was not a patient to any urologist or kidney specialist around the Peshawar area. With no kidney disorder, it was difficult to understand why he needed these medicines. On cross-checking with the Pakistani officials, we discovered this is the same Al Kuwaiti whom we had been trying to locate for years. He is now in a town called Abbottabad near Islamabad. It is difficult for us believe that Osama must be so close. Maybe Kuwaiti is now living a secluded life away from his previous sins. But our aim is not to locate Kuwaiti. The main target is still out of bounds. Concentrating on this particular Pashtun who had shifted our focus to Abbottabad, I tracked him down to a large compound house. This compound has some huge surrounding walls so as to hide its inhabitants. Now this is the compound that we need to investigate further.'

Lead 4

'After learning the real name of Al Kuwaiti, alias Ibrahim Saeed Ahmed, we started tracking calls of all his family and friends in Kuwait. Of the many calls we intercepted, he never revealed his present address to anyone, heightening our beliefs. We were waiting for him to make a mistake. He usually used to drive an hour or more from the suspected compound to make any calls. He used to change SIM cards to avoid detection. But we were equally determined.

'Last year we intercepted the call Al-Kuwaiti made to his old friend. "Where have you been? We've missed you. What's going on in your life? And where are you right now?" enquired the friend.

There was a long pause but the friend insisted. "I am back with the people I was with before," replied Kuwaiti.

'"May God facilitate," replied the friend.

'Kuwaiti is Osama's most trusted lieutenant. If he says he's back with the people he was with before, then we have a strong suspicion that he must be with Osama.

'Mazzi, intelligence gathering is a game of many aspects. Among these leads, we believe we have touched every piece of Osama's life: his social life, his past records and acquaintances, his family life, his medical condition, everything. We are not sure of his presence but that is what precisely you are required for. You have to help us join these dots and reach a conclusion.'

I was still half convinced.

'OK, if I agree to help you people and investigate the compound, if we succeed, I know what I get, but what if your most wanted man is not in the compound? What if he never was and my actions are under suspicion by the Pakistani Taliban? These Talibanis have a strong hatred towards the army officers who aid the US. What if they kill me? What would my family do in the US without me or any money? Will you support my family?'

'Yes,' said Brad in a thundering voice. 'God forbid, if anything happens to you and if we miss our mark, we will pay your family one million dollars in the US. Is that fine with you? Now will you help us in our mission?'

CHAPTER 38

The Final Movement

I was in the middle of world politics, surrounded by three of the most powerful nuclear-capable armies of the world. Entrapped, I could not reveal the facts encountered every day. I could not afford to goof up on any front. Any lapse would mean certain death, by some country or the other. I was walking the thinnest line possible between perfect execution and execution. Being in an extraordinary situation like me, it was foolish to expect conventional problems. But Camp Rovers prepared me for this. Not just physical trouble, it taught me to withstand mental toughness, belief in peers, and moreover the ability to deliver.

So let's do it. Let me dig in to find the most wanted man on the planet.

It was March 2011, second week. And as luck would have it, the defense ministry wanted me to lecture the fresh batch of pass-outs at the PMA (Pakistan Military Academy), Kakul in Abbottabad. Sometimes destiny gives us such definite indicators for the way life is going to unfold. A week ago, I was completely unaware about this institute. Maj. Gen. Anwar mentioned it once when he made a reference about his son's future plans. These Americans needed me to visit Abbottabad and I had no reason for the same. This town and the academy were so close to Islamabad but I had no calling. Today I have this opportunity to go back to India, making sure my Pak family is taken care of, and now when the Americans want me to investigate some locations in the town, I am being invited for a fortnight to this place for educating and motivating youngsters. With basically ample free time, I had a perfect setting to inspect and probe the place.

After receiving the official communication for the short stint at PMA, I immediately informed Maj. Gen. Anwar. He was already aware of it.

'Mazzi, I know you are invited to PMA for a lecture series. In fact it was me who suggested your name. With the vast experience in varied fields that you have garnered in the last year, the army is planning to make your lecture an annual affair. The cadets will not only be inspired hearing about your battle-line valor, but your experience with the tribals and the

Baloch will also give them an insight of rural Pakistan. Now you are a mentor to thousands of cadets who look up to you as a hero, my boy. Go and educate them about life.'

Sandra had lunch with me that afternoon where I informed her about this development and she was electrified. She assured me her support as and when needed. It would have been risky for the operation if she accompanied me. This town was not more than thirty-five miles away from the capital city of Islamabad. I handed over my responsibilities to the designated officer in Landi Kotal and left for Islamabad to spend some time with the family. We decided to celebrate the new bungalow with a continental dinner at an upmarket restaurant. We ordered some mouth-watering Italian delicacies at Pappasallis, Jinnah Super Market, where the kids enjoyed the mouth-watering pastas and pizzas.

I raised a query softly. 'What if we get an opportunity to leave this country forever to settle in some foreign location with no acquaintances or friends around, would it be OK with you? Are you guys fine with starting a new life in a new country?'

The kids were clueless and they hardly cared about it. Afaaz, taking the initiative replied, 'It doesn't make it difference to us, Papa, as long as you and Mom are coming along. Any place on the planet is fine with us. But if possible please take me to America or Britain. I want to visit these two great countries. They have the best possible life.' And he continued digging into his macaroni. Inshaa was completely a novice to any of such things. She was busy spilling the pizza toppings on her dress. Adaah heard me patiently, and knowing her, I knew she would not rake up the discussion in front of the kids. After the wonderful tiramisu, we drove back to our home. Adaah changed into a seductive nightgown, came over to my side, and then probed about the weird query I had put across on the dinner table.

'What is that you are withholding, Mazzi? Tell me. I can read it in your eyes. You are hiding something and you know you cannot lie to me. So speak your heart out and tell me what is troubling you.'

A wife is a very dangerous entity. I spend such wonderful times with Aafreen and Sandra but never tried to analyze my body language or facial expressions. It's impossible to conceal anything from a wife.

'Adaah, what did I achieve after laying my life in the line of fire for this country? Some media recognition, a medal, a plump posting? Almost lost my life for my motherland, and what is the assurance it won't happen again? After working with the administration, visiting the hinterlands, experiencing the people's wrath first-hand, I am sure this country and this army is heading down the drains. There is no soul and heart working here. Every individual is greedy and works for his own benefit. I am a dedicated soldier but even I have my own life and family. If I had not survived the blast, these politicians would have given you a medal, some money, and maybe a business opportunity. But the loss of life is irreparable. I am not scared of death but today I am scared of being separated from you and the kids. I can't imagine a life without all of you.'

'Come to the point, Mazzi.'

'I have an opportunity to work for an organization. You know I won't disclose to you the details. Working with them might give us a chance to settle abroad along with some good money. Just like regular days, I won't be able to spend much time at home but my family would be safe and financially secure. Are you ready to relocate with the kids to a completely new but much safer and secure environment?'

'Mazzi, your injury episode was not very easy on me or the kids. We have been through a horrid time seeing you in all that pain. Every moment we prayed for your recovery and a chance to run away from all these troubles. Your resurrection is nothing short of a miracle. You and the kids are my life. I would be more than happy to leave this chaos and settle in a safe place. Please make it happen as soon as possible. Take me away from this mess.' And we spent the night in each other's arms, reassuring the faith.

Next morning, I went to the army headquarters to meet a few officers who had been lecturers at the academy, trying to get insights about this new task. I called Yusuf for a chat, when he informed me that my courier with the information required had already been dispatched. He revealed it was in an unusual format and I would have to use my analytical skills to decode. He educated me about some decoding techniques to be used. An unsubscribed, unwanted international fashion magazine arrived home that afternoon. Adaah was busy ogling the designs and admiring the half-naked models. When I glanced through the fashion journal, I discovered that it was not a usual magazine. It had specific highlights, names, numbers, color codes, numerals aligned, all covert and furtive. I spent that evening trying to decode the markings, just as Yusuf had instructed. I managed to interpret one page and what it disclosed. One of the names provided by AD was of the 26/11 Mumbai terrorist attack planner and handler Abu Jundal. When I decoded the information provided by Yusuf, I discovered his name was Riyasat Ali as per Pakistani records, staying at Murike. Most wanted Abu Jundal in India was Riyasat Ali from Murike, a regular citizen. I had all the information required about this fugitive, his address, his bank accounts, and his forged passport details. This was enough for me. I called Yusuf.

'Bhai, I've received your courier. Many thanks.'

He chuckled. 'Brother, use it with caution. The data is embedded in a cryptogram to prevent misuse.

This kind of information is priceless and any country would spend a fortune to acquire that.'

Now I had the data the Indians were looking for. But I was not in a haste to inform AD yet. I had to execute this one last mission for the sake of my family, secure them, and leave with pride.

Next morning before donning the hat of a professor for the family and role of a spy for the Americans, I asked Adaah to keep her and the kids' stuff packed up and ready to move any moment.

'I will inform you as and when the time arises. All the necessary arrangements will be done. Just make sure you don't talk about this to anybody. Gear up, darling, a new life beckons you.'

CHAPTER 39

The Final Frontier

Named after British Deputy Commissioner James Abbott, 4,000 feet above sea level is the beautiful hill station of Abbottabad. Located in the Orash valley, close to three major cities of Pakistan, this place has a pleasant climate through the year and is a very popular tourist destination for the nearby cities of Islamabad, Peshawar, and Rawalpindi. This is the hometown of the country's premiere military training academy, Pakistan Military Academy (PMA). It has twelve companies and three training battalions, a very impressive institution offering courses in every department of academics.

I checked into the senior officers' guest house at the PMA, occupying one of the most impressive suites overlooking the massive institution. I was a guest of honor and the students performed a brief welcome skit on my arrival. Some participants of various nationalities accompanied the local cadets. I was glad to know this academy also trained students from thirty-four different countries. The first couple of days were occupied meeting the staff and inspecting the beautiful campus. Very much like the NDA or the IMA, this academy imparted training to raise meticulous army officers. Science, arts, adventure training, endurance building, combat training, crafts, drama, debate, and every facet was covered in the entire gamut of preparation.

A fortnight of activities was planned for me: addressing the new recruits, lecturing the pass-outs, motivational speeches for the staff, and some cultural activities. The good news was that most of these activities were planned during the day, the evenings relatively unoccupied. This was my first outing as an undercover agent. I took a couple of days to get acquainted with the staff and getting familiarized with the surroundings. Within the first few days, my driver, Mehmood, who was assigned to ferry me around became my confidant. The fastest way to build bridges amongst men is to open up to a few indulgences. I befriended him by enquiring about the sins available around. He grasped my intentions and offered me his services. For an amount, he provided me with a bottle of Scotch. It was an educational place so I refrained from making friends with the staff. I was skeptical about mingling informally with the employees, to avoid any suspicion. But this strategy worked wonders for me. Lonely enjoying my drink every evening, I had only Mehmood for company. He was a local who had been posted in the academy for more than three decades and lived all his life in this town. He was a devout Muslim so he refrained from alcohol. In the evenings, he would serve me my drink, sit on the floor, and chat with me about how the sleepy tourist village transformed into a bustling town. He shared experiences with the decorated alumni of this prestigious institution while filling up his marijuana chillums. He was hesitant about his indulgence in the beginning but I wanted a trusted aide for my mission so I encouraged him to smoke and open up. The stage was set and the duty was about to begin.

After the first few days at the institute, I asked Mehmood to ferry me around the city, show me some places of interest. The British-era grand Victorian church called the Central Church was astonishing; so were many historical buildings in and around the city. The town's rich historical lineage, pleasant climate, scenic backdrop of mountain ranges offered a European experience. I was amazed to notice the educational institutes strewn all over. This town had the highest literacy rate in the whole country. Beautiful schools and college campuses were abundant. Many high-ranking retired army officers also resided in this town. With all this education opulence and such enlightened citizens, I doubted Sandra's claims.

I would not be surprised if her assumption would turn out to be farce. It was difficult to believe that the most feared and hated face on the planet would be residing in such an educated, secure locality. But the success of this activity was very important for my future. Whether America managed to capture, kill Osama is insignificant. What matters to me is that my family gets citizenship, the money and I flee from this country. After spending a day admiring the tourist destinations, I decided to launch the hunt. Sandra and her team had provided me with specific location and details about the suspected house. Now I wanted Mehmood to work for me. I always tipped him handsomely for his services to strengthen the bond. It is better to have friends around in such dangerous missions rather than obedient servants. Mehmood was the best of both, a trustworthy friend and an obedient servant. It was time to embark the most coveted journey of my life.

The next day I asked Mehmood to drive to the south-west of the PMA, towards Bilal town. Around a mile away from the academy, I was looking for a house as Sandra portrayed. We drove around the area for some time where I noticed at the end of a dusty road, there stood a massive ugly structure. There was nothing unusual about this place apart from its mammoth size, an ugly heap of bricks and concrete. The place was on a much bigger piece of land compared to the houses nearby, was surrounded by a giant twenty-foot-high compound wall topped with barbed wire. I studied Sandra's claims; by all means this was the structure she was talking about. I asked Mehmood to stop the vehicle at some distance from the house, got down to observe the neighborhood. The locality was like just any other place of the town, nothing unusual or no atypical activity around. I always imagined an individual of such importance would be living in a fort-like structure surrounded by armed guards but this house, apart from its sheer size, was just like any other dwelling. Nonetheless, Sandra had all the reasons in the world to believe this was the location. And whether it was true or not, I had a duty to investigate it further. I was traveling in an official vehicle so I didn't venture close. But the place certainly had some indicators. The house had very few windows and there was an unusually huge wall on the upper floor. It was weird to see such a closed structure. One remarkable thing was that it had no wires running in. Apart from the basic electricity wiring, there was no other cable running into the house. No phone, Internet, or any television cables. It was odd to see such an enormous structure without any connection with the outside world. This supported one of Sandra's theories that Osama was holed up in a place with minimal electronic connections. I was intrigued. I decided to approach this task technically so I opted to dig into the official records of this house before venturing too close. My coordinates read 34°10'09.51"N 73°14'32.78"E, exactly what Sandra informed me. My target was in sight. I decided to code this place the N-34.

On our way back to the academy, I enquired with Mehmood, 'What are the prevailing land rates here? This place has many retired army officers residing. With such beautiful weather and educational abundance, I am also interested to build my retirement home in this town.'

Mehmood was an old hand at the academy; after his three decades of service here, he was a known entity in all government offices.

'Sir, I am very glad to know you want to build a house here. I will assist you completely. The local administrative office, tehsil office is en route to the PMA. I know a few staff members there. If you want, I will get you introduced and they will be the best guide to your aspirations.'

With ample time in hand, I asked him to stop by the tehsil office. The car halted in front of a small shabby structure; Mehmood made a dash inside to assemble some officers to welcome me. Being a known story in the country, I received a pleasant response everywhere. The tehsildar greeted me and all his staff was polite enough to offer me every help to buy a property. After enquiring about land rates and purchase formalities, I requested them to show me the records room and educate me about the documents required to purchase a piece of land. One of the officers led me into a small dingy room with thousands of files scattered around. I handed the officer a Rs. 5000 note asking him to help me with some specific document. The officer was taken aback at first and resisted the money, but when I insisted, he was humbled. I asked him to search for some documents of Bilal town area and the biggest house in that locality. After searching for a while, he handed me a file and informed me this was the biggest house in the area. Perfect for my expectations, it was N-34. I researched the documents to discover some anomalies. When I was allotted the plot near Islamabad as a part of the Hilal-i-Jur'at, I recollected that I had to submit my Computerized National Identity Card (CNIC). I recalled how the revenue officers then boasted about the computerization of their department and nobody could make a false entry or a bogus purchase. But in this case I noticed that a manual ID card was used for identification of the purchaser. The officer noticed the mistake but quickly shrugged off the responsibility, saying this was unusual. He excused himself, reasoning he was not the officer when the purchase was made. But nonetheless, I was here not to trap a dishonest government officer. Some irregularity in the records built my confidence. The purchase was made in the name of Mohammad Arshad Khan, a trader from Waziristan in the year 2003. The officer informed me that the buyer must have paid a good bribe to accept this manual ID card. Other documents pertaining to the buyer's personal information were not completely genuine. My suspicions grew stronger and I made a photocopy of the records. Since I had already paid the officer, his loyalty was at my disposal. I requested him to maintain secrecy and thanking the tehsildar, we moved on towards the academy. I was on track. Arshad Khan was the name of the courier that Pak officials had informed the CIA about.

On the records, I noticed Modern Associates was the architecture firm and Mohammed Younis was the architect of that hideous structure. The next day, we drove to the office of this particular architect. The town was abundant with beautiful vintage buildings and ugly modern structures. I was sure Younis was a contributor to the latter. I introduced myself.

'Hi, Mr Younis, I am Brigadier Mazhar Qureshi. I wish to build a bungalow in this beautiful town, some of my friends have suggested your services so I came here to see you.'

Younis was embarrassed and apologized for not recognizing me. He was beaming with pride, pompously displaying me his previous work. I displayed some interest in learning the scheme of things. I enquired in a while, 'Can you tell me which is the biggest and the most difficult project you executed? Any particular structure you built that provided the luxury of space along with privacy? I am keen to live a secluded retired life. Tired of all the attention, I want to build me a house that will keep the prying eyes of the public and media away.'

He then haughtily revealed about the Waziristan kothi. He informed me, 'Sir, around six to eight years back, I built a massive bungalow for a trader from Waziristan. Built on a plot of around 3,500 square meters, this structure was not very aesthetically designed but I built it according to some weird requests of this client. The Pashtun trader, Arshad Khan, originally sought permission for a structure of two floors from the local administration. During construction the third floor was added though the additional floor was never authorized. This Arshad Khan spent an obscene amount to built the additional floor. I myself bribed local officials to get the work done. The illegal third floor is completely isolated from the rest of the house. Built with an intention of maintaining complete privacy, it has windows only on one of the four sides and these are opaque. The windows are just a slit above the eye level. And a huge seven-foot wall covers the terrace leading from this floor. I was curious to know the purpose for such alterations but the client paid me more than my fees to stop enquiring. Sir, I built this house exactly as per the client's demands and the same could be done with your bungalow as well.'

Younis was an honest architect who was not concerned about the Waziristan kothi or its occupants. He was more interested in bagging my project so he started updating me about his other works around the city. Having the required information, I took a leave and assured him to get back in a few days after finalizing the plot.

By now I had enough reasons to believe that there was something fishy in the house. The suspicious documents provided to purchase the plot, the house being built with cynical, secretive intent, and an unauthorized floor gave me a rationale to trust Sandra's theory. I decided to call her and update her about all the information gathered about N-34.

CHAPTER 40

The Safe House

It was the third week of March; my days included lecturing the students on various facets of warfare. The disclosures were running to packed houses with soaring popularity. I established a connection with Sandra who was in Islamabad by then. She was working with the same NGO with whom she arrived in Landi Kotal. I called to inform her about the irregularities discovered while probing the official records of the house. She was ecstatic with the facts which helped built a strong case. She asked me to find the team a safe house and informed me the CIA was taking keen interest in this location and was ready to pursue my leads. She wanted me to rent the place in the name of the NGO Save the Child, which was fronting for the CIA. Relieved to know some support was arriving for my activities, I instructed

Mehmood to suggest a real estate agent who would help in searching for the right place for a retirement home and in turn the safe house as well. I met a few real estate agents, all of whom were very capable of finding me a plot of land. In between many such agents, a very interesting person named Nazar grabbed my attention. Very loud and boisterous, he mentioned how he brokered the deal for many immigrants who had come to the town after the 2005 earthquake, when the NATO operations made many flee their residences from adjoining areas to reside in this town. He was deeply interested in country's politics, NATO strikes, also enquired about my Baloch experience. With such copious knowledge in every direction, I decided to appoint him as my local search agent. He was happy with the responsibility and decided to show me some plots in the vicinity. We drove all over the town; while driving through the Bilal town area, the Waziristan house was unmissable.

'Nazar, if possible, I want to buy a plot of this size and build a house of this scale,' I said.

'Oh, sir. The Waziristan kothi is your liking. So you are fond of huge houses. Definitely, sir, a man of your stature deserves nothing less. I helped Arshad buy this plot, so don't worry, I will also help you find a similar piece of land.'

With the ease that he mentioned Arshad's name, I was on the right trail. After inspecting half a dozen plots all around the city, we stopped at a restaurant for evening tea. Here I innocently asked a question to Nazar, 'The residents of the Waziristan house must be very wealthy. They have a huge house indeed.'

Real estate agents are unofficial moles in their expanse of operation. They are required to keep tabs of every plot, house, shop, the owners, residents—who is moving out of town, who is shifting residences, business, and all data pertaining to land. This query was an opportunity for Nazar to shower all his knowledge.

'Sir, the Waziristan house is a very suspicious place. The search for this plot was initiated by a police officer. A few years back, some local police personnel spread the word amongst our agent community that ISI was looking for a big plot to build a guest house. We already have the PMA and many important government institutions here so this made sense. They were represented by an officer from Islamabad, Col Shah, whereas I brought the seller to the table. The one plot I suggested was smaller than their expectation so I convinced the owner of the adjoining plot, a doctor, also for the deal. The discussions were held by some English-speaking polished officer who finalized the plot on the first day itself. All of these deal meetings were attended by different individuals and we were not aware of the actual buyer. Nobody negotiated for the price and they paid the owners all money in cash. It was huge sum during those days and the spiffy bank notes were too alluring. Though the plot was meant for government purposes, it was bought under an individual name. We met Arshad bhai, under whose name the plot was bought on the day of registration formalities. He was uncomfortable visiting offices, so he paid a huge sum to complete the documentation formalities without appearing anywhere personally. Naturally the government official objected, but a call from ISI and generous earnings shut his mouth. All these proceedings were suspicious and confusing. Though the premier agency was involved in the purchase and was projected to build a guest house, they were not keen to let their name be used for official records. They could notice me and the sellers being wary about all this. But I was promised a commission beyond the official figure and the seller along with the doctor were provided with a parcel of land in the hinterland free of cost. Well, that sealed our doubts forever.

'Since I was the local connection, I was the liaison for the deals. Within a few days, construction started and the structure was built like a fort, a very closed building. Being ISI, they were not keen to disclose their visitors or activities. After official formalities, the proceedings were helmed by Arshad bhai. He built a huge guest house, big enough to accommodate thirty to thirty-five people, but also left a large area unused. The plot was then surrounded by an eighteen-foot wall. A family started residing at the place which put all of us agents into a tizzy. We suspected it to be the caretaker family. But since the ISI was involved, nobody had the guts to raise a doubt. After the construction of the house, they dug a well within the compound. The empty space surrounding this house was being utilized for farming activities. They started planting vegetables and also reared some cattle inside. Sir Arshad bhai is a very strange person. He resides there with his brother Tariq and two or three women. They also have an old uncle of theirs who is very ill. The oldie rarely comes out of the house and is in a piteous state but the brothers nurse him very religiously. May Allah give him good health and long life. I've also met his two kids, Abdur Rehman and Khalid. The women of the house always go out in their 1987 red Suzuki van every morning. Arshad bhai revealed me that they made a fortune trading in gold and foreign currency and they own a hotel in Dubai. But the locals suspect otherwise. The whole family is very reclusive and hardly interacts with anybody from the locality. Many crib about their high-handedness and inability to participate in community charity programs.

'Sir, I don't want to brag about my credentials but you are an honorable army officer so I am revealing to you all this information. I would like to disclose to you some secrets. In my line of work, we are required to keep track of people and their movements. We are expected to be informed about plots, apartments that are available for sale or lease, who lives where and shifts residences to which place. So I put this expertise for the best use of our country as well.

Since I was deeply involved in the whole process of building this fortress, I was commissioned by the local unit of ISI. One of their officers has been in contact with me and pays handsomely to make sure I keep the local administration and other officials away from this house. I have managed to get the house listed as *bechiraagh*, or uninhabited. The officials have never collected any taxes from here since its construction in 2005. I've also managed to procure not one or two but four separate electrical connections and piped gas connections for the family. The family is weary and reluctant to visit offices to pay bills. I do all this donkey work for them. Arshad bhai and his family are guarded by this ISI. The officer inspired me to carry out these tasks for the greater cause of national security. I am a small individual who is interested in earning some extra bucks. It also provides me a moral high of serving for the nation. I disclosed this information to you since you are a proud solider and can understand how elated a commoner feels to participate in such activities. I am strictly instructed not to enquire or disclose anything beyond my limits. But I am happy with my contribution towards the country.'

So here were some important bits of information: ISI being the lead in setting up the kothi, an old ailing uncle who rarely left home, an ISI officer who pays a local agent to keep the officials away. All this was very exciting. Why was the ISI trying to hide this house from other government entities? Why was it so closely involved with this particular address? Pakistan is a very distrustful place where no faith exists between government departments. Many residents were aware of the suspicious nature of this residence but nobody cared or dared to investigate. I contemplated enquiring with Yusuf about this but refrained. I didn't want to overlap two different initiatives. I didn't trust Nazar completely. He could be faking this whole set-up just to bag my project and prove his might. This whole country and its populace were full of suspicions. But still I wanted to keep Nazar engaged because he was a treasure trove of information.

'Nazar bhai, my friend, runs an NGO and wants to rent out a place close to Bilal town for three months. Can you help me find a place? She just wants one room to work from, so a shared residence or a PG also works well with her. But they need a separate room for their work and stay. Please inform me when you find something.'

'Sir, I can show you something right away. There is a farmer, Samrez, who resides in the Bilal town locality. He has a massive ancestral house but nowadays he's in a very meager state. He lives off doing small farming and gardening activities for rich residents of the town. His place is only a few blocks away from Waziristan Kothi and he also works on the farmland inside the kothi. Should I speak to him?'

'Finalize it. You have my permission. Just reach him as soon as possible and inform him that his spare room is on rent from this moment onwards.'

I immediately handed him two Rs. 5,000 notes as a token to confirm the deal. Nazar was surprised.

'Sir, I recommend you should at least see the place before you decide.'

'Nazar, this is an NGO. They are here to help people. They would be more than happy to know their rent is also helping some poor person and his family. So don't worry, I know them very well. They won't doubt my decision. Just inform the farmer that he has new neighbors.'

A farmer who was farming at Waziristan house, and very close to the target location as well—what better location for the safe house to be expected?

I updated Sandra about the developments. She was eager to join me and the team arrived the very next day from Islamabad. They alighted directly at Samrez's place. It was a humble abode with simple amenities. The team was under strict instructions not leave the premises and wander around the town. The target location was within reach. We decided to talk to Samrez later. I dumped all the information gathered over the past few days to the team. They set up their data center and the mission was on the way.

CHAPTER 41

Decoding the Data

After enlightening the students at the PMA with my lectures, I used to travel to Samrez's house. This spy occupation was exciting. We put our boards in place to analyze every lead and information. Nazar's information of an old ailing uncle was useful and it helped the CIA concentrate on the location. Sandra held the review meet.

'We have enough indicators to believe that OBL must be inside the house. I shared with the CIA and the White House all the information supplied by Mazzi. Armed with such specific data, they deployed our eyes in the skies to look into this compound. They engaged the National Geospatial-Intelligence Agency on the job and they have got back to us with some interesting information. They focused their highest penetrative lenses on the house and have observed some unusual activity. An ailing uncle as reported by Mazzi is definitely living within the house. This ill individual is in very poor health, it seems. He never leaves the premises. He daily emerges for an hour or two to take strolls in the courtyard. Our onlookers are calling him the pacer. Our lenses tried to zoom in on his face but the imagery is never clear. The analysts have been trying to estimate his height but it is difficult because of the lack of any reference points. This old sick uncle of the Pashtuns is our target. But still there is a strong possibility of us going wrong. We need concrete evidence to convince the White House. From here on, we try to gather ground facts and proofs to support our claims. Let's get closer to the house. My team can't do this since the sight of any non-resident near the compound might alert the target and he may escape. So we have to be extra cautious. Mazzi, you are our only hope. I've a clear communication from my government to provide you with everything you want, before and after the mission. So please help us. You are doing exceedingly well until now and we completely trust you to deliver.'

Such beautiful words from a beautiful lady inspired my confidence. But this was not a place to display affection. We were staying in the house of a conservative Pak family. Such felony might offend the hosts and spoil our prospects. Though we were flirtatious, both of us were aware of the gravity of the situation. I went back to the academy as always and contacted Nazar.

'Nazar bhai, I want to meet some contractor in the area to understand the construction cost and the time taken. Can you help me find somebody? Some officers here have recommended the name of Tahir Javed. Do you know him?'

'Brigadier sahib, Tahir is a good old friend and we have worked together in many projects. I also strongly recommend his services. I am traveling today but will contact Tahir. If you are in town, I will ask him to call you and then both of you can meet. He is completely trustworthy and he will do a good job.'

I continued with my daily activities and around midday I got a call from Tahir. We confirmed to meet in the evening at a Coffity, a coffee shop. Tahir was a regular resident who earned his living contracting civil jobs around the area. He was an outspoken person and very proud of his work. I enquired with him about the prevailing costs of materials and labor. After an hour of discussion, I asked him about his previous work and he bragged about a huge house he built in the Bilal town area.

'Brigadier sahib, you should see that house. It's almost like a fort with an eighteen-foot compound wall. The partitions and walls on the inside are also very bizarre. It is one of the weirdest works of my life. I was a little suspicious of these people and inquired the reason for such construction. They asked me to shut up but paid me handsomely. They rarely enquired about the expenses, paying me offhand for whatever I asked for. Leaders from the local terror outfit Harkat-ul-Mujahideen used to visit and make payments. Since the money was good, I refrained from asking too many queries. I am a simple family man and not interested in all these games of religion and politics. To tell you frankly, Pakistan is a very difficult place. Here we have many such creepy characters. Any success in this country comes with enmity. Many Pakistani businessmen make foes on their road to riches. We adopt a live-and-let-live policy here. But that is none of our concern. As long as the money is good, I hardly interfere. Let Nazar find a plot for you, sir. I assure you I will build you a house much bigger and better than that Waziristan haveli, and at half the cost.'

Thanking him for the time and assuring him of the civil contract, I made my way to the safe house.

En route to the academy, Mehmood asked, 'Sir, what do you think about these NGOs? Are they a boon or a bane? These are the same people who bomb our innocent citizens and then they come with their medicines to nurse them back. Are their actions justified?'

It was a difficult question.

'Mehmood, everybody here has a duty to perform. The soldiers kill because it's what their superiors ask them to do, you drive this car since it is your duty and your officers ask you to. We are small pawns in this big game. We don't question. We just follow orders. So don't worry too much. We should be happy that the NGO is here to do some good for our people.' I purposely deflected the question with a wayward reply. He was growing suspicious because of my daily visits to the safe house.

With all the inputs from the real estate broker, the civil contractor, it was time to move closer. All the data gathered was sent across to the command center for analysis. Since Mehmood was being edgy about my visits, I relieved him. I was scheduled to go back to Islamabad in the last week of March. The institute invited me for the pass-out parade which was scheduled around third week of April, a gracious event helmed by the army chief. Many senior officers graced the occasion along with their families. It was scheduled only weeks later, so I decided to go to Islamabad and come back some days prior to the event to get back on the mission. My days at the academy were limited and we were nowhere close to confirmation. I decided to take the plunge, stroll near the house to see there was something to learn. My official duties were almost complete but I continued to stay back in the guest house. Nobody at the academy had the courage to doubt my intent so I made the most of this trust. With Mehmood gone, the official vehicle was also given back. I decided to take the local transport to avoid any suspicions in the area, walked to the city center area, and from there hired a seat in a shared cab to the Bilal town area. Wearing a cap, a high-neck T-shirt and with a camera hanging around my neck, I tried to resemble a tourist. I casually strolled around the vicinity of the Waziristan haveli. It was a regular day where the residents were busy with their usual activities. Wandering around the area, I was intrigued to see a small kid play with some rabbits. I went up to him and started chatting. His name was Zarar Ahmed. Using some of my knowledge about rabbits, I got talking to this young fellow.

'So, Zarar, where did you get these rabbits from?'

'From the Wazisristan haveli.'

I nailed it.

'How? Did you go inside? I have heard that very dangerous people stay in the house and they don't interact with anybody in the neighborhood.'

'Uncle, these people look dangerous but they are very nice. Arshad uncle and Tariq uncle are very fond of me. I play with their kids. They have a huge garden in their compound. They have a lot of rabbits, hundreds of chickens, and also a cow. Abdur and Khalid are my friends. But there are many more kids in that house. They don't play with us and are confided on the upper floors. Arshad uncle is a very kind man. When kids play cricket in this area and if the ball is knocked into their compound, the kids are not let inside. Instead, the kids are paid a hundred rupees for every ball. So the boys in the vicinity have made this a trade. They purposely hit the ball into that compound to earn money.'

'Arrey waah, Zarar, you are a very intelligent boy.' I walked him to the nearby store to buy some chocolates. 'And who all stays in the house?'

'Uncle, I don't count who stays in that house. I am always confused with so many people around. There are around twenty-five to thirty people in there.'

'Have you seen their elderly uncle who stays with them?'

'Yes. I mean, I never saw him up close but he usually walks inside the compound for some time and then disappears. I think he is very ill. He always wears a cowboy hat while walking. I've seen that uncle eating chocolates with apple—strange food habit. But Arshad uncle is very kind.'

Well, I had the first encounter with somebody who had a chance to visit the premises. This on-ground activity was a gold mine for information. For a few chocolates worth some pennies I could collect information worth millions. I asked the kid about his family and he pointed me to the house.

'Who stays with you?'

'Ammi, Abbu, and Grandmom.'

'Can I meet them?'

Zarar led me to his house where his grandmother was sunbathing on a broken chair outside. He introduced me to her as a reporter and informed me her name was Khurshid Biwi. I greeted her, 'Khaala, Aet Salaam Waalekum.' (Greetings, Aunty.)

'Waale kum aet salaam.'(Greetings.)

'Khaala hum ek akhbaar ke reporter hain. Hum iss shehar ke bare mein duniyaa ko batana chahte hai.' (Aunty, I am a reporter. I am making a documentary about this town.)

'Bolo, mein kyaa kar sakti hoon?' (So how can I help you?)

'Kucch nahin, thodi jaankaari haasil karnii thi is area ke bare mein, rehnaa, khaana, peena, pehnaava, iss jagah kii saari baatein.' (Just generally wanted to gather information about this place, food, etc.)

I convinced her to enlighten me with the history, present, and other events in the area. Excited about her media appearance, she divulged to me details from the old times to the modern era. She informed me how this town saw an influx of people from different areas after 2005. The earthquake and the American bombings made a lot of people come to this silent town and spoil its serenity. She hated these immigrants who ruined the peace and essence of this town. I poked, 'Now you should be proud of staying in an elite neighborhood. Wealthy neighbors from far-off places like Waziristan are for company.'

But the very mention of that haveli enraged her.

'It is not a haveli, sir, it is more like a jail. I have accompanied Zaraar once to meet the neighbors, but they didn't let me in. They have huge gates fitted with security cameras. They view every person and let them in only after confirmation. The two owners are decent gentlemen but their elderly uncle is a very rude person.'

I was excited to hear somebody who knew all the residents inside.

'Why do you think so? Did you get a chance to talk to their uncle?'

'No. No way, nobody can. Once on a rainy day, Tariq dropped me off at the market. I asked him about the elderly sick person but he deviated from the topic. But that oldie is quite a personality. He has three begums in that house. He enjoys his time with the youngest begum on the top floor and discards the other two begums. Despite being ill, the oldie is so horny that he has a regular dose of *Avena sativa* syrup for potency enhancement. The eldest begum is very jealous of the youngest one. The eldest begum did not stay here since the beginning. She has come just recently. There is definitely something wrong with that house. With all the money in the world, they don't socialize. They live extremely frugally. They are so secretive that they refrain from putting their rubbish out for collection and burn it down to ashes. They avoid visiting any doctors and use Tibb-i-Nabwi for illness. Their kids never visit masjids. Their women don't even talk to the neighbors. They don't share their phone numbers with anybody. In fact their house has nothing: no phone, no television. I don't understand how they live. With all the money, they never contribute in social causes. It must be so claustrophobic inside.'

I concluded that women are unofficial secret agents of the planet. Women have all the information without any real purpose. They just love to know what's happening in the neighborhood and this has proven to be a blessing for me. The info of a newly arrived begum mirrored with Sandra's theory of OBL's wife released from Iranian custody. All pointers were supporting our claims. I took her leave, and walked closer to the haveli. At a stone's throw away from the haveli was Rasheed's general store. I went to the store and purchased a few packets of junk food to engage the owner in a conversation.

'You have rich customers now.' I made a gesture towards the haveli.

The owner did not respond much.

'Yes, they are big people, really rich. Arshad usually visits my place to buy chocolates, ice creams, and cold drinks.'

He was not very cooperative and continued his work. I refrained from probing any further. I walked further down and found Sajid's store. It was the biggest provision store in the vicinity with an adjoining bakery. I went inside to make some purchase and found the owner indulged in some work but when he saw a tourist like me entering, he came over to attend. I decided to make some heavy purchase to lure him. He helped me select articles which got us conversing.

'You are a very fascinating businessman, Sajid bhai. You take good care of your customers and I am very happy with your service. I am sure that your daily customers must be your friends and you must be treating them well.'

'Thank you, sir, for the appreciation. I am a simple businessman and want to serve my customers the best. Yes, many of them are my very good friends. I try my best to keep them satisfied so they come back to me.'

'So who are your most esteemed clients?' I enquired.

'Oh, many. All residents in the locality are very fine gentlemen but here Arshad and Tariq deserve a mention. These two wealthy individuals always stock the best of the supplies, all the best brands of soaps, shampoos, milk, all provisions, everything top notch. And they pay all cash. They never ask for any credit. But what makes them different is the pace in which they consume these supplies. They are ten to twelve people living together but guzzle articles of twenty-five to thirty people. I am puzzled how they achieve this. It seems they have an army staying inside. I love to provide them the best of the service. I also offered them free home delivery for their provisions but they refused. They even refused to share their contact number. But nonetheless they are thorough gentlemen and my best customers. All the shopkeepers in this area speak very highly of the brothers.' All this was a very crucial piece of information.

I had enough information to pass on to Sandra. All residents, shopkeepers, neighbors confirmed many of our suspicions. The hunt was narrowing down and the excitement was pulsating. I started dreaming about Saakshi and my country. It was my last day at the institution, and after a farewell, it was time to head back home.

CHAPTER 42

Cricket Again

I reached Islamabad in the last week of March. The past weeks kept me occupied in formulating and planning the capture of OBL, completely unaware of happenings around the world. On reaching Islamabad, I was surprised to see that the Cricket World Cup was already on its way. It had been two years since I followed the sport or watched a cricket match. The 2011 ICC World Cup was being played in India, Sri Lanka, and Bangladesh. Pakistan was also a co-host of the event but lost the opportunity after the cowardly terrorist attack on the Sri Lankan cricket team in 2009. After the astounding victory of the T20 World Cup, I was totally out of touch with this beautiful game. Islamabad made me realize euphoria around the tournament. I logged on to my laptop to track the Indian cricket team's performance in the past two years. The results were astonishing. Under the super-talented M. S. Dhoni, Indian cricket had soared to great heights. The team, with some refreshing new faces, reached the pinnacle of success, winning every tournament in India and abroad. I was amazed to know such stupendous achievements and couldn't wait to see India playing.

I reached Islamabad on 24 March 2011 and turned on the television to catch up with the latest news. The media was thoroughly unaware of anything these Americans were scheming but was completely engrossed in the World Cup. Pakistan had thrashed the West Indies on the previous day, 23 March, submerging the country in joy. The feared Pakistani bowling attack had wrecked the Windies batting line-up and the Paki openers sailed to the petite target of 112 without losing a wicket. This was the worst defeat for the Windies in their history of World Cup appearances. When I reached home, India was chasing a difficult target of 261 against the mighty Aussies, but I was ecstatic to see a thorough team effort and the target was almost in sight. Half-centuries by demigod Sachin and a cautious innings by Gambhir had set up the match for flamboyant Yuvraj to wrap it up. As soon as India won the match, the whole media turned their attention towards the impending semi-final between the two most hostile nations in the world, where defeat for any side is utter humiliation. During this week-long break between matches, the news channels of both the countries had nothing but the imminent contest to talk about. So age-old players were talking about old times, vintage matches were being replayed, experts were analyzing every minute detail. The television was flooded with cricket. The match scheduled on 30 March was like a festival or more like a war. Prime ministers of both the countries and many high-profile dignitaries were expected to witness the contest. The last match I witnessed was between the same opponents in the snowy camps of Nathu La pass. It was different format of the game but there is never a dearth of adrenaline when these warring nations are at loggerheads. This time, a grand dinner was organized at the senior officers' mess. I was fidgety. I was naturally an India supporter but watching the match with Pakistan army officers was a dangerous proposition. Any reason for celebration for the Pakis would be a moment of sorrow for the Indian in me and any dent to Pak prospects would make this Indian dance. Any sixer hit by the Indians would make me jump for joy but an Indian wicket will make me sulk. I was joyous at heart, sorrowful on the face, rejoicing outside and grieving inside. It was confusing and complicated. This whole outing was going to be as complicated as my life had been in the past twelve months. The family was very excited to attend the event and I couldn't refuse them. I was nervous to the core.

The stage was set for the biggest sporting event of the Indian subcontinent. The two nuclear martial countries were about to clash in what was touted as the greatest showdown of the tournament. Most businesses and offices in both countries were closed or declared a half-day. Governments in almost all the states and provinces of both the nations declared official holidays on 30 March because of this match. Thousands of screens were put in public places across both the nations and electronics stores experienced increased sales of television sets. The lives of more than a billion people across the subcontinent came to a standstill. The Pakistani PM traveled to Mohali, India on a special invitation from his Indian counterpart. The streets were empty, and the bars, hotels, homes were packed. Everybody was in front of some television screen. We traveled to the officers' club, which was brimming with excitement. I was happy to meet Gen. Anwar who came all the way from Peshawar for the match, glad to have a senior officer around whom I was comfortable with. The women and children had a separate hall and projector for themselves so the men with their glasses full were liberated thoroughly.

India won the toss and elected to bat. India's batting had been its strength forever and the Pakistani bowlers were always the toughest in the world. As the god of cricket, Sachin walked out to open the innings, the whole club gave them a standing ovation. Sachin is admired all around the world with equal enthusiasm. The match proceeded and Sehwag at his swashbuckling best hit the Pak bowlers all around the park. Every shot he hit made me giggle on the inside and somber on the outside, very difficult and complicated times on a personal front. The Master Blaster was rock solid at the other end. He was determined to deliver. With Sehwag gone, Tendulkar steadied the innings. While the whole world was busy enjoying the game, I noticed a bunch of senior police, army, ISI officers busy with their cell phones every once in a while. Gen. Anwar was also a part of this group. I was eager to know what they were up to. I struck up a conversation with Gen. Anwar. I was the general's blue-eyed boy; his mischievous smile made me suspicious.

'Want to make some quick bucks?' he enquired.

'Eh? How, sir? Everybody loves to make money and I am no exception. Please guide me, sir.'

'You ever bet in your life? How much can you spare?'

Bet! I was stunned. I was aware about the betting syndicate but participating in one was never in my scheme of things. Nonetheless, the past year was a complete revelation for me. So why not this? I concurred.

'Bhai has informed me that the master would score a half-century. So I can assure you this one feat will be achieved. And it's India's victory today. So tell me how much?' Anwar sir enquired of me.

'Five hundred thousand rupees. Done,' I consented.

Same as me, many officers put their money on India winning. Suddenly the atmosphere changed. I had many officers cheering for India. Though our gang was not loud about it, we exchanged a smile for every boundary or a six the Indians hit. As Gen. Anwar had already predicted, the Pakistan team performed as per instructions. Sachin was dropped not once or twice but a total of four times. Misbah-ul-Haq, Younus Khan, Kamran Akmal, and Umar Akmal all spilled their catches to help the legend carry on. There was real scare when he was given leg before by the on-field umpire and the whole lot of us were worried about losing our money. Gen. Anwar was calling somebody frantically. The Indians went for a review of the decision and the review was upheld. Tendulkar was declared not out by the third umpire.

'See how the matches can be controlled. Bhai can remote operate any game in any part of the world.'

'Who is this Bhai?'

'Come on now, Mazzi. Were you living under a rock for all these years? Bhai, the infamous don of the Indian underworld, who has been staying here with us under our security for more than two decades now. Do I need to provide you with more details?'

I figured out Gen. Anwar was talking about Dawood Ibrahim.

'So are the Indian players also involved in all this?' I asked him with a heavy heart.

'Maybe yes, maybe no. I cannot comment on them. But the BCCI is a multimillion-dollar organization. They pay their players handsomely. IPL, endorsements, and many things rake in huge amounts for the Indians. So I doubt their involvement. But our Pakis are the poorer lot. With a few exceptions of high-performing players, there are not many who make a decent amount. They seldom get a chance to represent their country so they are poisoned to amass when they have an opportunity. For important matches like these, the amounts offered are humungous. One night of non-performance can settle the players and their generations for the rest of their lives. So I don't blame these young minds. Not all players compromise and may falter naturally. But it's difficult to comprehend. That's the way life is, make hay while the sun shines.'

Now that explains the dropped catches. Some may be deliberate, some genuine mistakes, but who knows what. I hardly cared. I was on a double whammy. India was beating Pakistan and my money multiplied. The match progressed exactly the way Gen. Anwar and his ISI officer friends predicted. It seemed as if it was scripted. The Pakistanis started slow and they managed only 70 runs in the first 15 overs. India had made 99 during their innings in the same period. And this difference of 29 runs was exactly the margin by which Pakistan lost the match. Which means both the teams scored exactly the same number of runs in the next 35 overs. Misbah again came to India's rescue and his super-slow innings helped the run rate shoot up and pressure pile up. Finally, the Pakis succumbed; Indians emerged triumphant. It did not turn out to be as uncomfortable as expected since it had my share of Indian supporters around.

'Mazzi, see, I told you. Now if you want to make more, bet your money on India winning the World Cup. It's already decided. Earn while you enjoy the game. And I've known Bhai for years. He's been one of the biggest fans of the Master Blaster. But he's aware that he cannot even sniff around that great man. So to offer his love, I expect he will ensure that the Master will win every format of the last game he plays. So a piece of advice for the future: bet blindly on the Master's last ODI, IPL, Champions League, test match, or even the domestic league. I am sure Bhai will pay his tribute.'

India was declared the world champion on 2 April 2011.

CHAPTER 43

Mission Vision

After spending the month end in Islamabad celebrating the Indian World Cup triumph all alone, I was restless to go back to India. I was itching to party with AD and my family. Sandra made a strong case presentation to the CIA and White House. She was also in Islamabad to interact with her superiors. One morning, I received a call to report back in Abbottabad. The pass-out parade was scheduled on the twenty-third of April. I had no official reason to spend time at the academy but Sandra's sounded gloomy. I informed Landi Kotal about my rejoining after the pass-out parade. Adaah was excited since the time I had mentioned to her about the new citizenship. I assured her of the relocation and departed from Islamabad with a commitment.

This time in Abbottabad, I checked into a hotel to avoid suspicion, hired a rental cab, and made a dash to Samrez's house. The team was there with an evident frown.

'Why is everybody so drab today? Everything OK?' I enquired. 'I hope our cover is not blown.'

This put a smile on their faces. Brad confessed it would be their last day on this planet the day their covers were blown and everybody burst out laughing.

'Getting back to work . . .' Sandra was at her authoritative best. 'I compiled all leads, data collected over the years, and some very vital information provided by Mazzi, to make a presentation for the officials. They are very supportive of our endeavors and assured us continual assistance in every way. But even after all the data provided, they are not sure of OBL's presence in the compound. To make this mission a complete success, we need a thorough confirmation of OBL's presence. The evidence provided is not strong enough for the government to take an action. Any military offensive is a breach on Pakistan's sovereignty and with already strained relationships because of the drone bombings, the government is not ready to risk it any further,' Sandra clarified.

'So is this a deadlock and all our efforts are wasted?' I enquired with concern.

'No, Mazzi, in undercover missions, nothing is over until it's over. Some officials strongly support our theory and claims. They will urge for an action if we could provide them with some concrete evidence.'

'What better evidence can we provide? We have information from people living close to the house, the local shopkeeper, neighbors, the contractors have all concurred to the fact that there is something fishy about this house. What else can we provide?'

'A country cannot initiate action based on statements of some indiscreet neighbors and shopkeepers. There have to be undisputable facts to support any encounter. And today we lack that solid proof. We have all the indicators to believe he is inside but it's ultimately a belief, not a fact. Even I am lost for further course of action. Suggest to me, my friends, what do we do? How do we take this ahead?'

'What options do we have? How can we confirm OBL's presence? In what ways have you people carried out such missions before? I am already neck deep in this game and cannot give it up midway. You are undercover agents. Success and failure are a part of your job. You people succeed in a few missions and fail in many. Nobody knows of your true identities so such failures don't impact you or your profiles. But I've been a soldier all my life. We have been trained to succeed. Any mission failure is our personal failure and we are not used to defeats. I will deliver whatever is needed. Your team needs to provide me with a guiding light and I will tread that path.' I was desperate.

We spent the evening weighing various options available.

'The presence of any individual can be confirmed by obtaining pictures. But that is not remotely possible. We have observed this suspected ailing old man has never left the compound in years and does not interact with visitors. It will be impossible to penetrate his secure perimeter. So how do we do that?' asked Brad.

'Only three parameters are precise to every individual on this planet. If we can confirm the presence of any one of these three parameters, we will have a strong argument,' Sandra suggested.

'So what are they?' I enquired.

'Every person on this planet has unique fingerprints, distinctive corneal retina scan, and inimitable DNA strand. If we could confirm the presence of any one of these three features, I can convince my administration of OBL's presence in the compound. Obtaining the fingerprints or retina scan is next to impossible since for that we will have to actually visit the residence or interact with the person. But DNA strand is something that can be obtained, analyzed, and cross-confirmed remotely. One of OBL's sisters died of brain cancer in Massachusetts General Hospital last year. We have preserved her brain tissue for our confirmation in case we find him. This DNA strand can also be extracted from any of his family members staying in the compound. So even if we have access to his son's or daughter's blood strain, our genetics team will find a match and we can confirm our target. But the question remains of getting inside the compound and getting the blood samples.'

'Sandra, you and I cannot get this done but I am sure anybody who belongs to the medical field can help us with this.'

'We are at a very critical phase. We cannot risk involving any unknown person at this stage. Where do we get this Pakistani doctor from?'

I took some time off and then it struck me: Dr Afridi. I remember meeting him at events in my Khyber agency and he was quite a personality. He had a reputation for being ruled by the rupee.

'I know of somebody who might help us. There's a doctor in my administrative area who can do anything for an amount. If you are OK with roping in another associate, I don't mind introducing Dr Afridi to the team. He works under my jurisdiction and is spiteful. I guess we can take this chance.'

Sandra and her team were desperate by now, frantic to reach a conclusion. They firmly believed in their claim and were dying to prove it.

'I am fine with inclusion of another member as long as he's trustworthy. Mazzi, any slip-up from his side will not only tarnish your decorated service record but can endanger your life as well. We have nothing to lose. If he falters, we can disappear in a flash but all your life is at stake. Are you so sure of this person?'

I had faced enough perils in life and this could be one of the last risks to encounter. I was aware of Afridi and his acts and if an obscene amount was offered, I was confident he would help us.

'That we will have to discuss with him and confirm. Let me handle this. He won't dishonor my word.'

I called up Landi Kotal, and my office connected me to Dr Afridi. He was the chief surgeon at the Jamrud Hospital in the Khyber agency.

'Dr Afridi, this is Brigadier Mazhar calling. You remember around the month of January we had a team from NGO Save the Child. You along with many doctors had briefed them about the situation in our region. The same team is planning a health initiative and they would like to seek your guidance about the same. Can you spare some time to meet them? They are presently stationed in Abbottabad.'

Dr Afridi was a subordinate and this call was like an indirect order.

'Definitely, sir. I will present myself whenever and wherever required.'

The doctor traveled the next day to Abbottabad, where we had an informal introduction with the team at Coffity. I arranged for his stay at the same hotel so we traveled back together at the end of the day. A dinner that night, along with a few drinks, bonded us. I opened my can of worms to ease him. The more I got to know of him and his deeds, the happier I was. He was a carefree person with a zeal to explore life. I was confident to entice him with the offer.

'Doctor, what if I offer you an opportunity to make a million US dollars? Will you be excited?'

A million dollars—he was already in an inebriated state and the amount made him jump like being a winner at *Who Wants to Be a Millionaire?*

'Senior officers like you make fun of small people like us. Even if I put all of my life and sweat, I would never even reach somewhere close to a million dollars. One dollar is eighty-five rupees, you mean to say 8.5 crores. So, brigadier sahib, let's not waste our time in silly talks. I'm drunk, doesn't mean you can pull my leg,' he replied.

'No, genuinely I can offer you a task, on completion of which I will pay you a million dollars,' I said with a heavy grudge in my voice and a stern look on my face.

The doctor gauged the gravity of the situation and inquired, 'Is this true? Can I make 1 million dollars in this lifetime? Tell me, brig. sahib, I will do anything for it, sir. Please show me the way and I assure you every task will be accomplished.'

'Not tonight, doctor. We are not in the right frame of mind. Tomorrow morning, you will have answers to all your questions and also the key to unlock a million dollars.'

Early morning, the doctor was up and ready in the lobby before I reached it. I could gauge that he did not sleep a wink all night and spent the night dreaming of the dollars. We took a walk to the safe house. He did not speak much but his excitement was evident. He was pacing ahead then waiting for me to catch up. We reached Samrez's house, climbed to the first floor where the whole team was awaiting our arrival. I introduced him to the team. He recognized a few of them who had arrived at Landi Kotal during winters.

'Sir, I thought we were going someplace else. This is an NGO office, sir. I never knew NGOs make so much money to offer a doctor.'

Sandra took the initiative. She briefed him about their past work and future plans. He heard it all peacefully and replied, 'Madam, all that you are telling me is routine NGO work. In my twenty years of medicine life, I've seen thousands of volunteers doing these and many other activities. You don't need a doctor all the way from Khyber to help you out. I am sure there are a lot of doctors in this town as well. Brigadier sahib, can I know the reason for making me undertake this journey? Can I know the whole truth, please?'

Sandra gave a blank stare, expecting me to divulge further details. I took the doctor for a walk in the balcony, put an arm around his shoulders and informed him of the whole set-up, the leads along with the task in hand. It all sounded like a sham at first, but as I briefed him about the complete build-up to the particular address, he started taking interest. He paid attention, and as we went back to the team, the doc had a big smile across his face.

'So, Dr Afridi, what is your decision?' Brad enquired.

'All this is too fast for me to understand and comprehend. You guys are trying to tell me that the most searched person on the planet, the feared face of terror is staying in the backyard of the Pak military and nobody is aware of it? I find this ridiculous.'

'This is the human mind. Sometimes we overlook things which are right in front of our eyes and search for them around the world. All this is still a speculation so we seek your cooperation to help us conclude. We are ready to bear your charges, doctor. Will you help us?' asked Sandra.

'I will definitely. I would like to be a part of this investigation. I would do anything to help you find that man.'

His enthusiasm was reassuring and we shook hands for confirmation.

'I think I am at a greater risk getting into this muck. This is going to cost you.' Pat came the reply.

I was not surprised to hear this. Dr Afridi was famous for his antics and we asked him to quote a figure.

'Brig. sahib, that man is worth 25 million dollars. In spite of all the efforts, nobody can reach close to him. I can make this happen. I will give you OBL. I am risking my life, my career for this. So I want something that will settle me and my family forever.'

'Speak up, doc, speak up. Tell us your amount' Brad thundered.

'Five million dollars.'

I was left dumbfounded. I was aware of the Pakistanis being corrupt but this was astonishing; the figure he quoted was mind-boggling.

'Doc, if we succeed in this mission, there might be a security issue to you. We would like to relocate you outside this country,' said Brad.

'What is the point of making this money if I don't enjoy it with my friends and loved ones? I am not interested in going anywhere. Just pay me the money and I will deliver what is required.'

'Done. I assure you five million dollars if you succeed. Now can we work on some concrete plan?'

CHAPTER 44

The Ideation and the Implementation

On our way back to the hotel, Dr Afridi was beaming with happiness, smiling ear to ear. The Americans never reasoned for any amount that was quoted for helping them trace this HVT. Looking at this desperation, I am sure they might have splurged more than the declared figure. It was a matter of prestige for their famed intelligence networks. This capture would re-establish the diminishing faith in their president whose re-election was still uncertain. They had been squandering a fortune for years now to gather information and this was the closest they were to OBL. For me, monetary earning was not the only objective. I was keen to head back to India without causing any trouble to my past and present family and this was my best option available.

The next morning, we assembled at the safe house for a brainstorming session to decide the course of action. After much deliberation, it was concluded that some medical personnel would gain access to the compound under a false pretext and collect the samples. Many international NGOs carried out health initiatives in Pakistan. The team decided to capitalize on this and planned to mobilize a panel of health workers to execute the activity. For the money that Dr Afridi was being paid, Sandra asked him to advise and recommend the way ahead. The doctor asked for a day off to travel to Khyber. He probably applied for a leave from his official position and came back the next day with some iceboxes pasted with the UN logo. I and the doctor formed a team to work in tandem. We opted to update the team once in two days about any progress.

We approached some low-level health workers for the task. With a decorated army officer by his side, it was easier for the doctor to convince the ignorant staff. We informed them of an international agency that allotted funds to carry out vaccination programs in and around Abbottabad. We assured them high wages for their cooperation. The workers did not enquire much as long as the pay packets were heavy enough.

The pass-out parade at the academy was scheduled on the twenty-third of April. It was a day when the town would be flooded with important dignitaries. We decided to wrap up this activity before the ceremony. To make the ploy appear authentic, we started this vaccination program in a small hamlet near Abbottabad, called Nawa Saher. Promotional posters were put up around the village to publicize the authenticity of this activity. We hired a grey jeep and pasted the logo of the provisional health department on the door. My identity helped us bypass the senior doctors of the area.

With unending budgets at our disposal, Afridi made most of this opportunity. He ordered the vaccines from one of his close associates from Amson, a medicine manufacturer based on the outskirts of Islamabad and made a hefty commission on it as well. He also offered me a share of the profits but I abstained. I was interested in getting an outcome of this drive rather than making petty amounts.

The first round of vaccination was a roaring success. I accompanied the team of doctors and health workers. We visited every house in the small town; after testing them for the first round of infection, the workers administered the vaccine. The health workers were paid handsomely in cash at the end of the day. It was routine work for them to raise any suspicion. Hepatitis B vaccine is administered in a routine of three doses. But after this first round of the drive was successfully implemented, it was time to hit the nail. We were running short of time.

With the twenty-third approaching, security arrangements around the town of Abbottabad were to be beefed up. The team assembled in the safe house on the nineteenth of April. It was decided to shift the vaccination drive from Nawa Saher to Bilal town. This was the first attempt from the Americans to actually breach OBL's security perimeter. These were tense moments at the safe house. I was dissuaded from accompanying the workers this time. My identity would act as a deterrent and might alarm the target. The doctor and his team were on their own. Sandra crafted a special bag for this day. This vaccine carriage bag was fitted with hidden cameras along with other devices to capture images, voices, and other coordinates when in the house. But we were completely unaware about what was inside the compound. And then our host, our housekeeper, our friend came to our rescue. We called Samrez to join us for the afternoon lunch. We informed him about the inoculation drive and asked his help in getting people to cooperate. In getting feed about the area in general, I enquired of him about the Waziristan Kothi.

'Samrez, we have learned that the residents of the Waziristan Kothi are not particularly courteous and interact with only a handful of people in the town. I hope you understand the importance of this vaccination drive and how imperative it is to make our country healthy. You are one of the few people who have visited the kothi. Can you tell us what is it like from the inside? We want to include the residents of that kothi as well in this drive. Our aim is to drive this disease out of this town and country. So will you tell us something about the residents of the kothi?'

'Sahib, I never had a chance to enter the house. I always work on the farms outside. But I must tell you, sir, that it is a weird house. It has unusually high walls and almost no windows. I've always interacted with Rashid or Tariq. The house is a small town in itself. It has its own farm where I grow wheat, tomatoes, cabbages, cauliflower, and other vegetables. The compound also houses many rabbits, around 100 chickens, and a cow as well. They have a deep-water well allowing them a separate water supply from the local municipality. In a farther corner of the compound, there are also some cannabis shrubs, probably for their Miskeen Chacha. It is a self-sustaining house.'

'Miskeen Chacha? Who is this, Samrez?' I enquired enthusiastically and the team was equally excited.

'Sahib, he is an old relative of Arshad bhai. I think he lives on the upper floor of the house and never comes down. I've never seen him. But I know he lives within the compound. Rashid Bhai's nine-year-old daughter, Rahma, often speaks about him. Once while I was ploughing the farm, she enquired of her father, why doesn't the old uncle ever go to the market or come down and interact with others? Rashid bhai explained to her that the uncle is very poor to buy anything and is very ill to talk. So he prefers staying upstairs. *Miskeen* means poor in Pashto. Since that day, Rahma referred to Miskeen Chacha many times. I never had a chance to see this chacha. But the brothers speak very highly of this Miskeen Chacha and nurse him religiously. On Miskeen Chacha's instructions, I and Arshad bhai had discussions with Muhammed Issaq last year. Muhammed owns a bull and Chacha wished their cow to be impregnated by Issaq's bull. The chacha cares for the whole family.'

Samrez provided us with some very vital insights and information. We were sure this Miskeen Chacha was our target. The team was eager to carry out the mission and 21 April was decided to be D-day. On the twentieth, I accompanied the doctor to inspire his health workers. It was an informal session with the staff.

'I am very grateful to everybody for the cooperation. We are all here to make our country a healthy country. All of you have done wonderfully at the Nawa Saher camp. Tomorrow we are moving to Bilal Town area. I want each one of you to knock on every door and make sure we administer this vaccine. It is absolutely vital to make every person take this for a better future of our country. I won't take too much time. All the best for your work and may Allah bless you all.'

The staff was excited with the inspirational speech from a decorated army officer. At this meet, the doctor allotted separate areas to different workers. The nurses assigned the Waziristan Kothi were Bakhto and Amna. I personally interacted with both of them, handed them the CIA-designed vaccine bag, and exchanged wishes for the next day. Unaware of any treachery, the ladies were radiating with pride. We went to the safe house before heading back to the hotel where the doctor was given specific instructions for the mission. I couldn't sleep all night. I was sure none from our team did.

On the morning of 21 April, the medical team gathered at the entrance of the Bilal town area. I was at the hotel and the team was at the safe house. The doctor was our only soldier on the ground. We were biting our nails waiting anxiously for the doctor to return. Somewhere during mid afternoon, he returned to the hotel. He was smiling as he entered my room.

'Brigadier sahib, I think I have the samples.'

My heart was beating out of my mouth. 'Tell me exactly what happened, doc.'

'Sir, I accompanied Bakhto and Amna to the compound. On reaching the place, I parked my grey jeep near a property dealer's shack, at a short distance from the kothi. I hurried through the gravel path towards the two nurses, who were already at the gate. We knocked and waited at the forest-green metal gate as I spotted the security cameras. We waited long but there was no answer. Amna was inquisitive about the fact that I had personally come to administer the vaccine at this house. She asked me whether we can skip it, citing no response. I ignored her and crossed the road to a low bricked compound on the other side. I enquired with the neighbors; they were uninformed of the occupants. Unperturbed, I went back and continued knocking. Reasoning non-occupancy, now Bakhto wanted to proceed.

'Suddenly a middle-aged man opened the gates. Seeing me in the doctor's apron along with a nurse beside, he inquired the purpose of visit. I briefed him about the hepatitis disease and the necessity of this vaccine. He stood there listening attentively to the advice and inquired about the ill effects if the vaccine was not taken. I educated him about the drawbacks and how the family could be affected if they fail to receive the jabs. The door behind him was closed while he was talking to us. I tried to peep inside but he gave a stern look, after which I refrained. He patiently informed us that only one of us would be allowed to enter and administer the vaccine. Bakhto, being the most senior, decided to take the task ahead.

'First, a drop of blood would be drawn from the patient and blotted on a rapid-test strip, which would show, within minutes, whether the patient had been infected with hepatitis. If the patient was negative, the nurses were instructed to administer the vaccine. I was holding my breath, perspiring until she arrived. Amna continued on her task and went ahead to other houses. As Bakhto came out from the kothi with the vaccination bag and the samples, I took it away from her. She managed to acquire many samples. I handed her another bag along with the money of other workers for the day's labor and quietly escaped. I've many samples and I have no idea of which belongs to whom. But we definitely have headway. Let's pray to mighty Allah that we have the right samples.'

I looked inside the bag to see many blotted papers and glass panels smeared with blood neatly placed in plastic cases. We headed to the safe house where Sandra's team was eagerly awaiting our arrival. Brad was in the balcony on a lookout and waved from far away. As we ascended to the upper floor, the whole team was staring at us and the bag. The doctor narrated the incident. They heard the chain of events patiently then instructed us to disperse immediately. The doctor took the overnight bus back to Khyber. Adaah arrived the next day for the pass-out parade event and we occupied the officers' suite at the PMA.

CHAPTER 45

The Real Action

On 23 April 2011, an impressive parade was held in Pakistan Military Academy, Kakul. This was the 123rd batch of the PMA long course. The chief guest of the ceremony was the Pakistan army chief, General Kayani. During his address, the general lectured how the Pakistan army is aware of the internal and external threats to the country. He further disclosed how the Pakistan army was working against terrorism and divulged the efforts of Pak army officers and soldiers in their war against terrorists. The sword of honor was awarded to the officer Abdul Malik of 123 batch, and the president's gold medal was awarded to the officer Qazi Fasi Uddin.

I was seated in the front row for the event. Gen. Kayani's speech about the war against terrorism was a paradox. All throughout the ceremony, the blood samples and other theories occupied my mind. If the samples proved their worth, it was going to be a sham for the army chief and his hollow claims of fighting terror. But did Dr Afridi get the right samples? One thing I observed in the past month of working simultaneously with the Americans and the Pak army is that the Pak army was completely ignorant of this ordeal. Agencies like the ISI were aware and might also be hiding OBL. But the Pak army was busy being a puppet for the Americans, who were equally disoriented in this terror land. Or was I wrong? Maybe trivial officers were unaware and the higher officers were hand in glove with the ISI. Maybe these officers were aware of OBL's presence and they purposely shadowed him in open sight to avoid any suspicion? There were many such dubious questions unanswered. Either way, my task was completed and I was awaiting my family's flight to the US.

The ceremony passed smoothly. I was about to leave for Landi Kotal to resume my duties, when on the twenty-sixth of April, I received a call from Sandra. I met her over dinner, where she briefed me about the proceedings.

'Mazzi, I've a positive confirmation about some action. Our planned operation was a 100 per cent success and one of the blood samples collected at the compound was a perfect match with OBL's sister.

It was a blood sample from one of OBL's daughters, Safia, we suspect. The cameras in the vaccination kit also captured some important images. One of them resembled Khairiah Saber, Osama's third wife, and Siham, his fourth wife. If two of his wives are present simultaneously at one location, this heightens the chances of him being there. Many voice samples were also collected, but they are of not much use since we don't have samples to cross-confirm them. But nonetheless, we have enough evidence. This still doesn't confirm 100 per cent Osama's presence in the compound, but this is the closest that we have reached after OBL's narrow escape from the Tora Bora mountains. We have a fifty-fifty chance.

'I personally had a word with Ms Panetta and she asked me to proceed with the delivery of assurances we made. So I am here to inform you that your and your family's new life is about to begin in about a week's time. I am arranging for the new passports. All of you will fly to the US on your present identities. I guess something colossal is planned in the coming days. We are sending back a large number of our consulate staff in anticipation of any backlash. You and your family will fly on the same flight with the consulate staff so you will be in safe hands. The administration has informed me that if the news of this fake vaccination camp is leaked to the media, they will term it as a failure. They will agree to the activity but will publicize it as a failed initiative. They would be doing this to maintain the sanctity of real, trustworthy vaccination camps. Or else governments around the world will start doubting genuine medical camps and vaccination drives. Anyways that is out of our ambit. There is one last thing that I need you to help me with. I want some information on the radars, their utilization along the Af-Pak border. If the government plans any offensive, they have to make sure that it will be done discreetly. How can you help us with this?'

'Let me see, Sandra. I have never been posted in the communications domain so I cannot assure much help but let me figure it out. One more thing, I am not keen on proceeding on the same flight with my family. I would like to see them go with the consulate staff. I have some unfinished business here. If you can deliver to me all documents related to my citizenship, I will leave in a few days. And most importantly, if your mission is successful, please transfer half of my prize money to my wife's account in the US and other half to an account which I will inform you shortly.'

Sandra was a seasoned undercover agent and she understood the difficulty of a senior officer disappearing in thin air. She nodded in agreement.

'Mazzi, I will give you all documents pertaining to your citizenship in the next two days. And I will process the family's details later. Take care.'

I instructed Adaah to pack her stuff and get the kids ready for a new life. She was happy and sad. We had recently moved into this new bungalow, which she was very fond of. But she had to let it go for a better future.

On the twenty-seventh, I visited the army headquarters where I bumped into Yusuf, my good old friend. Engaging him in general discussion, I inquired about the radar capabilities of our country. Yusuf had spent considerable time with ISI phone tapping and surveillance. He informed me that Pak had the best of the tracking facilities. The radars were rested in the peace mode during peacetime, along the western border of Afghanistan. It was not economically feasible to keep them running 24/7. But the radars along the Indian borders were on a full-time alert. I passed on this information to Sandra when she delivered my documents. She was my mainstay in this endeavor and this was a time for departure. She hugged me tight and planted a kiss on my cheeks.

'Mazzi, you have been my angel. Your arrival resolved all my efforts. Thank you for coming into my life. I will never forget those beautiful moments we spent together. Thank you for everything. I will catch up once you are in the US. After such wonderful times, I don't think I can ever forget you. Goodbye and take care.'

When I reached home that evening, Adaah had some real estate agents coming over to inspect the property. She was a wise woman and was aware that with the present scheme of things, it was advisable to offload all immovable properties before taking up a new identity. She offered a 25 per cent discount on market rates but I still thought it was a good deal; the next day, our new bungalow was sold to some individual who paid all the money in one day. The kids were confused with all these activities, but they were just excited about going to the US. Suhail was traveling to his native town so I escaped answering uncomfortable questions. Sandra informed me 29 April would be the departure date. We spent the last day shopping and having fun in the little time we had. On the twenty-ninth, I dropped off the family at the airport. I hugged Adaah, Afaaz, and Inshaa a final goodbye. The kids had tears in their eyes and I couldn't hold back mine. I was feeling empty inside to let go of a family that brought me back to life. But such is life.

To keep myself aloof from the anticipated commotion, I planned to go back to Landi Kotal on the thirtieth of April. That very evening, I connected with AD.

'AD, my duties towards this country are over. Please take me back home. Tell me, what amount would be needed?'

'I am glad for you, my boy. I hope your family is not piggybacking with you. I will start the proceedings right away. Believe me, you will be back with your family in the next ten days. Keep around a million rupees handy. I am not sure of what would be the spend, but keep it handy.'

I reached Landi Kotal. Adaah called me from Kennedy airport, NY. She reached there safely with the family, thanks to the cordial staff. I was relieved. I rested for a day, and was about to resume my duties on the second of May, when the big news was transmitting all over the television.

'Osama killed in an American strike on the night of 1 May in a high-walled compound in Abbottabad.'

My heart skipped a beat.

CHAPTER 46

Back to the Front

After the Osama raid in Abbottabad, the whole country went in a tizzy. The embarrassed government had no courage to demean the Americans, neither the audacity to accept the fact that OBL was hiding in plain sight, less than two miles from their most acclaimed military institute, where thousands of army men train every year. For years the government had been denying any leads of this HVT; in fact, they shrugged off the responsibility on Afghanistan and Yemen for hiding OBL. And when the Americans, with their meticulous planning, dug out Osama from right under their noses, the government was humiliated and ridiculed in front of the world.

Empty claims of fighting against terrorism fell flat, and it was pandemonium all around the administration.

The force was completely demoralized. The discontent was clearly visible on the faces of the soldiers in Landi Kotal as well. They were angry with the government for letting the Americans get away with an attack on Pakistan's soil and sovereignty. But every soldier was as helpless as the government was, feeble and timid to raise any voice against the mighty world bullies.

The first few days passed with a shadow of gloom spread across the garrison. I refrained from interacting with the staff or moving outside the camp. The sure-shot success of the teams' efforts was commendable. I did all this for the well-being of my family and to go back to my motherland without any guilt. I was feeling claustrophobic in this country. My only responsibility was already across the shores and now I wanted to run away as soon as possible. I called Dr Afridi, but he was untraceable. The defense ministry called for an urgent meeting of all the senior officers to review the situation and boost the morale of the force. I decided to give this meeting the slip, citing health reasons.

AD's messenger approached me and asked me to travel to Quetta along with my Land Cruiser. With most of the army assembled in Rawalpindi for the review meeting, I had the chance to escape without too many permissions from superiors. My car was the only asset that was still with me. I drove to the same hotel where I stayed with Aafreen. As the last time around, a mechanic visited the hotel under the pretext of servicing the vehicle. Driving with him around the town for some time, I stopped in front of a shop. He collected a bag and we continued towards the hotel. I did not ask too many questions and neither did he interact much. On reaching the hotel, he handed me the bag along with a service bill of around 500,000 rupees. I observed this must be the world's most expensive car service. I went up to the room, removed stuff from the bag, and filled it with cash. The mechanic collected the bag and left without any acknowledgement. I hurried back to the room to see the contents of the bag: a Pathani suit and the typical Baloch skullcap. It also contained a note with some numbers scribbled. The numbers made no sense in sequence but I was sure they definitely made some logic. I was not trained in decoding puzzles but I had to. There were a few mathematical equations to be solved which took me back to my college days. I solved those jumbled equations to find 55 11 6600 in a scrambled format. But it was some specific message. Today was the fourth of May. Was this a specific date, 5 May 2011, 5/5/11? But then what was 6600? Was it time? Maybe. I decided to follow my instincts and take a risk. The date indicated was tomorrow. I experienced butterflies in my stomach. My journey was scheduled, back to the country which had already counted me dead. Would this travel, transformation, and tale be accepted by my people? The pressure was humongous. This was the longest night of my life. I donned my Baloch attire at 3 a.m., fiddling in front of the mirror making sure everything was perfect—the attire, the cap, the shoes. The tension was enormous.

I was down in the lobby at five, walking up and down the hotel. The minimal staff of the hotel that was present at such wee hours was a tad confused but it hardly mattered. The valet delivered my car at 5.30 a.m. and I was already on the road. Timing is of utmost importance in such missions. Too early could also spell doom. So I decided to wander around the town for a while. If all worked well, this would be my last day in this country.

At around six, I drove towards the service center, where a few people were already at the gates. Upon my arrival, one of them came over to the passenger seat and greeted me. He asked me to step down and join him for tea. I was not in a mood for formalities, refused the offer, but he insisted. It was a bitter cold morning. As we walked towards the tea stall, my car was taken inside the service station. The tea was helpful in battling the cold but I hardly spoke to the man. We went back to the place, waiting for the car. The car arrived and this time it was driven by somebody in army attire, with two people on the rear seat. I almost had a heart attack. It felt as if the plan had been compromised and I was being impounded. But it was nothing of that sort. The three inside were speaking local language and laughing amongst them. I occupied the rear seat and we drove towards the Chaman border. The two other occupants in the rear seat were dressed like me. AD had instructed me to keep mum and simply obey orders.

A few miles before the border gate, we three from the rear seat alighted and entered an old van cab that was used to ferry people across the border. The army man driving my car got down, gave a big hug to the other two guys, and drove away. I was at a distance watching, trying to understand. Our cab drove for a distance and picked up a family en route to the border gate. The family had five kids along with the parents. The cab was overcrowded and each one of us had a kid on our lap. I was perspiring as we approached the gate.

The driver went to the checkpoint to verify the documents. It was very early morning when the soldiers were half sleepy. As the driver was striding towards the checkpoint, the father of the kids inside our cab suddenly slapped three kids hard. It was very disheartening and enraging to see this kind of treatment but I was advised to be a mute spectator. The children were bellowing with pain and crying at the top of their voices. Hearing the commotion and the cries inside the car, the soldier at the gate hurriedly stamped the documents and the driver ran back to the car. We crossed into Afghanistan with the babies still howling. The guards on the Afghan side were perhaps informed about such cab and activity. They let us through without any checks. We drove straight to the car dealer's office. The cab halted and all the occupants went their way. I was left alone in front of a closed shutter, which suddenly opened up and out came AD.

'Jay Ambe Ambe Bhawano Maa, jai Durge, Durge Bhawani Maa' was the shout as we clung onto each other. We both had tears in our eyes.

'Bro, you are safe now. Today is the beginning of a new life. You are scheduled to depart for India from Kabul tomorrow morning. Your documents mention you as an Indian teacher who has been in Afghanistan for the past six months. Don't worry, the immigration officers will be cooperative. The officials in Delhi have been informed of your arrival and all formalities will be taken care of. The army will decide on your career if you can convince them of your story. You are aware of how complicated it would be. You are already decorated posthumously. Anyways, I have recommended you for a posting in R&AW. Your exhaustive experience of the past two years is priceless. I cannot commit you this but I've made the initiative. You can visit your family and friends in the meanwhile. It would be impossible for anybody to accept such facts but now the ball is in your court. I've completed my duty as a friend and a soldier. All the very best for your future life, hope to see you soon on such assignment. Take care, brother. Please hand me over the remaining 500,000 rupees to clear off the payments.'

A car was waiting to take me to Kabul. AD handed me some documents and I bid him a farewell as the car sped away. I checked into the guest house of the Indian embassy, had a little nap of contentment. That evening, the television was playing the big news, the death of Hilal-i-Jur'at Brig. Mazhar Khan in a car accident near Quetta. The brigadier was alone in the car, driving towards Landi Kotal when his car fell into a ravine. The massive explosion left behind a body charred beyond recognition.

I sank in the sofa, wondering about the impact. I immediately called Sandra in NY and asked her to notify Adaah the truth about the accident and an assurance I would catch up soon. I decided to stay back in the guest house to avoid any unnecessary complications. As I retired for the day, many thoughts were running through my head.

I was an Indian soldier killed by my own army, resurrected in Pakistan, decorated posthumously by India, hailed as a national hero by Pakistan, involved in locating the most dreaded terrorist of the world. I've been a brave soldier for India, protecting the borders. I've been a diligent officer for Pakistan, bridging relations with the tribes. I've been a deceptive spy for the US, helping to locate the most hated man on the planet. I've always been a sincere, earnest, hard-working warrior for any task I undertake. I am determined to deliver for any country which provides me with an opportunity. Today, I am an American citizen, an Indian teacher, and a dead Pakistani army officer. By the time you read this experience, I could be in the interior of the US of A enjoying life with my Pak family, I may be tracking the terrorists in Pakistan, or I might have to simply disappear from the face of the planet. I am en route back home, unsure how life will unfold. The fighter inside cannot be contained for long. One thing I can assure you all is shortly I will be *back to the front!*